HARD LANDING

D0860895

DAVID G. KEITH

Good Egg Press

Copyright © 2016 Good Egg Press
All rights reserved.

HARD LANDING

Library of Congress Catalog Number: 2016956509

ISBN: 978-0-9863706-2-5 (print)
ISBN: 978-0-9863706-3-2 (ebook)

No part of this publication may be reproduced, stored in retrieval system, or transmitted by any means—electronic, mechanical, photographic (photocopying), recording, or otherwise—without prior permission in writing from the author.

Hard Landing is a work of fiction. Names, characters, places, and incidents are the products of the author's imagination or are used fictitiously. Any resemblance to actual events, locales, or persons, living or dead, is entirely coincidental.

Cover Design by OMG Media
Interior Design by Lorie DeWorken, MIND*the*MARGINS, LLC

Published in the United States by Good Egg Press
www.goodeggpress.com

For my beautiful wife, Giselle.
My best friend and partner for life.

To Yvonne + Dave
Hope you enjoy Hard landing!
Best Wishes

PROLOGUE

Jonathan Timbers parked his car in the back alley and entered the small mom and pop market through a back door. The owner of the store, John Royster, had been a high school classmate of Timbers some twenty years earlier. The two had stayed in touch over the years, but were never great friends—more like business associates.

Marcos, standing behind the register, nodded at Timbers as he walked in. The young clerk was covered in ink, his long hair gathered in a ponytail that hung halfway down his back. A shiny red nose ring was a new addition since Timbers had seen him last.

"Is Royster around?" Timbers asked, grabbing a candy bar from the display case next to the cashier counter. He ripped open the wrapper and chewed off a third of the bar in one bite.

Marcos thought about informing Timbers that he owed a buck for the chocolate but thought better of it. Timbers had a temper and Marcos preferred not seeing it on display.

"Yeah, he's in his office."

Timbers made his way toward the back of the shop, winding through a couple of very cramped aisles of food and assorted household items. He passed by two young women in the beer aisle and brushed against the prettier of the two.

"Sorry."

The woman looked at the handsome Timbers and smiled, responding,

"No problem." He thought about stopping and and chatting up the woman but he had business to conduct.

The office door was closed so he knocked loudly. A few seconds later the door opened a crack and Royster peered out to see who it was.

"Jesus, just let me in. You are so paranoid."

Royster opened the door. "You'd be paranoid, too. I've been robbed three times this year. The last two I had a gun put to my head. So shut the hell up."

"Nice to see you, too," replied Timbers.

Royster closed and locked the door behind him and the two moved to chairs on opposite sides of a large and very cluttered desk.

"Do you have my stuff?" asked Timbers, getting right down to the business at hand.

"Do you have my money?"

"Yeah, but I need to see everything first, make sure you didn't screw it up."

Royster smirked, but didn't respond. He reached into his pocket and pulled out a ring with a couple dozen keys. He quickly located the correct key and opened the bottom drawer of his desk, pulling out a small canvas bag. He held it up and asked, "Where's my money?"

Timbers softened a bit. He could have insisted on seeing the contents before showing him the cash but thought better of it. It's not like Royster was going to rob him in his office. He reached into his jacket pocket and pulled out a roll of cash, rubber banded together. He tossed it on the desk.

Royster shoved the clutter on his desk off to one side, making room to count the cash. He removed the rubber band and quickly began laying out all the bills.

"It's all there, don't worry. Nothing bigger than a twenty, like you asked."

Halfway through, Royster was satisfied all the loot was there. He tossed the canvas bag to Timbers.

Timbers opened the bag and removed the contents. There wasn't much, but it was everything he had asked for. Fake driver's licenses and passports along with a fake American Express card. He looked closely at the forged documents, holding them at different angles to catch the small amount of daylight that filtered into the room. The quality was excellent, but he'd expect nothing less for the cash he had just handed over to Royster. It was all the money he had, but he knew there would be plenty more cash coming his way soon. The five grand was a down payment on his future and that future was just a few days away.

"So, what are you up to, big boy?" asked Royster. His curiosity had gotten the best of him.

"None of your damn business."

Roster looked at Timbers sitting there across the desk, thinking back on their high school days together. Timbers was smart and had received a full academic scholarship to Texas A&M, where he had majored in business. After completing college he returned to Colorado and had gone into banking. A fairly normal, if not bland lifestyle—a bit surprising given that Timbers always had a little bit of a dark side. Royster could never quite figure him out, and now here he was sitting in his dank, dark office with a fake ID, passport, and credit card. What the hell was he up to?

"You wanna count the rest of the cash or can I get outta here?" Timbers asked.

"Nah, we're good. I know where to find you if I find you shorted me fifty bucks."

"It's all there, pal. And by the way, you'd never fucking find me."

CHAPTER 1

"Let's break camp here for the night."

"Works for me."

Mark Heath looked at the scenery that surrounded him and his younger brother. "God, it's so beautiful here. I never get tired of it."

They stood there quietly, taking in the beauty of the Colorado forest.

"I'll set up the tent if you'll gather some firewood. We can have the trout for dinner."

"Sounds good."

"Looks like there might be some firewood off in those trees," he answered, pointing off a hundred yards or so from where they were standing.

David Heath set off toward the stand of trees while his brother, Mark, pulled the tent from his backpack.

It was Saturday, two days before Labor Day, and the brothers were enjoying their end-of-summer backpacking trip, a ritual they had carried out for more than fifteen years. The brothers had managed to stay close despite going off on their respective careers in different cities in different states. Each was married with a couple of kids and had become ensconced in his own life. The backpacking trip was something they each looked forward to every summer. As their lives became more complicated, the trips were getting more and more difficult to pull off, but here they were again, not a hundred miles from

Boulder—the place they had grown up.

Mark grabbed the tent from his backpack, found some level ground, and started the assembly. Once the tent was up he grabbed the fish they had caught an hour earlier and placed them in the small frying pan he carried in his backpack. It would be their third meal of trout in four days, but neither was tired of it. He then began getting an area ready for starting a fire. He gathered some pine needles and now just needed the firewood that David had left to gather.

Mark looked up to check on his brother's progress and saw David running toward him. He was empty handed and looked agitated, almost frightened.

"What's going on? Where's the firewood?" Mark asked as he approached.

David stopped in his tracks and motioned for Mark to come toward him.

"What is it? We need firewood if we're going to cook up the trout. It's not sushi, for God's sake."

"Come here," he responded anxiously, "You gotta check it out."

"What is it? What's wrong?"

"Down in those trees—there's a weird smell. I can't tell what it is."

"What are you talking about? What kind of smell?"

"There's a smell coming from the trees . . . I don't know what it is, but it's sickening. I can't stand it. I'll go find the firewood from somewhere else."

"That'll take too long. Oh, for God's sake, I'll get it." Mark headed toward the trees where David had detected the odor. Looking back over his shoulder he added, "Gather up some pine needles while I'm gone so we can get the fire going as soon as I'm back."

Mark loved his brother, but sometimes he lost patience with the guy. Go grab some wood, that's all he had asked him to do.

As he came upon the pines, he stopped dead in his tracks. David was right—it smelled like rotting meat. It was overpowering, making him feel slightly sick. But his curiosity was greater than the feeling in his stomach and he continued toward the trees, taking shallow breaths and covering his mouth with his sleeve. The smell grew stronger as he approached—he could sense that even with his shallow breaths. He looked along the ground near the base of the trees expecting to see a dead animal, but there was nothing. He walked quickly around to the other side of the trees and could see nothing that would generate such a horrible odor.

The pine trees were nearly a hundred feet tall and the aspens were half that, their leaves shimmering in the late afternoon sky. He gazed up, moving around while keeping his eyes glued to the thick branches reaching into the sky. The smell was pungent, and Mark wasn't sure how much longer he could take it before he would need to leave for fresher air. Just then something that caught his eye, about halfway up one of the thicker pine trees. He shifted a bit to his right to get a better look, and a few seconds later was running back toward camp.

CHAPTER 2

"I'm heading home. You gonna be long?" she asked, standing in the office doorway.

"Yeah, probably a couple more hours. I'm sorry, I'm just swamped right now."

"Sorry to hear that, Mr. Sheriff."

Mia Serrano quietly closed the door behind her and slowly walked across the expansive office. She slid in behind his desk and sat in his lap, wrapping her arms around his neck. Neither spoke as she kissed him gently on the mouth.

"God, Mia—you're killing me."

"What's a girl gotta do around here to get some alone time with the sheriff?"

"I'm sorry, Mia. I'll tell you what—give me one hour and when I get out of here we can head out for a nice dinner."

"Well, if that's the best you can do . . . " she replied, kissing him again, this time on the neck.

Newly-elected Rocklin County Sheriff Mick McCallister moved his hand onto Serrano's leg. She was wearing a black skirt cut just above the knee, and his hand moved easily northward to mid-thigh.

"Ah, hell."

"What—what's wrong?" Mick replied.

"My cell—it's going off."

Mia reached into the pocket of her matching black blazer and pulled out her phone. She had set it to vibrate, so while McCallister hadn't heard it, she had felt it go off.

The caller ID told her the call was from the on-duty watch commander.

"Serrano."

"Hey, Mia. It's Jim Bailey down at the CO's desk. We need you to respond to a 9-1-1 call over in the Samson Creek area. At this point we're not sure if it's a homicide, but it's what you might call a bit suspicious."

"What've we got?"

"A backpacker called in and reported something dead in a tree up in the hills off Highway 83. It's quite a ways up from the ground so he isn't sure, but says it stinks to high hell. Anyway, I talked to Commander Espy and he wants you and Keller to respond and check it out."

Mia took a moment before responding.

"Well, if it's something in a tree and it's too high to be easily identified, would it be possible to get the fire department to respond—maybe with a fire truck equipped with a ladder?"

"Len Phillips is the field sergeant at the scene. You might check with him about the feasibility of getting a ladder truck in there. I have no idea what kind of terrain we're talking about but that area is pretty rugged in places. The fire guys can be a little territorial when it comes to their equipment."

Mia responded, "Just tell them there's a little kitten stuck in a tree and that a crowd of young females has gathered. They'll be out there in no time."

"Yeah, no kidding."

"Okay, I'm actually in the office today getting caught up on a backlog of reports. I'll leave in a few minutes My ETA is probably a half hour."

"Lucky you, working the Saturday of a long weekend?"

"Yeah, it's a glamorous life."

Mia ended the call and returned her attention to her boyfriend of fifteen months.

“What the hell was that all about?” asked McCallister, looking at Mia with an intrigued look on his face.

“We’ve got a possible DB in a tree out near Samson Creek and they want me to respond to the scene. They’re sending Keller as well. Can I take a raincheck on that nice dinner you promised me?”

“Of course, but let’s remember where we left off here.”

Mia leaned in to the sheriff and gave him a lingering kiss on his lips.

“You got it.”

Mia headed downstairs to her desk in Major Crimes. She glanced at the sign-in board hanging on the wall at the entrance to the bullpen and smiled to herself. Seeing her name on that board brought her a lot of pride—it had been a long, difficult journey to earn the coveted position of homicide investigator. She had more than a dozen years with the RCSO, but had been formally given the job less than a year earlier. But the move into homicide wasn’t via the traditional route. From the patrol division she had moved into a traffic investigator position, often a deputy’s first foray into detective work. She worked traffic accident cases for nearly five years, excelling in the role. Then, through a series of unusual consequences she had become involved in a sensational murder investigation. Mia had taken the lead on the case, which at first was believed to be a fatal traffic accident. But before long it was determined that it was not an accident at all, and was, in fact, a cold-blooded murder. She and veteran detective Jack Keller were teamed together to work the case. Mia and Keller soon determined that Castle Springs businessman George Lombard had been murdered by his business partner, Scott Lennox. Lennox had been charged with the crime and was about to go to trial. The case had been a difficult one and had caused a significant strain on the relationship between Mia and Keller when she learned Keller had not been honest with her about some aspects of the investigation.

Mia passed by the large board and took a seat at her desk. She called dispatch and got the exact location of the call-out, along with the cell number for Sergeant Phillips. She dialed him up, got a quick rundown, and asked about the feasibility of getting a fire truck close to the tree. Phillips said he believed a truck could access the area, as the terrain was not particularly severe at the location. He also told Mia the crime scene was close to a fire access road and fire department personnel were likely familiar with the area. She asked the sergeant to call the fire department to get the ladder truck out there and gave him her ETA of thirty minutes. Her thoughts then drifted to partnering with Jack Keller on the call-out. She was tempted to head to the crime scene alone, letting Keller catch up to her there. But she fought that temptation and dialed Keller's cell number. The call went to his voicemail, allowing her to leave a quick message explaining that she would meet him at the scene. Relieved, Mia headed for the door.

It was nearly sunset by the time Mia approached Highway 83 from I-25 and it was turning into a beautiful Colorado summer evening. She turned onto the highway, traveled west about fifteen miles, and began to look for a deputy stationed at a dirt road. Phillips told her the area had been blocked off at that point, eliminating the possibility of anyone coming upon the scene. It was unlikely anyone would, but they couldn't take any chances. It was important to keep the scene as pristine as possible, at least until they knew what exactly they had up in the tree. As she approached mile marker 15 she slowed, looking carefully for the dirt road.

A minute later, she saw a RCSO patrol car parked at an angle across the entrance to the road. Yellow crime scene tape, anchored by small pine trees on either side, blocked access. Mia rolled to a stop and lowered the window of her unmarked unit. She didn't recognize the deputy.

"I'm Mia Serrano from Major Crimes. I got called out on this possible dead body. Do you know if Jack Keller has arrived yet?"

"Nope, you're the first person on scene since I got assigned to watch the road."

"Well, there will be a lot more personnel responding out here. Jack Keller, as I mentioned, as well as several members of our CSI team, and maybe a fire department truck."

"Okay, thanks for the heads up. The sergeant didn't tell me much."

"Were you the first deputy on scene?"

"No, that would be Kowalski. I was his backup—took me almost a half hour to get out here. I'm working beat three but they sent me 'cause they had no one else nearby."

Mia could sense a bit of frustration from the young deputy as he explained his role in the call-out.

"Yeah, I can believe that. Of course, not much of anything goes on way out here."

The deputy just looked at her and shrugged. He handed her a clipboard with the sign-in log. Mia quickly signed her name, badge number, and her time of arrival.

The deputy lifted the yellow crime scene tape, allowing Mia to drive underneath. She drove up the dirt road for a half mile or so until she came upon two RCSO patrol cars parked next to a small tent. She saw Sergeant Phillips and another deputy talking to what appeared to be a couple of campers. One of the campers looked pretty shaken and was leaning against a pine tree, while the other stood close to Phillips and Deputy Kowalski.

Mia approached the group.

"Hey, Mia, this is Mark Heath and his brother, David. They made the discovery and called it in."

"Hello," replied Mark, extending his hand to Mia. "My brother David is a bit unnerved. He's the one who first saw the body—or whatever it is—up in the tree," he added, nodding toward his brother.

David acknowledged Serrano with a half-hearted nod. Mia turned her attention back to Mark and asked him what had happened.

"My brother and I were backpacking and decided to make camp for the night. He went to gather some wood down toward that stand of trees," he said, pointing to an area a hundred yards away, "and came high-tailing it back, looking terrified. He told me there was a bad smell coming from the trees, so I went down there to check it out, and that's when I smelled it, too. Very powerful and very foul. I've never been around a dead body, but somehow that's what I thought of right away. It's way up there and the branches make it hard to see, but if you look up at just the right angle you can see something that looks human."

Mia stood there listening to Mark Heath tell his story. She didn't get any sense that he was lying or covering anything up, but her training and experience always kept her open to such a possibility. Mia had a pretty good bullshit meter and she didn't get any sense Mark Heath wasn't telling her the truth. And if he or his brother did have something to do with whatever was in the tree, they sure wouldn't be calling the police to alert them to it.

Mia looked toward Sergeant Phillips. "I'll go down there and take a look for myself. We've got a team on the way—they shouldn't be too much longer. Got CSI coming as well as Jack Keller from Major Crimes. Once the fire truck arrives we can get up on a ladder and really see what we've got."

Mia grabbed her Maglite from the car and walked toward the trees. It didn't take long for her to detect the foul, distinctive odor. It was human, all right—she was sure of it. She had been around enough dead bodies to know: the sick, putrid, almost-sweet smell was like no other. Her nose didn't lie.

She stood at the base of the trees and shone her Maglite up into the branches, doing her best to breathe through her mouth. She moved the ray of light from tree to tree, craning her neck to see if she could find the source of the smell. But the thickness of the branches made it difficult to make out what she was seeing. She shifted her position on the ground to get a better angle—and then she saw it.

"How in the hell . . . ?" she wondered out loud to herself.

She took off her blazer and placed it on the ground, marking the spot where she was standing, and headed back to the area where the two backpackers had pitched their tent.

CHAPTER 3

Jack Keller was headed to his daughter's place in the tiny town of Rosebud for a visit when he got the call from Commander Bailey about the possible body in a tree. He had made a quick U-turn and was heading for Samson Creek when he saw the call from Mia pop up on his cell. Screw her, he thought, he knew what she was calling about. Bailey had told him the two had caught the case together. He let the call go to voicemail, content with letting Serrano stew a little bit.

His thoughts turned to the call from Bailey. A body in a tree? Why the hell not, he thought, as he drove out Highway 83 toward the scene—he had seen just about everything during his nearly forty-year career.

Keller was a tall, handsome man with hair that was more gray than black. He was sixty-three years old but looked younger, despite carrying an extra fifteen to twenty pounds around his midsection. Keller had a great sense of humor, a rather dry wit that was lost on some people. He could also be biting and acerbic if a particular situation called for it. He didn't have a lot of friends outside the department, or inside, for that matter, but the few friends he did have would do virtually anything for him. Divorced twice, he swore he'd never go down that path again. Women found Keller attractive, but he had rarely dated in the fifteen years since the last divorce, which had left him both bitter and broke.

He had arrived in Rocklin County ten years earlier after doing a thirty-year stint with the police department in St. Louis, Missouri.

At SLMPD, Keller spent more than half his career working homicide cases, investigating more than 300 murders and posting an astounding conviction rate of nearly seventy-five percent. But burnout among detectives was commonplace in his old division at SLMPD. The late night call-outs, drive-by shootings, and drug-fueled murders pushed many good, hard-working detectives to early retirement. Jack Keller lasted longer than most but ultimately went the way of the others.

His first marriage was to his high school sweetheart and for the first few years things went well. The marriage produced a daughter, and Jack and his young family settled in a nice, middle-class St. Louis neighborhood. Life was good for the Kellers, and the future looked bright.

But over the next couple years, as Jack became more and more involved with his career at the PD, things changed dramatically. He landed a coveted position within the department working undercover, but the assignment took everything he had, both physically and emotionally, leaving him with very little time or energy for his young family. The time he did spend at home was used for self medicating, with Southern Comfort being his drug of choice. As time went by, Jack's drunken spells became more and more prevalent and the result was a very troubled marriage. Finally, on a cold January night, Jack returned home from working a double shift to find the women in his life were gone, never to return. So, Jack Keller worked harder. The department was all he had.

It was dark by the time he reached the dirt road turnout. He didn't make any small talk with the deputy, quickly identifying himself and signing in when handed the clipboard. A few minutes later, Keller could see flashing red and blue lights coming from the light bars atop the patrol cars parked near a tent. The bright, pulsating lights created an eerie backdrop with the trees and nearby mountains. Next to the marked units he saw an unmarked unit and guessed that Mia had beaten him there.

Mia motioned to Keller and they walked back toward where the marked units were parked to get some privacy.

Keller started the conversation, skipping the small talk. "So, what've we got here?"

"I briefly interviewed one of the two brothers who called it in. The other one is a bit spooked, so I left him alone, at least for now. The one I did speak to told me there is a very foul smell coming from a stand of trees over that direction," Mia replied, pointing. "I went over and could smell it right away—I have no doubt we've got a DB. The crazy thing is that the smell is coming from probably forty feet up the damn pine. It was almost dark, but I think I saw a leg and a foot."

Keller shook his head, almost imperceptibly. He didn't say anything for a few moments but then responded.

"How sure are you of what you saw? I mean, it's dark and you say it's maybe forty feet up?"

"Pretty sure it was a leg and a foot, but I'm one-hundred-percent sure the smell is human."

"Well, let's go take a look."

Keller grabbed his Maglight from his unit and the two walked quietly past the others, making their way down to the trees.

"Here's the best vantage point," she said to Keller, as she pointed to her blazer on the ground.

Keller looked at the blazer and then at Serrano.

"I put it there to mark the spot—so we'd be able to find it easily. It's dark and I didn't want to lose my place."

"How very Nancy Drew of you."

"Shove it, Keller. I figured it would help you, given your advanced age and all."

Keller shot her a half smile. It was a small victory for Serrano.

Keller grabbed his Maglite and pointed it toward the tree.

"Look about halfway up and you should be able to see it. It's a leg and a foot—I couldn't tell if the rest of the body was attached or not. Maybe you can tell."

Keller slowly worked the beam of light up the tree, a few feet at a time so as to not miss anything. After thirty seconds or so the beam was halfway up the pine and he stopped. Looking more intently, he shifted a bit and craned his neck to get the best possible angle.

"Damn, I think you're right. We've got ourselves a leg and a foot."

Keller took out his cell phone and pointed it up the tree. He clicked a series of photos; the flash cast an eerie look to the scene. Then, using his thumb and index finger, he zoomed in to enlarge the photos he had taken. It was a long shot, given the conditions and the tree branches obscuring the view from the ground, but he thought it was worth a try. The first several photos were worthless and he quickly moved through the series, but then caught a break.

"Look at this one—tell me what you see," Keller said, handing Mia the phone.

"Oh, yeah, there's no doubt," responded Mia, shaking her head.

"Jesus, but how in the hell . . . ?" Jack replied, looking up at the tree. He stopped when he heard voices back at the tent.

"Sounds like Larry Voss and the CSI team has arrived. Let's get over there and figure out the best way to proceed."

Mia and Keller started the trek back to the tent.

Before they reached the others, Mia turned to Keller and said, "Nice one using the zoom feature on the camera. Very MacGyver of you."

"Thanks, Mia. That's the nicest thing anyone's said to me all day."

Larry Voss was a highly capable member of the RCSO Major Crimes Unit. For several years he had worked with Mia Serrano in the Traffic Investigations Unit, but with her ascent into Major Crimes, he happily made the move with her. It meant a little more money in his paycheck, but more importantly it gave him a sense of purpose, something he could point to with pride—he was part of the elite Major Crimes Unit—often coordinating the efforts of the crime scene crew. As a widower with no children, the RCSO was pretty much his whole life.

The group turned their attention toward Keller and Serrano as they approached.

Keller motioned to everyone to gather together.

"We need to call the medical examiner and have them respond. And let's get an ETA for the ladder truck. We've got ourselves what looks like a dead body some forty feet up a pine tree. Gonna be a challenge, but let's pull together and get it done. Right now we need to get some light on those trees down there. If a couple of you CSI guys could set up the portable lights, that would be hugely helpful."

Larry Voss nodded at Keller and motioned to two of the CSI techs. They headed off to get the lights set up.

Phillips responded, "I'll handle the fire department and the ME."

Serrano answered, "Thanks, Len, and I think we're going to need the command post vehicle out here. Would you mind giving them a call?"

"Not at all."

Turning her attention toward the Heath brothers, Mia said, "I'm sorry, but you'll need to pack up all your things. We'll have one of our deputies take you wherever you'd like to go for the evening."

The Heath brothers both nodded but didn't speak.

"Deputy Kowalski, can I have you handle that, please? Take them back into town to find a hotel, or wherever else they want to go. You are at their service."

"Sure, no problem."

"Gentlemen, I'm sorry you had to experience this. But thank you for your cooperation."

The brothers began gathering up their things and taking down the tent.

A few minutes later, Sergeant Phillips walked back toward the group. "I spoke with the fire battalion chief in Castle Springs and he said the ladder truck has been dispatched. I also called the ME and their ETA is an hour. The command post will also be coming out, but their ETA is a little longer, probably about two hours."

"Okay, that all works," Keller confirmed.

Once the Heath brothers had gathered all their supplies and climbed into Kowalski's patrol car, Keller turned toward the group.

"Okay, listen up everybody. This scene is going to be a huge challenge. We've got the terrain, the darkness, and the difficulty of a body forty feet up a tree. Evidence could be all around us, and given the situation, there could be evidence for miles around—we just don't know yet. It'll be virtually impossible to find everything, but that doesn't mean we won't try. Normally, we draw a perimeter around a crime scene and focus all of our attention inside that perimeter. Here, we have something different. Tonight and until daybreak, let's focus our attention on the trees where we have the body, and leave the surrounding area as undisturbed as possible. Tomorrow morning when we have sunlight we'll have our Explorer Scouts come out and help canvass the area. Now, once the fire truck gets here, Mia and I will go up the ladder and see exactly what we've got. The ME won't want anyone touching the body, but we can do visuals and see if there's anything obvious. Once they arrive, they'll want to take over the scene, at least initially, to do their thing. Does that work for everybody?"

"How do we know it's a crime scene at this point?" asked one of the CSI techs.

Keller responded, "We don't know for sure, but people don't just die up in trees. At the very least, we've got a suspicious death, and that's something Major Crimes always takes a look at anyway. I think we should know more when we get a close-up look at our vic. And if that doesn't tell us what we need to know, then the autopsy should give us some answers."

The faint sound of a siren could be heard in the distance. The group fell silent for a moment as they listened to the siren approaching.

Keller continued, "The fire department is almost here. Sergeant Phillips, we'll need for you to keep your deputy stationed at the dirt road entrance. We don't need any looky-loos coming up here. Which reminds me—we need to use band two for all of our communications tonight, or use your cell phones. We're lucky we have service, given the remoteness of the area. There's probably a cell tower on one of the mountaintops around here. The last thing we need is for the media to get wind of any of this; they'd have a field day with it and we just don't need the extra hassle. But, just in case, I'll call Mark Archer and have him respond to the scene."

Mark Archer was the media relations officer for the RCSO. His job was to communicate with reporters on significant events that occurred within the RCSO jurisdiction. If the media heard about a body in a tree there would no doubt be a huge amount of interest. Archer routinely responded to crime scenes and having him there in the event that word leaked out was a prudent strategy.

Mia looked down the dirt road and could see the headlights of the fire truck. "I'll go down and meet them and direct them to the tree."

Mia walked down the dirt path and flagged down the truck. She spoke to the firefighter riding shotgun.

"I'm Mia Serrano from the RCSO. Thanks for coming out tonight; we appreciate the assist."

"Sure, no problem. I'm Captain Nick Juarez. My chief says you've got a possible DB in a tree. Did I understand that right?"

"Yeah, a couple of backpackers called it in. Said there was a very foul odor coming from some trees and so our Major Crimes Unit responded. My partner and I did an initial look but it's tough to see through the branches and now the darkness. We were able to see what we believe is a human leg and foot. Your truck will let us to get up close and see exactly what we've got."

"Lucky you."

Mia ignored the comment.

"How high up can we go on that ladder?"

"About sixty feet or so, provided we can find somewhat level ground to park the truck. If it's really uneven then not quite as high."

"Looks like the body is about forty feet off the ground."

"Shouldn't be a problem. Who'll be going up in the bucket?"

"My partner and me initially, and then, depending on what we find, we'll have the medical examiner go up afterwards."

"I'd be happy to go up with you if you think that might help," responded Juarez with a smile.

Jesus, firefighters are all the same, thought Mia as she dismissed the offer.

"No, thanks. My partner and I can handle it."

"Okay, if you change your mind, just let me know. I do this kind of thing all the time."

"You put your ladder truck into pine trees to examine dead bodies on a regular basis, do you?" Mia replied, in an effort to cool off the young firefighter.

"Well, no—not exactly."

"We need the truck down by the trees that are lit up over there," Mia continued, moving the conversation forward.

"Okay, I'll see what we can do."

Once the fire truck was in place the ladder with the bucket was lowered to the ground so Mia and Keller could climb aboard. Both did their best to hide their discomfort being together in such tight quarters. Soon they were lifted from the ground and the bucket began climbing through the air. Once they were at the correct height, Mia motioned to Captain Juarez to move the bucket toward the tree. She and Keller could hear the gears shift from the truck as the bucket moved inch by inch into the branches of the tree. Both she and Keller trained their lights into the tree, hoping to locate the body, being careful to shield their faces from the branches as they moved closer.

Mia had seen plenty of bad things over the course of her life, but this experience gave her the willies. She wasn't sure if it was the darkness or the more obvious issue—she was very likely to encounter a dead body in a pine tree.

"There, follow my light," said Keller, interrupting her thoughts.

Mia composed herself, moved her beam over to where Keller was pointing his—and then she saw it.

CHAPTER 4

Jonathan Timbers had hardly slept the past three nights, and when he did manage to sleep, it was filled with nightmares about Vanessa. He wasn't sure which was worse—lying awake thinking about her, or dreaming about her once he drifted off. Thinking about her while awake was probably better—at least he had some control over his thoughts, unlike the terrifying stuff going on in his nightmares.

His wife, Diane, had no idea what he was going through. How could she? She was blissfully unaware of the relationship her husband of twelve years had been having with the young and beautiful Vanessa. Diane had only met her once, at Jonathan's office Christmas party some nine months earlier. She had certainly noticed her; Vanessa was hard to miss. Jonathan had made the introduction, but he had introduced his wife to everyone they encountered that night at the Denver Four Seasons Hotel. Diane certainly didn't pick up on any vibes between the two, and the subject of Jonathan's co-worker had not come up since.

But now his world was caving in and he felt like a tiger in a cage. He was perspiring heavily on the hot August Colorado night, and his mind was racing, trying to determine the best course of action. He was working through all the possible scenarios in his head, playing the what-if game. He needed to be ready for what was coming next, because he knew it wasn't a matter of *if*, but rather a matter of *when*.

Mia gasped and grabbed Keller's arm. The sudden movement caused the bucket to shift and they both fell heavily against one side, pinning Keller between Mia and the wall of the bucket. She immediately righted herself and apologized to Keller for the fall. He didn't respond, but quietly turned his attention back to the subject at hand. Mia was embarrassed; she didn't need to have Keller see her flinch—it was an unwritten rule among homicide investigators: don't let your emotions get in the way. But what hung in that tree, not five feet from them, was enough to make anyone flinch. Except Jack Keller.

The victim was young, white, and female. She appeared to be almost sitting in the tree, in a primarily vertical position, with her legs straddling a large, thick limb. She was naked, except for a very tattered pair of black panties. Most of the panties were gone, and what remained was in shreds. The woman's body was covered in dried blood that had turned a brown color. There were patches of hair missing from her head, apparently torn from her scalp. Her eyeballs were both gone, leaving deep, hollow sockets.

Mia had seen enough and turned her attention to the tree itself, looking closely at the branches around the victim's body. Keller didn't speak, but took out his phone, activated the flash, and began snapping photos of the body, zooming in on various parts of her body. Mia noted that many smaller tree branches above the victim were broken, and that the young woman was actually suspended in the tree on the large limb. The limb likely had kept the woman from falling through to the ground.

From Mia's perspective the evidence was clear: the victim entered the tree from above. She didn't climb up the tree; she somehow fell into it. Mia was interested in hearing Keller's thoughts, but he was busy snapping away. The two stayed in the tree for several more minutes while Keller took more photos. Finally, he turned to Mia. "I'm about done. Is there anything else you want to do while we're up here?"

"No, I think we can let the CSI team and the ME take things from here."

"Agreed."

Keller looked down from the bucket and waved at the fire captain. "We're ready to come down now."

A few seconds later, the gears on the truck engaged and the ladder began moving Keller and Mia away from the tree. Once the bucket was on the ground Keller climbed out first and then gave Mia an assist as she crawled out.

"Well, any luck up there?" asked Captain Juarez.

Keller responded, "Yeah, I guess you could say that. We're going to need your truck the rest of the night and into tomorrow, possibly. Can you check with your superiors and make sure they're okay with that?"

Juarez looked at Keller and then at Mia. "Sure. I'll give them a call." The tone of the cocky young firefighter had turned somewhat solemn as the weight of the situation sunk in.

Keller turned to Mia. "Let's head back and brief the team on what we found."

"We'll be back once the ME arrives," Mia said to Juarez.

"Okay. I'll be here."

Keller and Serrano didn't speak as they walked up the hill toward the command area. It was important to develop their own ideas and theories about what they had seen before sharing their thoughts with each other. This reduced the chances that either would be swayed unnecessarily by the other's observations. It was a common investigative strategy, much like separating witnesses of a crime. A good investigator would always interview witnesses separately to hear each person's unique perspective before the witness could be persuaded by someone else's viewpoint. It's human nature to be influenced by other people's accounts of an event that person witnessed firsthand. The tendency is to abandon or at least question one's own memory of events if someone else who witnessed the same event remembers it differently. This rarely helps an investigation.

"Do you want some more time before we brief the others?" Keller asked.

"No, I'm good. Let's fill 'em in."

As Keller and Serrano reached the top of the hill, they could see the ME's white van parked several yards away from the group. Mark Archer had also arrived and was talking with Larry Voss.

"We can include Archer and the ME in our debrief," offered Mia.

As they approached, everyone zeroed in on Keller and Serrano.

"All right. Mia and I will fill you in on what we've got so far. Mia, you want to start?"

"Go ahead, Jack. I'll follow you," Mia responded, offering the senior investigator the floor.

"Okay, we've got a deceased white female suspended about forty feet up in a pine tree. She looks to be in her twenties and is essentially straddling a pretty good-sized branch. The branch appears to have broken her fall, otherwise she would likely have hit the ground. She's naked except for a very torn pair of black underwear. She's pretty bloodied, but we weren't close enough to determine if the blood came from a specific wound or wounds. The blood could just be superficial—scrapes and scratches from falling through the branches of the tree. It's just too early to tell. There are chunks of hair missing from her scalp and both of her eyes are gone. I don't think she's been in the tree all that long—there isn't much decomp taking place. All in all, it's like a scene out of some fucking horror movie."

Mia took the reins. "I saw it the same way Jack did, and don't have much to add about the condition of the body, but I did note some things about the tree branches around her. The branches immediately above her are broken, indicating that she entered the tree from above. That could mean a lot of things, but it does eliminate—at least in my mind—the possibility that our victim climbed up into the tree. I mean, that may sound obvious to all of you, but how she got into that tree is going to be a crucial piece of the puzzle. She entered from above and in all likelihood came down onto that tree with a significant amount of force—enough force to break a lot of branches. So you think of all the obvious things—did she fall from a plane? Is this a skydiving accident? If it's an accident, then where is the failed parachute? And why wouldn't the pilot or whoever report it to authorities? Obviously, it's too early to know what exactly we have here, but I think it's very likely we will find some clothes in the area, unless stuff fell into other trees in the area and is stuck in the branches. So a canvass of the area will be really critical."

Keller stepped in. "Voss, can you contact dispatch and see if there were any missing persons reports filed over the past ten days or so? I seriously doubt she's been in the tree that long, based on the level of decomposition, but let's go back that far to be safe. Also, have them run a query to see if the department received any calls about any possible skydiving incidents over the same time period. I think we would've heard about it if someone called something like that in, but let's check just to be sure. Also, could you let Commander Espy know we'd like to have as many police Explorer Scouts as possible out here first thing tomorrow morning to assist with the canvass?"

"Sure, no problem," Larry responded.

Mia turned to Archer, who had arrived a few minutes earlier.

"Mark, have there been any inquiries from the media?"

"No, nothing at all. There was a double-fatality traffic collision earlier tonight off I-25 and so their attention is focused on that for the time being. But make no mistake about it—if they get wind of this case, they'll be all over it."

"Thank God for small favors," quipped Keller.

Archer, a twenty-five year veteran of RCSO, understood Keller's acerbic sense of humor. They had worked closely together on more than two dozen homicide cases. Keller did the detective work and Archer kept the media at bay. The last thing the RCSO needed was Keller talking to the media—not that he'd ever give a reporter the time of day. It was a good arrangement and Keller, loath to trust anyone, did trust Archer.

The two had an understanding of what information could be released to the media and what needed to be played close to the vest.

Mia turned to the ME.

"Dr. Mora, it's great to have you out here tonight. It's not often we get the ME himself responding to our crime scenes."

"No problem, Mia. I take a couple of shifts each month, just to keep my hand in the game. I gotta say this case seems a bit more intriguing than most of the cases we usually handle. Looking forward to helping out in any way I can."

"Thanks for the support, Doc," answered Mia.

Keller jumped in. "You ready to go down and check out what we've got? You can do your thing if you're ready."

"Yes, that sounds good. Let me get my stuff, and—oh, let me introduce Becky Placer. She's a new tech in our office."

Placer, a woman in her mid-thirties, nodded at the group and everyone offered a quick hello before Mora and Placer collected their gear and headed down to the trees with Keller.

Larry Voss made his calls to dispatch and reported that there had been no missing persons report filed with the department in the past ten days. Nor had there been any calls regarding possible skydiving accidents in the county.

After Keller returned, he suggested to Mia that most of the RCSO personnel on scene be released so they could go home and get some rest. It was nearly midnight and there wasn't much more anyone could do until morning. It would take some time to get the body out of the tree. Mia agreed and told everyone to return at six the next morning so they could start canvassing the area. Jack asked Sergeant Phillips to keep patrol personnel at the dirt road and requested at least two deputies be assigned to protect the integrity of the crime scene.

Finally, after more than two hours of effort and the assistance of several fire and sheriff's personnel, Dr. Mora placed the body of the young victim into the back of the ME van.

"Can we get an expedite on the autopsy?" asked Keller.

Mora looked at his watch. "It's almost three now. It's Sunday so I've got nothing scheduled for today—how about I open her up when we get back to the office. Does that work for you guys?"

"That would be a huge help. How much time do you need before you get started on her?" asked Keller.

"Give us a couple hours. Meet at five?"

Jack looked at Mia and she nodded.

"That'll work. See you then."

After Placer and Mora left, Jack turned to Mia. "We've got the cut at five and our guys will be back here at six to start the canvas. Voss can get them started and we can come back out here once the autopsy is complete. Meanwhile, I'm hungry—you want to grab some breakfast back in town and talk about where we go from here?"

"Yeah, that sounds good. I can drive if you'd like—no need to take two cars."

Keller nodded. They climbed into Mia's unit and drove back to town. They found a coffee shop that was open all night and grabbed a booth near the back. Mia allowed Jack to take the seat facing the front of the restaurant, knowing it was instinctive for him to want to keep an eye on what was happening in the place, although 3:30 in the morning wasn't exactly a high-traffic time for the coffee shop. While it was a bit uncomfortable for Mia to have her back toward the door, she would deal with it. She wasn't going to slide into the booth next to Jack—it could give people the impression they were a couple, and they were anything but that.

The waitress came over offering coffee and they quickly pushed their empty cups in her direction. Both had been awake for nearly twenty-four hours and they knew they quite possibly had another full day ahead with no sleep. As homicide investigators, they were used to the grind, but that didn't make it easy. Keller was sixty-three years old, but adrenalin always kept him going.

Mia, more than twenty years younger than Keller, was confident she could keep pace with him. She knew if she didn't, Keller would leave her in his dust, and she wasn't going to let that happen.

Once the waitress poured their coffee and left the table, Mia looked at Keller. "So, what do you think?"

"I need to hear what the ME has to say, but in my mind it's clearly a homicide and when the victim is young and female, it's generally a crime of passion. Pissed off boyfriend or husband—something along those lines."

Mia nodded in agreement. Young females weren't often victims of homicide, but when they were, it was almost always at the hands of someone they knew.

"So how did she get in the tree?" Mia asked, looking at Keller from across the table. It was the million-dollar question.

"I think your earlier observations were spot on. With the broken branches above her, she most likely did fall into that tree. But with no skydiving accidents being called in, and with no missing persons report filed, who knows. The most likely scenario is she was pushed out of a plane and landed where she landed."

Mia did her best to hide a shudder. The thought of being pushed out of a plane and having your last moments filled with terror was almost too much to comprehend. She hoped to herself that the young woman was already dead when she was pushed out.

She continued, "Any chance her killer put her in the tree? Killed her somewhere else then decided to ditch the body by hiding her in a tree forty feet off the ground where no one would likely find her for a long, long time?"

"I guess that's a possibility, but it would take the cake. I mean, the killer would get an A-plus for ingenuity, at least in my book. The problem with that theory is that we didn't see any evidence of it tonight. When we have some daylight we can take a closer look at the tree. If someone did that there should be plenty of blood evidence. And the other problem with that theory is how would someone physically do that? She didn't look like a large woman based on what we saw, but getting even a relatively small person up a tree? I don't think that's a one-person job. So, unless they called Captain Juarez and had him bring out his ladder truck, I don't think it's very likely."

Mia jumped in, "Hopefully the autopsy will tell us more."

The conversation came to a stop as the waitress brought the food they had ordered. Jack and Mia started in on their omelets and didn't speak for several minutes. Mia broke the silence. "So, the Scott Lennox trial starts in a couple weeks."

Keller continued working on his omelet.

She hadn't talked to him about the case for months, but the DA was ready and things would be soon underway. Both she and Keller would be on the stand testifying during the trial and Mia had some significant concerns. Both knew the case would attract a lot of attention. A couple of Denver-area news stations had expressed interest in covering the proceedings gavel to gavel. It would be the biggest trial in Rocklin County history and would certainly shine a huge spotlight on the RCSO and their handling of the case. Mia wanted things to go well, not only for her and the case, but for her boyfriend, the newly-elected sheriff of the RCSO.

It was clear that Keller wasn't interested in discussing the case, so she sat quietly and finished her omelet.

CHAPTER 5

The Rocklin County morgue was located in a nondescript, bunker-like building in Castle Springs, just a half mile from the RCSO Justice Center. It looked nothing like the morgues featured on television crime shows, lacking the fancy lighting and high-tech equipment often displayed in the glossy world of television crime dramas. But the facility was highly functional and Dr. Mora and his staff cranked out nearly two hundred autopsies a year. To an outside observer an autopsy could look like a violent assault on a body, but to the physicians who performed them and the investigators who witnessed them, it was a fascinating look into the science of the human body.

Dr. Mora and Becky Placer were waiting for Mia and Jack when they tapped on the entrance door. It was still still dark and well before normal working hours. Mora unlocked the door and let the two in.

" Come on in, guys. We're ready to go."

"Thanks again for doing the cut so quickly, Doc. We appreciate it."

"No problem, Jack. I know you guys want to get a jump on this case and with the Labor Day weekend we'd have to wait till Tuesday otherwise."

Dr. Mora pointed to a small room adjacent to the autopsy tables. "Grab some coveralls in there—you know the routine. Join me when you're ready."

A few minutes later, Keller and Mia joined Dr. Mora at table number three. There, laid out on her back, was the body of their young victim. The overhead lights beamed down on the woman, who was sprawled naked, face up. The environment of the autopsy room was sterile, with harsh lighting and hard, stainless steel surfaces. It didn't offer the opportunity for anyone to look their best, but if you were lying on one of the tables, you probably had bigger things to worry about. Even with the harshness of the room, both Jack and Mia could see that this young woman had been quite beautiful.

Keller took out his cell phone and snapped some photos of the victim as Dr. Mora began to speak.

"First off, before we get started with the procedure, let me run down my findings so far. The general condition of the body and the blowfly larvae found on her body show that she has been dead for twenty-four to thirty-six hours. I was able to do a preliminary examination of her body before you arrived and could find no obvious wounds typically inflicted by a knife or firearm. She definitely has some broken bones, but we won't know the extent of those injuries until we open her up. But the most telling thing I found pre-cut was a ruptured femoral artery, probably from the force of hitting that limb that we found her on. Her arrival onto that limb was not a gentle one—she hit it with enough force to cause the artery to rupture, so there is zero chance she went up into that tree and sat on that limb. As you know, a ruptured femoral artery can be fatal very quickly. With an injury such as this, the body could lose virtually all its blood in about five minutes. Here, I can show you."

Dr. Mora directed their attention to the victim's groin area, pointing out the wound.

Keller jumped in. "If she bled out that quickly, and lost all that blood—there should be blood in the tree or on the ground below, correct?"

"Yes, but keep in mind that the blood could be over a wide area. On the limb where we found her, down the trunk of the tree, on the ground; and no doubt with the way animals forage, they could have disturbed the blood as well. Which brings me to her hair and eyes."

Dr. Mora moved toward the top of the table and motioned for Keller and Mia to join him there. He pointed to the victim's head. "There are clumps of hair missing from the victim's scalp. These clumps were almost certainly plucked from her head by birds. This is not uncommon at all; I've seen it in many cases where a body is found outdoors. Birds pluck the hair and use it for their nests. It works much better than pine needles and the other stuff they use. Now, both eyeballs are missing as well. Again, you can blame birds for that. You might be surprised to learn that eyeballs are very high in protein and the birds will consume them. Again, something we see with some frequency in bodies discovered outdoors."

Mia looked at Jack and shook her head slightly. More than she wanted to know. She could feel her breakfast stirring in her stomach.

Dr. Mora caught her gesture. "Gross, I know. But it's all just nature and the way things work in the wild. These things both happened postmortem, so obviously she didn't feel anything."

Mora grabbed the overhead magnifying glass suspended above the table. He moved it close to the victim's eye sockets.

"Look closely and you can see small wounds around each socket. This is where the birds used their beaks to pick the eyes out. Again, not unusual."

Both Mia and Jack looked through the magnifying glass and could see very small wounds with droplets of blood around the sockets.

Mia had seen enough and quickly changed the subject.

"Anything under her fingernails indicating she might have been in a physical struggle before she died?" asked Mia.

"No, which makes me wonder if she was even conscious when she left the plane."

Mia chimed in, "For her sake, I hope she wasn't. So, the blood on the other parts of her body—is that just from superficial cuts and scratches?"

"Yes, most likely from the branches as she plummeted through the tree, prior to hitting the limb which stopped her fall. There's nothing substantial there; it's just as you described, Mia."

"Makes sense," added Jack.

"Now, there was another interesting thing I discovered about our young victim."

"And what was that, Doc?"

"Look here, at her hair, and on her arms and upper chest—I know it's difficult to see because of all the dried blood—but look really closely . . . there, do you see it?" Mora asked, pointing to a patch of hair.

"Yeah, I do . . . is that glitter?" asked Mia.

"Yes, I believe it is. I took several samples from her body and I'll have the lab run tests on it, but yes—I would say that it's very likely glitter."

"What the hell?" asked Keller.

Dr. Mora continued, "I've seen this a few times before with young female victims. Evidently, putting a little glitter on your body and in your hair is something many young women do, especially when they are in a party environment."

Mia nodded at the doctor, while Keller just shook his head.

"Wow, Jack. I think you need to get out more. Do a little clubbing, big guy . . . live a little," Mia teased.

"You know, I feel a little bit older every day."

Mora smiled and continued, "It does suggest that our victim was possibly doing a little partying on her last night. We should know more about that when I get her blood results back. They'll tell us if she had any alcohol in her system when she died. I've requested a full blood panel work up on her, which will also tell us if she had any drugs in her system at the time of death."

"And you think the TOD was maybe two days ago or so?" asked Mia.

"Yes. Based on what I see with the blowfly larvae . . . that's about right."

"That would put us around Friday, then. That could fit: our vic goes out and does a little partying to start the weekend," continued Mia.

Both men nodded.

"How about an age for our Jane Doe?" asked Keller. He found the older he got, the more difficult it was to determine someone's age, especially if they were young.

"I'd say about thirty. Just a guess, but I'd say that's about right," responded Mora.

"How about the panties?" asked Keller

"Well, there's not much left to them and the part that was still there didn't have a label. I checked them for semen, but found nothing. That doesn't mean she didn't have sex right before her death, it just means any semen that typically leaks onto the panties was simply not there given the shredded condition of the panties. The autopsy will give us a more definitive answer on that. I did ask Becky last night for her opinion about the panties, if she saw anything unique or telling about them."

"And . . . ?" asked Keller.

"Nothing. . . just looked like a regular pair of woman's panties to her. So I don't think they'll be much of a lead for you."

"Bummer," sighed Mia.

"Hopefully, the canvass we do this morning produces some articles of clothing. Our victim sure as hell had more on than this at the start of her day," added Keller.

"You would think so," replied Mora.

It was shortly after eight by the time Mia and Jack left the office of the medical examiner. The autopsy had not given them much beyond what the pre-cut examination had yielded, and they still lacked the most important thing—her identity. They were also very interested in getting the results of the blood tests Dr. Mora had run, but those would take a few days.

"Let's drop the prints off at the station before we head back to check on the canvassing efforts," suggested Mia once they were back in the car.

Jack had taken the victim's fingerprints at the autopsy. With no one reporting her missing, she was essentially a Jane Doe, but they hoped that running the prints through the RCSO in-house system would reveal her identity. If she had ever been arrested by RCSO, her prints would be in the system, but if she had a clean record, they'd get nothing. They could run her prints through AFIS if necessary—the national database for fingerprints, but for now they'd start with RCSO and see where that got them.

"I called Larry Voss. He said things were going well with the canvassing. They've spread out over a half-mile area and the search has already produced a couple of things," Mia added.

"Okay, cool—we should be there in an hour or so."

They dropped the prints off at the lab at RCSO and headed back toward Samson Creek. At the dirt road cut off, a different deputy waved them under the crime scene tape and they headed toward the trees. As they approached the area, they found twenty or more RCSO units, marked and unmarked, parked in the vicinity of where the Heath brothers had pitched their tent the day before. Now, the RCSO command vehicle was parked there instead. The forty-foot long, specially-equipped motorhome would provide them with many of the tools they'd need, as well as a place they could be comfortable for meals and bathroom breaks.

"It looks like we've got a whole brigade out here to canvass," Mia observed.

"Good. We've got a lot of area to cover," Jack replied.

Keller and Mia headed over to Larry Voss, who had a clipboard in his hands.

"Hey, how'd it go with Dr. Mora?"

Mia filled Larry in on what they had learned about their Jane Doe, letting him know her fingerprints were at the station being run through the in-house system.

"Hopefully that will yield an ID on our vic; if not we'll run it through AFIS. Without an ID we're really hamstrung on the investigation," she added.

"Well, let me tell you guys what we've done so far. We have twenty-six RCSO personnel out here today doing the canvassing. It took some effort getting this many folks out here over a long weekend but we managed to find the resources. I've created a search grid spanning out in all directions from the tree where the body was found. The terrain is a bit difficult in places, so it's taking us a little longer than I'd hoped, even with all these resources. But so far we've only covered about a quarter of the area. We've found a lot of stuff, but it's difficult to know for sure what, if anything, belonged to our vic."

"Any signs of a parachute, or parts of a chute?" asked Keller.

"Nope, nothing" answered Voss.

"Okay, I think we can rule that out. I think we'd have heard about someone plummeting to their death on a failed skydiving jump. So, what did the team find?"

"Some articles of clothing, or at least parts of clothing."

"Like what?" asked Mia.

"A woman's shoe, a somewhat shredded black dress, and a gold necklace," answered Larry.

"Where are they?"

"I had the team leave them where they were found. I didn't want to further disturb the area. I wasn't sure how much investigative value there would be, but thought it was best to just mark each spot with a small flag. There—you can see one of the flags on the side of that hill over there," he explained, pointing to an area a couple hundred feet from where they were standing.

"Good. Always better to be safe than sorry," Mia affirmed.

"Anything else of interest?" interjected Keller.

"Not really, just trash that backpackers or campers might leave behind. People can be pigs."

"Let's check out the stuff your team found. Can you walk us out to them, Larry?"

"Sure, let's go."

Voss led Mia and Keller away from the command post and into the gridded area. Studying his clipboard, he directed them to the first find, a woman's shoe.

Keller took a pen from his shirt pocket and used it to pick up the shoe. He held it out for Mia to examine.

"This is probably something you're a little more familiar with than me. Looks like there's a name on the inside. Here—take a look."

Mia took hold of the pen and brought the black shoe toward her face. "Yeah, it's a Jimmy Choo pump, pretty high-end stuff."

"What does a pair of those run?" Keller asked.

"I'm not a hundred-percent sure . . . don't have any in my closet. I would guess maybe five hundred bucks a pair."

Voss gave a low whistle.

Keller took the shoe back from Mia and placed it in an evidence bag he had brought from the command post.

"What's next, Larry?"

Voss checked his clipboard. "Grid one-ninety-eight. It should be about a hundred yards from here, over in that direction," he added, pointing to an area just south of where they were standing.

The three carefully walked the hundred yards in silence. They saw another small flag stuck in the ground and zeroed in on it.

"This should be the necklace," Larry commented, looking closely at the grid layout on his clipboard.

Once again, Keller reached into his pocket for his pen and squatted down to pick up the necklace. It was broken at the clasp so he had to carefully balance it on his pen to keep it from sliding off.

"Mia?" Jack said, again extending the necklace toward her so she could take a close look.

"Nice piece of jewelry. A gold chain and a decent-size diamond.

I'm no expert, but it looks real to me, and based on the Jimmy Choos, I'd be a little surprised if our vic was wearing a cubic zirconia around her neck."

Keller dropped the necklace into another evidence bag and slipped it into his coat pocket.

"Next," Keller said.

They followed Voss for nearly a quarter mile to the next flag stuck in the ground. There they found remnants of a black dress, but it was too damaged to tell much about it. Keller bagged it and the three headed back to the command vehicle where they grabbed sandwiches and sodas, parked themselves at a conference table, and started to discuss their findings.

"Any ideas at this point, Jack?"

"One possibility is that our victim is a high-end call girl. Picked the wrong john, possibly. Or, who knows, maybe she had a boyfriend and he found out what she was doing in her spare time."

"I had the same thought," Mia added, thinking about the beautiful young woman splayed out on the stainless steel table at the ME's office just a few hours earlier.

"Our vic was beautiful, and the high-end shoes and jewelry lend themselves to that theory. And the fact that no one has called her in as missing . . . " Mia's voice trailed, "that fits the prostitute angle as well."

"If her prints aren't in our system, that blows a little bit of a hole in our theory," Jack noted. "Unless she's new to the profession and hadn't been arrested at this point for plying her trade."

Mia replied, "High-end girls don't do street corners; it's all an Internet game now. The client picks out one he likes from some X-rated website and they send her right over. There's way less chance for police contact, so a lot of these girls can go a long time without any scrapes with the law. Just keep your customer happy, take the money, pay a thirty- or forty-percent charge to the Internet madam, and move on to the next one."

Keller responded, "Well, unless she's got rich parents or a sugar daddy, women her age aren't usually wearing shoes that run five bills. The call girl angle seems the most likely, at least at this point. Let's hope we get a hit on her prints. In fact, I'll give Bobbi a call right now, she's the on-duty records clerk today . . . see if she's got good news for us."

Keller dialed the number to RCSO and asked for Bobbi Hogan. Mia sat quietly eating her turkey and cheese sandwich. She was starting to fade; she had been up for nearly thirty-six hours. The adrenalin rush you got from handling a homicide call-out lasted only so long.

"Hey, Bobbi, this is Keller. Did you have a chance to run those prints yet? Oh, great—what did you find?"

Keller hung up the phone and looked at Mia.

"We got nothing. No prints in our in-house, so Bobbi's going to run it through AFIS."

Mia looked at Keller. "Could be she's not from this area. If she fell into that tree from the sky then something in the air dropped her there. Just because she landed in a tree in our county doesn't mean she's from here. She could have taken off from anywhere and just happened to land within RCSO jurisdiction."

"Lucky us."

"So, what else do you want to get done today?'

"Until we get an ID we're flying blind. I say if Bobbi comes back with something then we push ahead into the evening and night. If she comes up empty then maybe we should call it a day and get some rest, then hit it big time tomorrow morning."

"Sounds good."

Both sat and finished their sandwiches without talking.

"Hey, we found something," said Larry Voss, peeking his head inside the command vehicle.

"What is it?" asked Mia.

"A bracelet. The cool thing is that it's got a couple of initials dangling from it."

Mia and Keller stood up from the table, tossed their sandwich wrappers in the trash, and headed out of the command post.

"Where is it?"

"It's in grid three-oh-eight, which isn't far from here. Come on, I'll walk you down."

The three headed back out toward the trees and quickly arrived at 308, where another small flag marked the spot. Jack removed the pen from his shirt pocket, crouched down, and used it to scoop up the bracelet. He held it up for him and Mia to examine.

"Looks like gold. Matches the necklace we found earlier."

Mia responded, "Yeah, and the initials hanging from it look like a T and a V. So, it's possible our victim has the initials T.V. or V.T., or it could be the initials of someone special in her life—possibly kids, or a husband or boyfriend—who knows."

"So, it's really of marginal help at this point; although if we get a positive hit on the prints it could help confirm her ID," Keller added.

He took out a plastic evidence bag and dropped the bracelet inside just as his cell began to ring. He glanced at the caller ID and saw it was Bobbi calling from RCSO.

"Hey, Bobbi. Got some good news for me?"

"I wish I did, Jack. I came up with nothing. I'm sorry."

"Damn. All right, thanks for running it . . . we appreciate it."

Jack clicked out of the call and looked at Mia.

"Nothing in AFIS either. How about we call it a day?" he said to her.

"Okay. Let's get an early start tomorrow and figure out where to go next."

Jack nodded and the three headed back to the command post.

CHAPTER 6

It was just after four in the afternoon when Mia arrived home. A hot shower, a quick dinner, and some time with Mick—that was the plan, she thought. She and Mick hadn't had a chance to have dinner the night before since she was tied up at the crime scene all night. She was exhausted so she and Mick had agreed that he'd come over and have dinner at her house. She knew it would be a struggle to stay awake for more than a few hours but she missed her boyfriend and wanted to see him.

"Hey, stranger—been a bit busy, have we?"

Mia looked up and saw her father, Chuck, standing in the kitchen as she walked in. Sasha, Mia's Jack Russell/Beagle mix was eating from the bowl near where Chuck was standing. Sasha hardly looked up when Mia entered—nothing came between her and her food at dinnertime. The dog was the definition of a chow hound.

"Hi, Dad. Yeah, it's been a crazy twenty-four hours. God, I feel grungy—I'm going to run up and take a shower. I'll figure out dinner when I come back downstairs."

"Want me to get something started? I can whip up some pasta and a salad if that sounds okay to you."

"That would be fabulous, Dad. Mick will be joining us," she replied and moved in to give her dad a quick hug.

"No problem at all. We've got some leftover sauce I can use, and—hell—even I can boil the water for the pasta. And you know what a wicked salad I make."

Mia smiled. It was great having her dad living with her. Mia's mother had died several years earlier and it had been very difficult for Chuck. He moved in with Mia, his only child, a year after the death and it worked out well. When Mia started dating Mick, her father was thrilled, and the two men had grown very close. Mick's dad walked out on the family when he was eight years old, leaving his mom to raise him and his younger brother. Chuck was like the father Mick had never had and Chuck considered Mick to be the son he had always wanted.

"So what kind of case did you catch yesterday?" asked Chuck.

Mia often discussed details of cases with her dad. He proved to be a great sounding board for her thoughts and theories as she put together her strategy for working homicides. She knew discussing cases with her father wasn't in keeping with RCSO policy, but she felt there was more upside than downside to talking with him. Chuck had spent more than thirty years in the aerospace field before he retired and was a graduate of Caltech in California. He was a brilliant scientist and his logical approach to things often helped Mia sort through her investigations. The only time there had been an issue was during the Scott Lennox case, when Chuck had tailed Jack Keller, who was teamed up with Mia to work the case. Mia had serious concerns about her partner's conduct during the investigation, and Chuck put a GPS tracking device on Keller's truck. That led to Chuck following Keller and a confrontation between the two that took place in a supermarket parking lot. Things between Mia and Jack had gotten off to a rocky start, and the fact that Chuck had followed him hadn't helped the situation.

"A homicide," responded Mia. "I'm teaming up with Keller again on it."

Chuck looked at Mia and didn't say anything. They were both thinking the same thing.

"And you never told Mick what Keller did during the Scott Lennox investigation?"

"No, Dad, I didn't. I don't like keeping things from him, but I really think it's for the best. If he knew, it would place him in an untenable position, and as the newly-elected sheriff I just don't want to burden him with it."

"But Mia, what if it gets out somehow? It would undermine not only Mick, but it could have a huge impact on the Lennox trial. If his attorney ever learned about the relationship between Keller and the woman turning state's evidence . . . well, I think we both know what could happen."

"I know all that, Dad. But if Mick doesn't know then he won't have to deal with it. The case will just proceed to trial and it won't be an issue. The important thing is that Scott Lennox pays for his crime. If I keep what happened to myself, then justice will be served."

Chuck looked at his daughter and knew it was useless to push it. The two had already had this conversation countless times. She had made up her mind, so he dropped it.

Keller had every intention of heading straight home after leaving the crime scene, but as he came back through Castle Springs he decided he'd stop by the station and see if their sketch artist might be working.

Scott Berman was a veteran RCSO deputy who worked sex crimes cases. He spent a great deal of his time on the internet posing as a thirteen-year-old girl. It had earned him the nickname "Tiffany" among his co-workers—the alias he used when trolling for perverts on various social media sites. Keller knew Berman often worked odd hours—perverts didn't just troll for underage kids Monday through Friday, so he often worked weekends and evenings. Berman had been working this detail for nearly a year and was looking forward to moving on to his next assignment. At first he found it interesting and satisfying, taking child molesters off the streets. But after a while it became tedious and downright depressing. His kids were all grown but he shuddered to think about the minefield that kids today faced—so many predators looking to take advantage. Maybe there were just as many when his kids were young, but somehow he doubted it; it seemed to him the numbers were much higher now. He had no empirical data, just anecdotal evidence.

In addition to his sex crimes assignment, he also served as the RCSO sketch artist. The department didn't have the need for a full-time artist; only the largest law enforcement agencies employed someone full time in that role. He was called upon when the need arose, typically a dozen or so times a year. He had always been artistic, and when that talent had been discovered by the RCSO brass some fifteen years earlier, he was sent off to a two-week seminar to learn how to be a sketch artist. He was very good at it and enjoyed a high success rate with his drawings. His shining moment in the role had come a dozen years earlier when he drew a picture of a suspect in a cold case. A six-year-old girl had witnessed the murder of her mother and and nearly twenty years later, after getting past some suppressed memory issues, had described the suspect to Berman. The rendering he provided was circulated among law enforcement personnel throughout the state and within a week they had a suspect in custody. His skills became legendary in Colorado.

Keller was in luck—Berman was at his desk.

"Hey, Jack. Heard you caught an interesting case last night. A body in a tree, is that right?" Berman asked when Keller showed up at his desk.

"Yeah, that's why I'm here. Our victim is a Jane Doe right now. She had no ID and we've had no luck running her prints through the system. I attended the autopsy this morning and took several photos of her. If I send them to you, would it be possible for you to draw her up? The face is missing her eyeballs and some hair, but other than that I think there's enough for you to go on. If you can do that we can get the drawing out to the press and see if someone recognizes her and comes forward with an ID."

"Sure, I can probably have something for you in a couple hours."

"That'd be great, but look—I'm running on no sleep right now, so I'm heading home. If you could just get it to me by the morning that would work fine. I'm working the case with Mia Serrano; she and I are going to hit it hard again tomorrow."

"Sure, Jack. No problem at all."

"Thanks. I'll email you the photos. I really appreciate it."

When Jack arrived home he popped a frozen dinner in the microwave and grabbed a tall can of caffeine-free soda from the fridge. He was exhausted and didn't need anything keeping him awake.

He sat at the kitchen table and watched as the microwave timer counted down. He thought about the case that had kept him going for nearly twenty-four straight hours. It was unusual, that much was clear. He had never handled anything like it during his time at St. Louis PD—a career that had spanned nearly three decades. He had now been at RCSO for over a decade, returning to law enforcement after being forced to retire by the brass in St. Louis when his drinking had spun out of control. The drinking, which had always been a struggle, had become his crutch following a divorce. It wasn't until the death of his teenage son, Brian, in a drunk driving accident, that he was able to give up the bottle. He had been sober for more than ten years.

A little after six o'clock, Mia heard Mick pull his car into the driveway and went out on to the porch to greet him. She was feeling better after her shower, but exhaustion was quickly setting in.

Mick didn't say anything as he stepped onto the porch, but just extended his arms toward her. She folded herself against his chest and just enjoyed the moment.

"God, I could stay right here forever," she said, with her head resting against him.

The two had been dating steadily for fifteen months, and their relationship was exclusive. Both felt marriage was in the future, but with the Lennox case and then Mick's election to the position of sheriff, things had been so hectic they hadn't had time to do much else. They maintained separate living quarters, with Mia living in Castle Springs with her dad, and Mick at his home in the mountains a few miles away.

They let go of their embrace and walked into the house. Chuck was there in the kitchen, dressed in an apron and working on the salad.

"Hey, Mick—hungry?"

"I am. What's on the menu tonight?"

"Pasta, salad, and possibly some homemade garlic bread. Still putting that part together."

"Sounds great, Chuck. Can I help with anything?"

"No, I've got it covered. Why don't you guys just relax a bit before dinner? I'll call you when it's ready . . . should be about twenty minutes."

"Can I interest you in a glass of wine?" Mia asked Mick.

"Sure, that sounds great."

Mia poured a couple of glasses of pinot noir and the two headed off to the living room.

"So, tell me about the woman in the tree. I've been getting periodic updates from Commander Espy, but I want to hear more. Sounds pretty bizarre."

"Yeah, even Keller is shaking his head on this one."

"And we've got no ID on the vic?"

"Nope. Not yet, at least. She's young, white, and very pretty. Or at least she *was*."

Mick looked at Mia.

"How long had she been in the tree?"

"Dr. Mora thinks only about a day, maybe a little more, which puts her death around Friday. She was well dressed, like she had been out somewhere nice. Keller is leaning toward her being a call girl—maybe she got in with the wrong john."

"So her client didn't like her services and stuck her in a tree?" Mick conjectured with a quizzical look on his face.

"We don't think she was put in the tree, we think she fell into the tree."

"Fell into the tree? Like, from an airplane?"

"Very possibly—or a helicopter, or who the hell knows."

"I'm surprised the media hasn't jumped all over this one yet. They'll love it."

"We had Mark Archer respond to the scene but no media calls came in about it. They'll figure it out sooner or later," Mia answered.

"Yeah, no kidding. And when they do it'll go big."

Just then Chuck poked his head into the living room. "I don't want to interrupt, but dinner's ready."

The three made their way to the kitchen and grabbed their plates. They sat at the dining room table and enjoyed the pasta. Mia was in bed an hour later.

CHAPTER 7

Mia woke early the next morning and found a text message from Keller on her cell. He told her he had asked Scott Berman to do a sketch of the victim and that they should put together a plan on getting it circulated that morning. Mia stared at the screen of her phone. She couldn't help but think back to a year earlier, when a very aggravated Jack Keller blasting her for "riding solo" on the Scott Lennox investigation. It would have been nice to discuss this with her before he had asked Berman to do the sketch, she thought. It was a good idea to have him work up a headshot of the victim, but courtesy between partners would have called for him to talk with her before he commissioned Berman to do the drawing. But she didn't want to allow petty feelings get between her and Keller, so she put her thoughts aside, took a shower, and left for work. She was in her office before seven o'clock.

A few minutes after she had settled into her cubicle, she heard movement in the bullpen area. She poked her head above her partition and saw that it was Keller.

"Let me grab some coffee and then we can sit down and go over our plans for today. How about we meet in the detective conference room in five minutes?"

Mia nodded but didn't say anything. She waited a full ten minutes and then walked to meet Keller. They took seats across the table from each other.

"Berman should have the sketch of our vic by ten this morning. We need to get Mark Archer to have it circulated by the media. It won't be hard to do; the media loves a good missing-person story and our victim is a young, attractive female. They'll be all over this like white on rice."

Mia responded, "So you haven't already brought Archer in?"

"No, Mia—I wanted to meet with you this morning to set our strategy for where we go from here," Keller responded, looking at Mia for an extra second or two once he had finished his sentence. He could sense that she was a bit put off, most likely for the steps he had taken on his own in getting Berman to do the sketch drawing and not letting her know right away.

"Okay, that's fine," Mia responded with just a hint of defiance.

"Something else you want to say, Mia?"

Mia paused for a second and considered how best to respond to Keller's question. No doubt Keller knew she was peeved. She didn't want to sound like some whiny woman complaining that she hadn't been consulted. She knew putting the sketch out to the public was a good idea, so she decided to let things go, at least for now. She had made her point.

"Nope. Let's get Archer on board. What else do you think we should do today?"

"Getting her ID'd is job one. Hopefully the drawing will yield some calls. We need to figure out what phone number we should use for the public to call in on. I'm thinking we can put one of our investigative aides on the line and have them screen the calls. Monica Schoenfeld is working this weekend—maybe she could do that for us."

"I'll check with Commander Espy about it," Mia offered.

"As soon as I get the sketch from Berman I'll call Archer and brief him. Does that all work for you, Mia?"

"Yes, sir," she responded.

Yeah, Keller had gotten the message.

They parted ways and agreed to meet again in an hour to finalize their plans for the morning.

Keller walked back to his office and fired up the computer on his desk. An email with an attachment from Berman was waiting for him. He clicked on it and the message popped up.

> The sketch of your one-eighty-seven victim is attached. I guessed on the eye color, but given her skin tone and other physical characteristics I would say the likelihood of her eyes being brown is about 95% so that's what I went with. Let me know if I can be of any further help. Good luck with this one—I hope you catch the prick that did this to her.

Keller clicked on the attachment and looked at a drawing of a beautiful young woman. He studied the sketch for a half minute or so and clicked out of it. He picked up the phone and dialed Mark Archer's cell. Archer worked in the administration section of the RCSO, giving him easy and frequent access to the elected head of the RCSO. Mark Archer knew how important it was to keep his boss apprised of things going on with the media. The last thing the sheriff wanted was to be surprised. That meant giving him news—all the news, whether it was good or bad. It was far better that the sheriff heard the bad stuff from Archer before he heard it from a reporter.

After a few seconds, Archer picked up.

"Mark Archer."

"Mark, it's Keller. I need your help on the woman in the tree case. Any chance you could come in a for a little bit this morning?"

"Sure, I can do that."

Archer was used to getting called out at all hours of the day, weekends included.

"That would be great, Mark."

"I'm actually close by—I can be there in fifteen minutes."

Keller turned back to his computer and opened the attachment again. He studied the sketch, just letting his mind wash over it. He found that sometimes things popped into his head when he allowed a stream of consciousness to take place. He didn't know why it worked, but it was something that had proven worthwhile in many of his past homicide cases. Nothing came to him immediately, but he left the sketch of the Jane Doe displayed on his computer screen. He got lost in his thoughts.

"Hey, Jack."

The voice startled him back to reality; he looked up to see Mark Archer standing outside his cubicle.

"Hey, Mark, come on in."

Archer took a seat across from Jack's desk.

"We're having trouble getting our victim ID'd. I took some photos of her at the autopsy and had Berman put together a sketch of what she probably looked like."

"'Probably looked like?' How long had she been in the tree?"

"Probably twenty-four to thirty-six hours, that's Mora's best guess. Berman had to improvise a bit on the sketch—our vic was missing both eyes. Plucked out by birds, Dr. Mora said. High in protein."

"Glad I've already had breakfast. So do you want me to put out the sketch to the media?"

"Yeah, I think that's our best bet right now. Mia is checking on having Monica handle the phone calls that are sure to come in once they run the sketch. Our victim was a looker and the press will jump all over this. Here, take a look."

Keller shifted his computer screen toward Archer.

"Oh, yeah—they'll love this. Nothing whets a reporter's appetite like a young, white, attractive female. And when you tell them we need help with an ID, they'll go nuts. How much do you want me to say about the details of her death?"

"Not too much. Certainly nothing about finding her in a tree. Just say she was found in a remote area near Samson Creek."

"Can I talk about TOD? It might jar some memories."

"The TOD is fine. So basically just show the sketch and talk about where we found her. Oh, and steer clear of the cause of death," answered Keller.

"And what *was* the cause of death, exactly?"

Keller looked at Archer.

Jack had worked with Mark Archer on virtually every homicide case since Jack's arrival at the RCSO some ten years earlier. He had total trust in him and knew he would never spill the beans to the media on any facet of an investigation. But still, the investigator in him liked to play things close to the vest. It was always a struggle—what to share with the guy who was charged with telling the world, through the media, about a case.

Conversely, Mark Archer, who had nearly twenty years under his belt as the media relations liaison for RCSO, felt it was best if the investigator told him everything. Then a discussion could take place, much like the one underway at Keller's cubicle, and everyone would get on the same page as to what to release publicly and what to keep quiet. It cut down on the possibility of any kind of misunderstanding. These conversations were always a bit of a back and forth, a sort of unspoken ritual, but Archer knew Jack would eventually come clean and fill him in. Archer had earned the trust.

"Our victim bled out. She landed in the tree with such force her femoral artery burst and she was dead within minutes."

Archer looked at Keller, shaking his head slowly, taking in what he had just heard.

"And how exactly did she come to fall into a tree?"

"That's the million-dollar question, but it's likely she either fell or was pushed out of an airplane or helicopter."

"Jesus. Email me the sketch so I can get it released in time for the noon-time TV newscasts. With it being Labor Day we should get some good air time—not much happening today except for parades and picnics."

Keller nodded at Archer.

"I assume Sheriff McCallister is up to speed on this case?"

"I don't know that for a fact, but I'd say it's a pretty good bet Mia has filled him in. But you might want to run it by him, let him know what we plan to do. This case will cause a stir," answered Keller.

"Okay, I'll give him a call and brief him. I'll also send you and Mia a draft of the press release I'll be attaching to the sketch. Does that work for you?"

"Yep."

"Okay, I'll have it to you within the hour."

Keller forwarded the sketch to Archer then put together a quick email to Mia telling her about Archer's plans. He also reminded her to check with Commander Espy about securing Monica to monitor the phone lines, and suggested they meet once the press release had been drafted by Archer so they could make sure everything was covered. Keller stood and went down to the cafeteria on the first floor to grab a cup of coffee and something to eat.

Mia was in her office when she heard the familiar chirp coming from her computer telling her she had a new email. She saw it was from Keller and quickly opened it, read the contents of his message, and looked at the attached sketch.

She sat there, looking at the drawing of the dead woman displayed on her computer screen. How could someone just disappear and have nobody notice? No one had called in a missing person on this beautiful young woman. Mia had checked again with their missing persons bureau when she arrived at the office that morning. It made no sense, unless the victim was from out of town and her family and friends had contacted the law enforcement agency in their own area. That was a distinct possibility, she thought—and something she would mention to Keller when they met later. Maybe this sketch should be distributed internally to all the Colorado law enforcement agencies, asking if it met the description of anyone reported missing in their jurisdictions. If this Jane Doe had been reported missing in another county, they would have no reason to assume she could be dead somewhere else. At least not early on. Getting the victim's face on TV and in the newspapers was definitely their best course of action.

Mark Archer returned to his office and checked his computer for Keller's email. He clicked on the attachment and a few seconds later the woman's face was displayed on the screen. Archer had handled media inquiries on more than two hundred homicides for RCSO and there wasn't much that disturbed him at this point in his career. But he found that looking at the dead woman's photo was a bit haunting. He wasn't sure if it was the bizarre circumstances of the case, the beauty of the victim, or the fact that he had a teenage daughter. Maybe a combination of all three, he thought.

He didn't have time to ponder these things for long, since Keller needed the sketch distributed ASAP. He quickly put together a media alert, listing what he could about the circumstances of the case, the contact number for people to call Monica if they recognized the victim, and his personal contact information at the bottom of the page. He sent it off to Keller and Serrano, asking for a quick turnaround on their review. He mentioned in the email that if he could get it back by 10:30 he would likely be able to get it out in time for the Denver noontime TV newscasts. The Denver newspapers would be even quicker—they would probably have it up on their websites within an hour of receiving it. It would be in the printed edition of the papers the following morning.

Archer did a quick search of several media websites, both local and national, to get an idea of what they were covering that day. He wanted to see if it was a busy or slow news day. The timing of RCSO news releases were often geared accordingly. His search showed there wasn't much going on in and around the Denver area that morning. It was Labor Day weekend, the typical dog days of summer. He sat at his desk, contemplating the amount of play his Jane Doe might get. Seeing the lack of any big stories, he felt that it could be the lead on the TV newscast, unless, of course, something bigger came along in the next two hours.

Archer picked up his phone and quickly dialed the cell number for Angela Bell. He still knew the number by heart, even though he hadn't dialed it in months. It began to ring and he had the sudden urge to hang up before she answered. Then he heard her voice.

"Mark, is that you?"

"Hey, Angela. Yeah, it's me."

An awkward pause hung between them.

"Is there something I can help you with?"

"Yes, actually, there is. I wanted to give you a heads up about a press release that will be coming your way in another hour or so. It's a pretty interesting case and I wanted to see if you could give it some play at or near the top of your newscast at noon."

"What's it about?"

"We've got a deceased Jane Doe and we're looking to get her ID'd. I can't tell you a lot, but her body was found in a remote area near Samson Creek a few days ago. She had no ID on her and no one has called her in as missing. We've put together a sketch of her face and we'd like to get some coverage in the hopes someone will recognize her and call us. Our homicide guys are pretty stuck without an ID."

"Sure, I think we can do that. I'm co-anchoring the noon cast. I'll make sure our producer gives it a sufficient amount of play."

"That would be great, Angela. I appreciate the assist. When you see the drawing of her . . . I don't know, it's kind of haunting."

"Okay, I'll be sure to get it in before the first commercial break. Are you sending this out to everybody, or just Channel Eight?"

"I'm sending it out to everyone—I'm sure you understand. We can't be partial to one media organization over the others."

"So, you just wanted to give me an early heads up, is that it?"

"Yeah, exactly. Well, I better run—look for the release, maybe around eleven."

"Okay, I will."

Mark Archer hung up from the call and sat quietly at his desk. He missed Angela, and it was good to hear her voice. They had met a few years earlier at a victims' rights rally in Denver; Mark was there representing RCSO and Angela was there in memory of her father, who had been murdered in 1994. The relationship formed quickly and the two dated for almost two years, but they ultimately parted ways and had agreed it was best that they not contact each other.

Mark wasn't exactly sure why he had called her, and now he felt a little foolish for letting his impulses get the better of him. He shook off the feeling and dialed the cell number for Sheriff McCallister. He needed to bring him up to speed on the distribution of the Jane Doe sketch in case the sheriff got any calls from reporters asking about the case. He needed to keep his boss apprised, and it would serve as a good way to get his mind off the phone call he had just made to Angela.

"I think we should send our Jane Doe sketch to all Colorado law enforcement. If she isn't from Rocklin County, it's possible that some other agency is spinning their wheels looking for her," Mia said as she and Keller went over the media alert that Archer had forwarded to them.

"Yeah, that's a good point. But, in reality, if that's the case, that other agency isn't doing much with it right now. Unless it's considered an endangered missing, they would pretty much just pin up the flyer in the squad room for the time being. Over a million people in the US are reported missing each year and more than ninety-five percent turn up within twenty-four hours. So unless the person calling it in had reason to believe that the person was in danger, it's probably not being actively pursued."

Mia responded, "All the more reason we should put it out."

"That's fine, like I said—there's no harm in it."

Mia continued, "I talked to Commander Espy and he gave us the clearance to use Monica as our call taker. I see that Archer listed her direct line on the release—which will allow people to avoid going through the hassle of our switchboard."

"I agree. And Monica needs to be ready at noon in the event her phone starts to ring. Let's buy her lunch so she can sit at her desk and handle the first few calls that come in," added Keller.

"Good idea. I don't think she'd mind doing that. She was pretty excited when I told her what we needed her to do."

"So, we're good to go on it?"

"Yep, let's do it."

A few minutes before eleven, Archer pressed the send button on his computer and the media alert, along with the attached Jane Doe sketch, was sent electronically to more than forty media organizations in the greater Denver area. From the biggest TV stations and the *Denver Post* to the small community newspapers—everybody received it at the same time. The marvels of technology, Archer thought. It used to take an hour or more to send these kinds of releases via fax to the media. And typically a third of them never made it to their destinations; they ended up lost in busy newsrooms. What a headache it used to be, but now Archer had an electronic timestamp on the releases, eliminating or at least reducing the likelihood of a pissed-off assignment editor asking, “Where the hell is the release you sent to everyone but us?”

In addition to listing Monica Schoenfeld as the person the public should call with information about the missing woman, Archer had listed himself as the primary contact at the bottom of the release. This was standard procedure as the investigators were typically too busy with the investigation to take the time to do interviews with every reporter who called. It was also a tricky business unless you knew what you were doing—reporters could at times be a bit conniving, and Archer was able to recognize such shenanigans, while someone with less experience might not. Archer had conducted more than five thousand interviews during the course of his career and had seen most, if not all, of the tricks some unscrupulous reporters played.

Within five minutes, his office line rang. His caller ID showed the call was from Dara Berman, a long-time crime reporter from the *Post* and someone Archer had talked to hundreds of times.

“What took you so long, Dara? You’re losing your edge.”

“Up yours, Archer. I’ll bet no one ever asked *you* what took you so long . . . ”

“Oh, touché, Dara . . . feeling a bit frisky this morning, I see.”

“So, what gives with this Jane Doe you guys are looking for? Your release was a bit cryptic and short on information. Not like that’s anything new.”

Typical Dara, thought Archer. The woman was older than God and had been at the *Post* for almost as long as he’d been alive. She had seen it all and then some. He had a very good relationship with her, partly because he gave her as much crap as she gave him. Dara liked that.

“Hey, I wrote that brilliant bit of prose. Don’t be criticizing my work.”

“Your work is seriously lacking. Come on, Mark—no cause of death, nothing about the crime scene, nothing about how was she found? Inquiring minds want to know that stuff, especially when they get a look at what Jane looked like.”

"We aren't releasing any of that right now, Dara. You know the game; we play these things pretty close to the vest. We just need someone to come forward and tell us who she is. She's got to be someone's daughter, sister, girlfriend, wife, neighbor . . . something. Run the photo, include the RCSO contact info, and if someone calls it in, then we can talk a little more."

"Your release says you think she died sometime around Friday. What makes you think that?"

"The medical examiner established the TOD based on his findings. We included that in the release to perhaps jog someone's memory and generate a call. You can say in your article that getting her ID'd will provide us with a huge investigative lead, something we need before we can really get the investigation going full steam ahead."

"So you're saying the investigation is stalled?"

"Dara, don't put words in my mouth. Getting an ID on a victim is something that is obviously important in any case. Our investigators have been working on this pretty much non-stop for the last thirty-six hours. Once we get her ID'd, that potentially opens several more avenues for us to pursue, greatly enhancing our chances at finding the person responsible for her death."

"Any chance this was an accidental death?"

"There's very little chance of that. We are proceeding with this case as a murder investigation. We're confident in that assessment."

"Okay, I should have something written up and posted on our website within the hour. I suppose Channel Eight will be leading with this at noon?"

"Well, I don't make decisions at Channel Eight or any other news organizations, but they received the same media alert at the same time that you did."

"Okay, Mark."

The call ended and Archer sat at his desk thinking about the last few seconds of the conversation. It didn't have a good feel to it—was

Dara Berman insinuating he gave Channel Eight some kind of advantage over other media sources?

God, he hoped not.

CHAPTER 8

By two o'clock that afternoon, Monica had fielded more than a dozen calls from people who believed they could identify their Jane Doe. Most of the calls were, "Oh, I'm sure she works at Starbucks in Aurora," or "She really looks like my son's ex-girlfriend." Not overly helpful, but each call had to be checked out. Patrol officers were sent out to talk with the reporting parties, but by five that evening nothing had panned out and no ID had been made.

Mia and Keller spent much of their day contacting the six regional airports around the greater Denver area. Working under the theory that their victim had fallen into the tree, they were exploring the possibility of some kind of accident. They knew the odds of something like that going unreported were highly unlikely, but they needed to do their due diligence just the same. Not surprisingly, they came up empty handed.

Mia decided to check in with Monica when she and Keller returned to the station.

"Well, how'd it go? Any new calls since we spoke last?" Mia asked as she sat across the desk from Monica.

"Not really. We got a total of fourteen calls; patrol has checked them all out and they tell me they came up with nothing. Sorry I don't have better news."

"That's okay. Things may pick up this evening when people get home and turn on the TV news or jump on their computers and check what's going on in their world. Typically that generates another round of calls . . . they should go until about ten thirty or so tonight, when the last newscast airs. And then our computer-illiterate residents will see it tomorrow morning in the newspaper and we may get another round of calls. But with newspaper subscriptions down so dramatically in recent years, that tends to be the smallest wave of calls we get."

"Wow, you've done this before, huh?"

"Yeah, a few times."

"So, who'll answer the calls that come in after I leave?"

"I'll take the phone calls for the next few hours and then Keller will take them until maybe eleven or so. Then we'll just forward the line to ring into dispatch."

"If you don't need me any more, I'll get out of here. The commander doesn't like to pay overtime."

"That's fine. Have a great evening, Monica, and thanks again."

Mia sat at the desk and sent Keller a text telling him she was now handling the call-in line. He responded to tell her he'd be there shortly so they could discuss putting together the murder book.

It was a widespread practice in law enforcement to compile a case file consisting of crime scene photographs and sketches, forensics, transcripts of investigators' notes, and witness interviews. Referred to simply as the murder book, it essentially captured a complete paper trail of the investigation, from the time the murder was first reported through the arrest of a suspect. This compilation assisted police and prosecutors in their efforts to keep everything related to the homicide in one place and was carefully guarded by investigators.

As Mia was typing a text back to Keller to confirm their plans to work on the murder book, the tip line rang. Mia leaned over to the phone to look at the readout on the display of the phone. *Private Caller.* She reached over and answered it.

"This is Investigator Serrano. Can I help you?"

"Yes, I'm calling about that woman I saw on the news a few minutes ago."

The caller was female and sounded young.

"Okay, I'm handling that investigation. Do you know the woman?"

"She looks a lot like one of my co-workers. But I don't know if she's missing."

"What do you mean?"

"I work with someone that looks just like her. Oh, this is crazy—I'm sure it's not her. I'm sorry to have bothered you."

"No, no . . . hold on. Let's talk a little more about this. First off, what's your name?"

"My name? Why do you need my name?"

"Just for the record. You don't have to give it to me, but it's easier if you do. In case we get disconnected or I need to follow up with you later about the case," answered Mia.

She knew she had to be careful or the caller might just hang up at this point without warning. She wasn't sure if this tip was going anywhere, but it was a bit more promising than the other calls that had come in earlier that day.

"Well, I think I want to keep my name out of it for right now."

"Okay, I understand. Can you at least tell me where you work?"

Just then Keller appeared and Mia motioned to him that she had a tipster on the line. Keller nodded and took a seat.

"I work in Denver at the payment processing center for Tower Bank."

"Okay, great . . . and the woman in the sketch, she works there with you?"

"Yes, but I'm really not sure it's her and I don't want to cause any problems for her. I'd be so embarrassed if the woman in the sketch turned out not to be her. I mean, I hope it's not her, but . . . "

"I understand what you're saying. Don't worry if you're wrong about it, we can check these things out very quietly and without anyone ever knowing it was you that called it in."

"Well, I haven't given you my name . . . " she added, her voice trailing off.

"Exactly, so you have nothing to worry about. Now, what is your co-worker's name?"

The caller hesitated for several seconds before responding.

"Vanessa Tolken."

"Okay, and what's the address where you work?"

As Mia talked with the caller, she scribbled the initials *V.T.* on a piece of scratch paper on the desk and passed it to Keller.

Keller sat up a bit straighter in his chair. Mia and the mystery caller had his full attention.

"Okay . . . it's one-eleven East Eighteenth Street in downtown Denver."

She motioned for Keller to write down the address as she continued to speak.

"And the name of your co-worker is Vanessa Tolken, correct?"

"Yes."

"Are you sure you don't want to give me your name? Or at least a contact number I can reach you at if I need to?"

The line went dead.

"Damn it."

Mia turned toward Keller, "She hung up. Vanessa Tolken—*V.T.* It matches the initials on the necklace we found yesterday."

"Maybe we should head over to the address on Eighteenth Street," replied Keller.

"From what she said, it's some kind of payment processing center. Not too sure we'd find anyone there on Labor Day." Mia looked at her watch—it was almost five thirty.

"It's worth a try, it could be a twenty-four-hour-a-day operation. Traffic going into downtown shouldn't be too bad . . . we could be there in less than thirty minutes. I say we give it a go."

Mia responded, "All right. Let me print out the sketch before we go."

Keller was right about the traffic and they found themselves in downtown in a very quick half hour. They located the Tower Bank processing center and found parking in a public lot less than a block away. They walked toward the building and saw that it was largely dark. There were, however, some lights on in the lobby. They pushed on the entry doors, expecting them to be locked, but were surprised when the doors opened. They walked inside and saw a lone guard standing at a security station near the elevators.

"Can I help you?" asked the guard, who looked to be in his early sixties.

"Yes, my name is Jack Keller and this is my partner, Mia Serrano. We're investigators with the Rocklin County Sheriff's Office in Castle Springs."

"Shit, Jack—how're you doing?"

Keller looked at the guard and then at Mia.

"Geez, you don't remember me. And I'm the one getting old."

"I'm sorry, how do we know each other?"

"I'm retired from Denver PD. Hung it up a few years ago. You and I worked together on a one-eighty-seven that took place down your way, but was committed by some of our fine little gang bangers here in Denver. We got a couple of life without paroles out of that case."

"Oh, yeah . . . I remember now. I'm sorry I didn't recognize you sooner."

"No worries, Jack."

"So you pulled the plug a few years back?"

"Yeah, about three years ago, I guess. Got a little bored so I took this job about a year ago. Keeps me out of trouble and gives me a little mad money, you know?"

"Sure, makes sense. I retired from St. Louis PD about twelve years ago and found myself a bit bored as well. I signed on with RCSO a year or two later, and the rest, as they say, is history."

"Yeah, RCSO was lucky to land you. Your reputation as a top-notch one-eighty-seven investigator was well known. You were a huge help to us in getting those pricks convicted."

"Well, thanks . . . Randy," Keller said after stealing a quick glance at the guard's name badge.

"So, what brings you to Tower Bank tonight?"

"We've caught a weird one, Randy. Got a dead body and no ID. But we were able to get a pretty good sketch drawn up of our vic. Here, let me show you."

Mia handed the drawing to Keller, and he handed it to the guard.

"Wow, such a pretty little thing. So, what's the connection to the bank?"

Mia stepped forward and joined the little reunion her partner was having with Randy.

"We circulated this sketch today and got an interesting call. A woman said our Jane Doe looked a lot like one of her co-workers here at the processing center. She said the woman in question, her co-worker, was named Vanessa Tolken. Jack and I thought we'd take a chance and run up here and see if we could find anything out. But it looks like things are pretty closed up right now, with the holiday and all."

"Well, hold on a minute . . . maybe not all is lost. Let me see what I can find out on my computer."

Randy turned toward a desk a few feet away from where they were standing. He reached over and began working the keyboard.

"Vanessa Tolken, you said?"

Mia responded, "Yes, that's the name the caller gave."

"Well, you're in luck—we do have someone by that name working in accounts receivable. Let me see if I can get her ID badge photo to display. We've got nearly six hundred employees here, but unless she's new, we should have her photo in our database."

"That would be great, Randy. We really appreciate the assist," said Keller.

"No sweat. Happy to help out a fellow investigator."

Randy turned the computer screen toward Mia and Keller so they could see the display.

"Is this your girl?"

Jack and Mia looked at the screen for a few seconds and then looked at each other.

"Bingo," replied Keller, reaching into his coat pocket for his notebook and a pen.

"Can you get her personal info from that database?"

"Yep, I sure can . . . hold on a sec."

Mia and Keller stood by while Randy continued tapped away on the keyboard.

"Yeah, I've got her file here. All the contact information, et cetera . . . "

"Great, can you read it off to me?"

"Sure. Her name is Vanessa Marie Tolken, DOB is nine seventeen eighty-eight. Home address is ten-eight-five-one Tarzana Place in Lone Tree. Cell phone is 303-527-7869, no home phone listed, hire date was November of oh-eight. That's all I've got access to at this point, I could probably get a lot more, but it would have to wait till tomorrow when the HR folks come in."

"No, that's all we really need tonight. We can't thank you enough, Randy."

"No sweat—hope it helps."

"Hey, do you mind giving us your contact information? In case we have any follow up questions later?"

"No, not at all."

Randy scribbled down his information and handed it to Keller.

Keller nodded and he and Mia left the lobby and headed back to their car.

Outside, Mia asked "Do you want to call her cell or drop by her place in Lone Tree?"

"I'd rather go in person. You never know who might have her cell phone now. Don't want to tip anyone off by making a phone call—better to go straight to the residence."

"Okay, sounds good."

Lone Tree was located about halfway between Denver and Castle

Springs. It was normally an easy twenty-minute drive, but with the Labor Day traffic moving south it took Mia and Keller nearly forty-five minutes to reach the address Randy had given them.

The home was in a new development just west of I-25, and, from the looks of it, a fairly pricey one. Lone Tree was known as an area where many young, affluent singles lived. As they pulled up in front of the home, Mia and Keller radioed into the RCSO dispatch center, letting them know their location, given the two weren't sure what, if anything, they might encounter at the home. Both checked their weapons, then climbed from the car and headed toward the door.

As they reached the driveway they paused, giving each other quick sideways glances. The signs were all there—a couple newspapers on the driveway, the entry light on the porch was on even though it was still daylight, and mail was sticking out of the front of the mailbox.

Mia rang the doorbell. Half a minute passed; nothing. She rang it again and Keller banged on the door for several seconds. Still no answer.

Keller looked at Mia and said, "I don't think we have probable cause to force entry. We have no reason to believe she's in any immediate danger—just the opposite. I don't think we can justify it."

"I agree. Let's poke around and see if any of the neighbors will talk with us."

The two walked back down the driveway and made their way to a neighboring home. They rang the doorbell and a woman answered.

"We're from the Rocklin County Sheriff's Department. We are trying to reach your next door neighbor, a Ms. Vanessa Tolken. Would you happen to know her?" Mia asked the young woman, as both she and Keller displayed their badges.

"Vanessa? Sure, I know her. Is everything all right? Is she in some kind of trouble?"

"We just need to speak to her. We knocked on her front door but there was no answer. Any idea where she might be?"

"No, not really. I haven't seen her in a few days. But that's not unusual; she sometimes takes off on little vacations or long weekends with her boyfriend."

"Do you know the boyfriend's name, by chance?"

"No, I've never actually met him. She mentioned that she was seeing somebody and I see him sometimes when he comes to the house. But I don't know him."

"You wouldn't have a key to her place, would you?"

"No, we aren't that close. Just friendly with each other, you know—like neighbors do."

Mia replied, "If you happen to see her, would you give us a call?"

"Sure, no problem."

Mia gave the woman her business card and she and Keller made their way back to their car.

"So, where do we go from here?" asked Mia.

"We have her cell number. I'm thinking maybe we should give Ms. Tolken a call and see what happens."

"Worth a try."

Keller reached into his coat pocket for the phone number Randy had given to them and punched the number into his cell. A moment later the call went through and it began to ring. After the sixth ring it went to voicemail and he pressed the speaker button on his phone so Mia could hear.

"Hi, this is Vanessa. Leave me your number and I'll call you back as soon as I can."

Beep.

Keller quickly disconnected the call before anything could be recorded.

Mia spoke first. "Maybe we should check back with Randy and see if we can get a number for the HR department at Tower. We can call them first thing tomorrow morning."

"She's either dead or she's fine. Either way, waiting till tomorrow morning when we can get easy access to the right people at the bank is the best way to approach it."

"Okay. So we call it a day, then?" answered Mia.

"Yep, let's get some rest and hit it again hard tomorrow."

"Okay, but I'll call in to see if there's been any activity on the tip line. Who knows—maybe we're chasing our tails here."

Keller looked at Mia and nodded, but they both had the same feeling. The dead woman in the tree was Vanessa Tolken.

CHAPTER 9

The minute Jonathan Timbers arrived to work the next day he was told by his administrative assistant, Catalina Alcala, there had been an urgent call from the HR department.

"What's it about—did they say?"

"No, just that you needed to contact Rob Adjakian as soon as you came in. I asked if I could be of some assistance but he gave me a firm but polite no."

Adjakian was the HR director for the Tower Bank payment processing center and not someone who typically called on routine personnel matters. The fact that he was asking for Jonathan to call him back concerned him.

"Want me to place the call for you now?"

"No, give me a few minutes."

"Okay, boss."

Jonathan sat in his office pondering the various scenarios. It was possible that it was some kind of personnel matter, maybe something private or delicate that Adjakian didn't want to explain to an admin. Maybe he was calling to ask a favor—perhaps the HR director was looking to get his niece or nephew a job. It wasn't unheard of; lots of favors occurred between managers at the bank. But then again, Adjakian was the HR guy—he could pull those strings himself.

Only one way to find out, he thought. He took a deep breath, picked up his phone, and pushed the button for Catalina. "Go ahead and get me Adjakian."

The call rang through and Adjakian picked up the line.

"Rob Adjakian. Can I help you?"

"Hi Rob, this is Jonathan Timbers, returning your call. How're you doing today?"

Adjakian skipped the pleasantries. "Hey, I got a call first thing this morning from an investigator with the Rocklin County Sheriff's Department asking me some questions about an employee who works in your shop."

Jonathan paused for a half second, his head spinning. He composed himself and then replied "Who are they asking for? And did they say what it was about?"

"She was a bit vague with me on the phone; just gave me the employee's name and said they needed to talk with someone about her."

"So, who are they trying to contact?"

"Vanessa Tolken. Our records show she's a supervisor there in your department—in accounts receivable."

Jonathan's hands began to shake.

He calmed himself before speaking. "Yes, she works for me. Who's calling about her?"

"The investigator's name is Mia Serrano. Her contact number is (303) 555-1869. She seemed anxious to speak with someone—can you return her call?"

"Sure, no problem, Rob. I'll take care of it right away."

"Great, thanks much."

Jonathan hung up the phone and contemplated the phone call from Adjakian. It could mean only one thing — Vanessa's body had been discovered. He had hoped that it would be some time before that occurred, but the plans to move the money were in place so he grabbed his laptop and fired it up. His and Vanessa's passwords were all that he needed to by bypass the dual control system and he had obtained hers a few days earlier. The transactions were complete in less than a minute. He carefully placed his laptop in his briefcase, walked into the outer office and calmly told Catalina that he had to run out to a meeting. She asked him when he would be returning and he replied, "After lunch."

She thought it was strange, since she showed nothing on his calendar, but didn't question her boss as he left the office. She shrugged, took out the latest edition of her favorite gossip rag, and sat at her desk reading quietly.

Jonathan walked quickly to the elevator and hit the button to take him down the forty-six floors to the lobby. Three minutes later he was in his car and on his way out of the secured garage. He entered I-25 south and drove to his home in Littleton. It was just after nine and he knew his wife would be at work and the kids both in school. He went to the basement and grabbed a hidden suitcase packed with all the things he needed, climbed back into his car, and headed for Denver International Airport.

As Jonathan drove north on the I-470, he considered his situation. A recent and unexpected turn of events had caused him to put his plans into overdrive. He could pull it off, he was confident of that, but now he'd be doing it without Vanessa.

Rocklin County Prosecutor Luke Dominic was thoroughly engrossed in his preparation for the biggest case of his career. The trial date was quickly approaching and he still had a lot to do to get ready. He had been personally assigned the case by District Attorney Dave Baxter and he knew it was the trial that could make or break his career.

The murder of George Lombard had not only captured the imagination of the residents in and around Denver, it had captivated the entire state of Colorado and beyond. The case had a little bit of everything—greed, sex, deception, betrayal, and a beautiful accomplice who had escaped capture for months before mysteriously turning herself in one day, saying she was tired of living life on the run. That woman, Lisa Sullivan, was now the key witness for the prosecution, having turned state's evidence against her former lover Scott Lennox in exchange for a plea bargain deal that kept her from serving any time behind bars.

Dominic needed to meet with Mia Serrano and Jack Keller to go over the testimony they'd be providing on the stand. As the lead investigators on the case, they would play a critical role in the trial. He'd been discussing aspects of the case with them for several weeks, but he wanted to go over everything one last time before the start of the trial. The judge on the case was the Honorable Richard O'Brien—a decent draw for the prosecution, but Dominic did have some concerns that the judge was a bit of a publicity hound. He had already ruled that one camera would be allowed in the courtroom, with the resulting footage shared among all media, something that could cause crazy and unexpected things to occur. The lawyers and judges always denied it, but having that camera present did change the dynamics of what went on in the courtroom. This case was already going to be sensational, and now the world would have an eye on the day to day proceedings. Dominic was a young law student during the O.J. Simpson case in Los Angeles and had watched hours of the trial on TV. Little did he know that some twenty years later he'd be the lead prosecutor on Colorado's juiciest murder trial.

He picked up the phone and dialed Keller's office number. It rang through to voicemail so he left a message explaining that he needed to meet to go over the final preparation for the trial. He called Mia Serrano, getting the same result and leaving the same message. He was unaware that the two were busy working another homicide; he hadn't seen the news coverage and the sketch of Jane Doe that was playing out in the Denver media.

"Now that we have a possible ID, we can run Jane Doe's fingerprints against Vanessa Tolken's prints in the DMV system."

Keller was standing outside Mia's cubicle and Mia nodded in agreement with Jack's suggestion.

Keller was almost certain that the DMV system would have Token's prints on file. If she had a Colorado driver's license, they had her thumb print, and that would register a hit. It was a tactical error on his part to run her prints in the criminal databanks at first—but he was feeling confident in the call-girl angle and was sure her prints would pop up under some previous arrests. It didn't work.

"I have a call into Tower Bank. I spoke with the HR director this morning and he said someone would get back to me ASAP. By the way, I got a call from Luke Dominic wanting to set up a meeting to go over our testimony in the Lennox trial. Did he contact you?" asked Mia.

Keller nodded, but didn't say anything. He picked up the phone on Mia's desk, called the records division, and asked them to run the DMV print comparison.

Mia continued, "Luke sounded a bit anxious on his message. I'm sure he's feeling a lot of pressure with this case."

Keller didn't answer. Mia looked at him. She was trying to get a read on him, weighing how he felt about testifying now that the case was just days away. She got nothing.

"Okay, just heard back from records—the print is a match. Our victim is Vanessa Tolken."

Mia looked at Jack, "No big surprise . . . where to from here?"

"We need to get her emergency contact information from Tower Bank. Have they called you back yet?"

"No, which kind of pisses me off—they said they'd have someone get back to me right away," responded Mia, glancing at her watch. It was nearly eleven.

Mia grabbed the phone and dialed up Tower Bank.

"Mr. Adjakian, this is Investigator Serrano again. I haven't heard back from anyone regarding Ms. Tolken. It's urgent we speak to someone—can you please make that happen?"

"Really? I spoke to her manager and he was supposed to call you right away. That was over two hours ago. Let me call his office right now and see if I can patch you through on a conference call. If I can do that, I can bow out of the conversation and the two of you can speak privately."

"Thanks, I'd appreciate that."

A minute later Adjakian came back on the line. "His administrative assistant tells me that Mr. Timbers left for the morning and won't be back until after lunch. There must be some kind of mixup. I certainly thought I conveyed the urgency of this situation to him when we spoke earlier this morning. Look, I can give you his cell phone number so you can contact him directly—would that work?"

"That would be fine. But, in the meantime, could I have Ms. Tolken's emergency contact information?"

"Oh, that doesn't sound good. But I certainly can give that to you under the circumstances."

Adjakian queried the computer on his desk. He gave Mia the information on Tolken and a cell number for Jonathan Timbers.

Keller was busy on his cell phone, but looked over at Mia when he was done.

"I just called Lone Tree PD, explained our situation, and asked them to run her address. It came back clean—there have been no calls for service from the residence."

Mia answered, "Well, if she's a high-end escort she'd be going to the client's place, not the other way around. Just the same, did they check to see if anyone had called in complaining about anything going on at her address?"

"Yeah, I had them run that, too. Nothing."

"Sounds like Ms. Tolken was a nice, quiet neighbor."

"So it appears."

"Okay, let me call the bank guy's cell and see what I can find out. Then I think we need to notify Tolken's next of kin."

"Agreed."

Mia dialed the number. Six rings later it kicked over to voicemail and she left a message with her callback number.

CHAPTER 10

Jonathan Timbers heard his cell phone ring. He glanced down at the display and saw that it was the RCSO calling. He let it go to voicemail—no big deal, he thought . . . it really wouldn't matter much.

He needed to make a quick stop before arriving at the airport. He exited Interstate 470 and began to drive around the surface streets in Aurora, just east of the interstate.

After a few minutes he located a large, run-down shopping center, pulled into the parking lot, and drove toward the back. He looked around to see if there were any security cameras on the light poles or the nearby store roofs. Seeing none, he pulled up to some cars parked in an area away from where most of the shoppers were parked. He guessed this was likely employee parking. He pulled to a stop and sat quietly in his car, waiting. After several minutes of no activity he climbed from his vehicle, went to the trunk, and grabbed a screwdriver from a repair kit he kept there. He walked to the row of parked employee cars and removed the front and rear plates of a late-model vehicle. He returned to his car, removed his plates, and replaced them with the plates he had just stolen. He put his plates onto the other car and climbed back into his car. He left the shopping center and drove down the main street of town. He knew it wouldn't take long and he was right. A minute later he came to a stop light and saw a homeless man standing at the corner, holding a sign asking for money. Jonathan chuckled as he read the sign: *Why lie—I need a beer.* He rolled down his window and motioned for the man to approach.

"I like your sign—at least you're honest, huh?"

The man smiled but didn't speak. He was missing both his front teeth.

"Look, I'm not going to give you any cash, but I have a cell phone here that I don't need any more. It works—do you want it?"

The man smiled and nodded, then took the phone from Jonathan. No one had ever given him a cell phone before.

Jonathan gave him a little wave and said, "Have a good day."

Two minutes later he was back on Interstate 470, closing in on DIA.

"I called Tolken's boss but got his voicemail, so I left a message."

"Geez, what's it take to have a conversation with that guy?" Keller responded.

"I don't know, but in the meantime, let's do the death notification. Tolken listed her sister as her emergency contact. She lives in Parker. You want to drive or would you like me to?"

"I'll drive. Meet in the back parking lot in five minutes?"

"Sure, that'll work."

The drive out to Parker was a relatively short one, less than twenty minutes from Castle Springs. The address they were given for Tolken's sister, a woman named Erin Faith, was in a brand-new development of single-family homes situated on one of the many golf courses that had been built in the fast-growing city of Parker. The neighborhood was upscale and they found the home on a cul-de-sac buffered up against one of the lush, green fairways.

Making a death notification was something Mia had done many times during her time as a traffic investigator, but delivering the news that a loved one had been killed in a traffic collision was a bit different than delivering the news that a loved one had been murdered. Both were tragic situations, but when a loved one has been taken from you at the hand of another, it was just another layer to wrap your head around in coping with the loss. Mia had never handled a 187 notification so they decided on the ride out to Parker that Keller would break the news and Mia would carefully watch the sister's reaction. There was no reason to believe that the sister was involved, but homicide investigators were trained to observe such things. Sometimes it paid dividends.

The two walked up to the front door of the home and rang the doorbell. A half-minute later, the door opened slightly and a young woman spoke through the opening.

"Can I help you?"

"Are you Erin Faith?"

"Yes, I am. Who are you and what's this about?"

Keller and Mia displayed their badges.

Keller answered, "We're from the Rocklin County Sheriff's Department and we need to speak to you. It's about your sister, Vanessa Tolken."

The door swung open and the woman stood in the doorway without speaking.

"May we come in?"

The woman nodded. "What about my sister? Why are you here?"

"I'm afraid we have some bad news. There's no easy way to say this—we're homicide investigators, and I'm afraid your sister—"

The woman covered her mouth and shrieked, "Oh my God, no, no . . . "

She staggered backward and for a moment both Keller and Mia though she was going to pass out. They rushed in and grabbed her by the arms.

"Can we sit down somewhere?" Mia asked.

The woman didn't respond, but Keller and Mia led her gently to a sofa off the entry and sat her down.

Erin Faith suddenly looked defiant, "This can't be—this is some kind of mistake."

"No, I'm afraid not. We're very sorry for your loss, ma'am," responded Keller.

"How did this happen? You're telling me someone killed her?"

"Yes, that's what we believe. It's our job to find the person responsible for your sister's death. I know this is a shock for you, but if you're up to it, we'd like to ask you a few questions."

"How did it happen?"

Mia looked at Keller. It was too early to be sharing any specific details of the crime with anyone outside the investigation.

"We're still piecing all that together. There are a lot of unanswered questions; that's why we were hoping you might be willing to tell us a little bit about your sister," Mia answered, quietly taking a seat next to Faith on the sofa.

"Oh, my God—I can't believe this," she replied, as tears began rolling down her cheeks.

Mia reached into her purse for the packet of tissues she had brought from the station. She handed the packet to her.

"I haven't spoken to Vanessa in a few months. We had a bit of a falling out back in the spring."

She began crying more loudly, with the tears turning into sobs.

Keller and Mia sat there quietly, letting the emotions pour out.

Once she had regained a bit of her composure, Keller continued.

"We know it's difficult but anything you can tell us might help with the investigation."

She looked at Keller and nodded.

"You say the last time you saw your sister was in the spring and that you had a falling out. Can you tell us what that was about?"

"It was just stupid stuff. I can't even remember now what we fought about."

Mia nodded. She touched the woman's arm and asked, "Do you know if she had been seeing anyone? Any special men in her life?"

"My sister was beautiful and there were always plenty of men interested in her. She could pretty much have any man she wanted. But, no, I don't know of anyone recent—but, again, I haven't had any contact with her in months."

"Tell us a little bit about your family—parents, siblings, et cetera."

"Our mother died when we were young. We were raised by our dad and our stepmom. It's just Vanessa and I; we don't have any other siblings . . . " her voice trailed off, the realization of what was happening taking hold. The tears began again.

"It's okay," Mia responded softly, "Take your time."

"I can't believe this. My God, I feel so bad . . . we hadn't been in touch for so long."

Keller took up the questioning. "Did she ever mention any enemies to you? People who she was worried about, maybe someone she felt could harm her?"

"No, not really. She was really a sweet person. Everyone liked Vanessa."

CHAPTER 11

Jonathan Timbers pulled into the long-term parking lot at DIA and found a space as far as possible from the shuttle stop. He'd park his car on the moon if he could, but the long-term parking lot was the place that would draw the least amount of attention. He hoped no one would discover his vehicle any time soon. The bigger the head start, the better.

He grabbed his suitcase and briefcase, locked the car, and walked toward the shuttle station some fifty yards away. A few minutes later, the shuttle pulled up and he climbed aboard, throwing his stuff onto the shelf inside and taking a seat. The shuttle was empty and the driver asked what airline he was flying.

"United."

Jonathan pulled out the fake passport, credit card, and driver's license his friend Royster had provided to him. Things were going smoothly, but he'd feel a whole lot better once he was out of Colorado. He checked the UAL flight schedule on his phone and saw a flight that would work nicely. The shuttle pulled up in front of Concourse B and Jonathan collected his things. He handed the driver a ten-dollar bill and headed for the check-in area for United Airlines. He walked past the baggage handlers and directly into the terminal.

The line was short and within a few minutes it was his turn to approach the United clerk.

"Good morning. What can I do for you today, sir?"

Jonathan smiled at the young woman and said, "I'm headed to Miami. Is there room on the twelve forty-five flight?"

"Yes, there is. We have economy, business-class, and first-class seats open right now. What's your pleasure?"

"Let's do first."

"Okay, can I see some ID, please? And will you be paying by credit card?"

"Yes, American Express," he replied, handing the clerk his passport and the card.

"Will that be one way or round trip?"

"Round trip, but I'd like to leave the flight home open for right now. Not sure how long my business in Miami will take."

Jonathan knew he'd never use the return ticket but he didn't want to draw any attention from authorities if they came looking. A one-way ticket would draw suspicion. It was much safer to buy a round-trip ticket.

"Okay, that'll be $3,770, taxes included."

"That's fine," he replied. After all, he'd never see the bill, much less pay it.

"Okay, Mr. Houston. I've got you in first class on our flight to Miami, leaving at twelve forty-five from gate twelve. Please be ready to board thirty minutes before the flight. Would you like to check your bag?"

"Yes, that would be great."

"I'm happy to do that for you. Have a great flight and thanks for flying United."

Christopher Houston, formerly known as Jonathan Timbers, took his ticket, nodded politely at the clerk, and headed for gate twelve.

Keller and Mia spent another twenty minutes talking to Erin Faith, but they weren't able to glean much from her. They left her with their business cards, expressed their sympathies one more time, and headed back to their car.

As soon as they were en route to the station, Mia checked her cell phone. She had silenced it while she and Keller were delivering the news to Vanessa's sister. She didn't want her cell going off at a time like that. She checked for messages or missed calls. There was nothing.

"Geez, what a prick."

"Sorry?" asked Keller, giving Mia a sideways glance as they pulled onto the highway back to Castle Springs.

"The guy from the bank—he still hasn't called."

Keller looked at the I-25 connector ahead of them.

"Well, I could go south and head back to the station, or I could go north and head to Denver. You know, kind of drop in on him."

"I vote for the drop in. It will give us a chance to talk with her co-workers—maybe one of them has some idea of what happened to our victim."

Keller merged onto the northbound 25 and traffic was light. Twenty minutes later they were in the lobby of the Tower Bank building. They looked around in hopes that Keller's security guard pal might be working, but he wasn't there. Another security guard was manning the post in his place.

Keller and Mia approached.

Keller began, "We're here to see Mr. Jonathan Timbers. Can you direct us to the right place?"

"Do you have an appointment?" asked the guard.

He couldn't have been more than twenty-two years old, and seemed to relish his role as a gatekeeper of sorts.

Mia stepped forward. "No, but we've been trying to reach him all day. We thought we'd come by and try our luck."

"Well, you really need an appointment. Maybe you can give him another call."

Keller badged him and the guard changed his tune.

"He's on the forty-sixth floor. Go on up."

"Thanks. See that wasn't so hard, was it?"

The guard shrugged and Keller and Mia walked to the elevator.

"Kids . . . where do they get the attitude?"

Mia snorted, "Tell me about it. I was a high school teacher for five years before I came to the RCSO."

They stepped onto the elevator and Keller pushed the button. The ride up was quick and smooth. As the doors opened onto the forty-sixth floor, they stepped out to a beautiful atrium with large, plush offices located around the perimeter. There was a receptionist standing guard at a desk adjacent to the elevator.

"Can I help you?"

"Yes, my name is Mia Serrano and this is my partner, Jack Keller. We're investigators with the Rocklin County Sheriff's Department and we are here to see Jonathan Timbers."

Keller and Mia flashed their badges at the young receptionist.

"Is he expecting you?"

Mia continued, "I was put in touch with him by your HR director, Mr. Adjakian. Mr. Timbers and I seem to keep missing each other, so we thought we'd drop in and pay him a visit."

"Let me contact Mr. Timber's administrative assistant. You may take a seat over there if you'd like," she said, pointing in the direction of a reception area.

Mia and Keller walked over and took their seats.

"I'd forgotten you were a high school teacher," said Keller, looking to pass the time while they waited for Timbers to be tracked down.

"Yep, I did it for five years. Taught English to juniors and seniors, mostly."

"What made you quit and become a cop?"

Mia paused before answering. Very few people within the RCSO knew the real reason she left teaching, and she certainly wasn't going to let Keller in on her past. So she gave her standard response to the question—one she had given many times before.

"I don't know, I guess I just wanted a change . . . something a little more exciting. You can get in a rut with teaching, but life as a deputy—well, you know—it's never dull. It's been a good thing for me."

"There's no way I could do that. All those know-it-all teenagers. I don't think I'd last very long."

Mia chuckled and replied, "Well, there aren't too many people who could do what you do for a living. So I guess to each his own."

Mia didn't allow herself to dwell on the real reason she left the teaching profession. She still couldn't bring herself to drive by the campus. Witnessing firsthand the events unfold at Columbine High School and seeing several of her students die that day still left a hole in her heart.

April 20, 1999 had changed her forever.

Just then, a pretty, young woman, very professional in appearance and demeanor, approached them in the reception area.

"Hello, my name is Catalina. I'm Mr. Timber's administrative assistant. I understand you're trying to meet with him?"

Mia began, "Yes, I was referred to him by Mr. Adjakian. I've been trying to reach Mr. Timbers today, but have had no luck. It's very important that we speak to him ASAP."

"Well, he's out of the office right now, but he's due back after lunch. It's nearly one o'clock now, so I suspect he should be here any minute. If you care to wait here, I can come get you once he arrives."

"Perhaps you can call him? Maybe get a confirmation on his arrival time? As I said, we've been trying to reach him all day."

Catalina shifted a bit on her feet, looking a little uncomfortable for a moment, like she was concerned about Mr. Timbers. Keller and Mia both picked up that vibe from her.

Sensing this weakness, Keller jumped in and pushed hard. "We're here on official police business. It's imperative we speak to him. Who is Mr. Timber's boss?"

Catalina responded, "I'm sorry for the inconvenience, but I'm really doing the best I can."

Keller looked at Mia and then back at the young woman. Satisfied that he had made his point with her, Keller nodded and said, "If he's not here in ten minutes then I'm going to the president of this outfit. He's gotta be around here somewhere. I'm sure you're doing everything you can, but we need to speak to your boss, like right now."

Catalina nodded and turned to go back to her office.

"Gotta love the good cop, bad cop routine," whispered Keller.

"Yeah, gee . . . funny how we somehow always play the same roles. Someday I want to be the bad cop. I can be a jerk too, you know."

Keller chuckled, "Yeah, sure, Mia. We can do that.

CHAPTER 12

Jonathan Timbers, aka Christopher Houston, walked through the terminal and found a seat near gate twelve. His flight wouldn't be boarding for at least twenty minutes, so he took the time to carefully study the people waiting in the terminal. He saw business people, couples, students, families—and he knew he had to select carefully. After several minutes he made his choice—a man who appeared to be traveling alone. He looked to be in his mid-thirties, had a couple of large and very visible tattoos and a ponytail that went halfway down his back. His luggage consisted of a tattered backpack, and the shoes on his feet were well worn. Most importantly, he looked like a guy who wouldn't turn down a few bucks to do a favor for a stranger.

Houston stood up and took a stroll, keeping his eye on the man with the ponytail. He was sitting at gate ten, and appeared to be waiting for a flight to Toronto, scheduled to leave just a few minutes before the flight to Miami was scheduled to depart. Perfect, thought Houston, he's heading out of the country. He walked around for a few more minutes, and then casually took a seat directly across from ponytail man.

From his vantage point, he was able to get a much closer look. The more he looked the more he liked, with the kicker being the large tattoo on the man's right bicep which read *Fuck the Cops*.

Perfect, Houston thought. We have a winner.

"Okay, it's been ten minutes. Time to raise some hell."

Keller stood up and walked back toward the receptionist. Mia followed.

But before Keller could begin voicing his displeasure, Mia jumped in. "It appears that Mr. Timbers has once again been detained. Would it be possible for you to contact Mr. Adjakian and let him know we need to speak to him right away?"

The receptionist looked at Mia and then at Keller. Sensing that Keller was near the end of his rope, she looked at Mia and said, "Certainly, I'll call him right now. I'm sure he'll be with you shortly."

Keller and Mia returned to their seats on the sofa and waited. A few minutes later, a man appeared and introduced himself.

"Hello, I'm Rob Adjakian. You're Mia Serrano, I presume?"

Mia stood up and shook Adjakian's hand.

"I understand Mr. Timbers still has not contacted you?"

"Nope, and we're tired of getting jacked around," interjected Keller.

"Maybe there's something I can help you with . . . what, exactly, do you need to know?"

Keller continued, "We need to find out when Vanessa Tolken last worked. It's very important we get that information."

"Okay, I can pull up that information from payroll. Why don't you come with me to my office? I can make the call from there."

Keller and Mia followed Adjakian around to the other side of the atrium to a large, very nicely-furnished office.

Keller muttered under his breath, "Now I see why they only pay a quarter percent on their CD accounts."

Mia elbowed him in the ribs. "Behave."

Adjakian motioned for them to sit while he called payroll. A minute later he hung up the phone and turned toward Mia and Keller.

"The last day she worked was this past Friday, but she didn't come into work this morning. No call, she just didn't show up at her report time. At the risk of being out of line, can I ask what it is that you're investigating?"

Keller and Mia looked at each other and Keller spoke. "I'm afraid we have some bad news. Ms. Tolken is dead and we strongly believe she's been murdered. We're the investigators on the case and the questions we're asking are critical for us to establish a timeline for her death."

Mr. Adjakian took the news hard.

"Oh, my God—that poor woman."

"Did you know Ms. Tolken?"

"No, I didn't. This is a pretty large operation and she worked under Mr. Timbers. But still, this news is very upsetting. I can't believe it."

"We've notified her next of kin, but at this point we'd prefer it if you kept it quiet. Most people who are murdered are killed by someone they know, especially when the victim is female. We don't know what happened at this point, but we can't rule anything out."

"You think it was someone she worked with?"

"At this point we just don't know, but that's certainly something we'll look at carefully. We always do."

Adjakian looked out the window and didn't speak for several seconds.

"I understand, but I think I need to let my boss know. Would that be all right?"

"Sure. Do it quietly, and ask him to keep it to himself, at least for now."

"Where you headed today?"

Ponytail guy looked at Houston sitting across from him, paused momentarily, and replied, "Toronto."

"Ah, I love Toronto. It's a beautiful city," replied Houston.

It was a lie; he had never set foot in Canada.

"Going up there on business or pleasure?"

Ponytail guy looked at Houston, not really sure why he was having a conversation with this stranger, but it seemed harmless enough.

"I got some family up there so I guess it's for fun, although my family can be kind of a pain in the ass, you know?"

"No kidding."

"How about you—where you headed off to?"

More lies. "Seattle. On business, unfortunately, although I may take some time for myself. It's beautiful up there in the late summer."

"Never been."

"Well, if you ever get the chance, jump on it."

Just then the first boarding call for the flight to Toronto was announced over the PA system.

Ponytail guy stood up and grabbed his backpack.

"Well, that's me. Nice talking with you."

Houston stood up, leaned into him a bit and said, "Hey, listen—I know this might sound a little odd, but I'm wondering if you could do me a favor?"

Ponytail guy looked at him, but didn't speak.

"There's a couple hundred bucks in it for you if you'll help me out."

That caught ponytail guy's full attention.

"What do you need?"

"I have something I'd like for you to take on the plane with you and when you arrive in Toronto, just leave it in the seat, kind of half-tucked down in the cushion."

"Jesus, what is it—a bomb?"

Houston laughed, "No, nothing like that. Here, I'll show you."

He handed ponytail guy his Jonathan Timbers Colorado driver's license, his medical insurance card, his MasterCard and two one-hundred-dollar bills, all held together by a rubber band.

"You want me to leave this on the plane, in the seat cushion?"

"Yes, but you can keep the money—that's for you, for your trouble."

"That's it? That's all I need to do?"

"Yep, that's it."

Ponytail guy looked at Houston and a small smile spread across his face.

"I don't know what game you're playing my friend, but I like it."

Houston smiled back and replied, "Have a good flight."

"You know it."

Adjakian picked up the phone in his office and dialed the number to John Crombach, chief executive officer for Tower Bank operations. He quickly delivered the news to his boss and then turned back to Keller and Mia.

"My boss said to cooperate with you fully. What else do you need?"

"Is Jonathan Timbers Tolken's supervisor?" asked Keller.

"Not directly, he's the VP of accounts receivable. Vanessa worked in that division, but she had a manager and that manager, in turn, reports to Mr. Timbers."

Keller sat a little more upright in his chair. He looked at Adjakian and said, "And now, Mr. Timbers is nowhere to be found and one of his employees is dead."

"Oh my God, you don't think . . . "

Mia spoke next. "We'd like to go to his office; do you have any problem with that?"

"I don't suppose there's any harm. My boss said to cooperate fully. I'll take you over there."

The three made their way to the other side of the atrium and stopped at Catalina's desk.

"We need to get into Mr. Timbers office. Is it locked?" asked Adjakian.

"Yes, he always locks it when he leaves. I'm not sure Mr. Timbers would approve of you going in there . . . it might be better if you waited for him to get back," she answered.

"No, we aren't waiting any longer. Open it up," demanded Keller.

Catalina looked at Adjakian and he nodded.

She stood up, grabbed the key from the top drawer in her desk, and led them to the door. She unlocked it and the four of them entered.

The office was large, similar in size and layout to Adjakian's office, only decorated in a more modern style. Keller and Mia walked around, taking it all in. They both had the same question running through their minds: was Timbers somehow involved in the murder of his beautiful employee?

Adjakian and Catalina stood near the doorway, not sure what to do.

"Do you have a key to his desk?" Mia asked Catalina.

Catalina again looked to Adjakian, who nodded.

"I'll get it," she replied, then turned and left the office.

"We may need access to his computer and his phone records as well. Does he have a company-issued cell phone?"

"Yes, everyone in management does."

Catalina reappeared and walked to the desk. She unlocked the top drawer and pulled it open for the investigators.

As Keller and Mia walked over to review the contents, they both saw it at the same time. Keller reached over and picked up a framed photograph from the desk, holding it up for the others to see.

"Would this happen to be Mr. Timbers?"

"Yes, that photo was taken a few months back," replied Catalina, standing off to the side with her arms folded.

"Looks like Mr. Timbers is a pilot, huh?"

"He flies almost every weekend," Catalina answered.

"Is this his plane?"

"No, he doesn't have his own plane. He usually rents one at the airport in Centennial."

The photo depicted a man standing proudly in front of what appeared to be a Cessna 182. It looked like the picture had been taken on the tarmac of a small airport. The tail number of the plane was clearly visible in the photo, and Mia quickly googled it. The search revealed that the plane was registered to a rental company at the Centennial Airport, twenty miles south of Denver.

Jack said, "We'll need to bring in our forensic people to look at his computer. We'll also need a photo of Mr. Timbers. I'm sure you have some nice head shots of the guy."

Catalina became defiant. "With all due respect, he's just late returning from a meeting this morning. So what if he's a pilot? A lot of people have their pilot's license. You're going to look awfully silly when he comes walking in here any minute."

Keller and Mia ignored her.

Mia continued, looking at Adjakian, "We're going to seize this office as a possible crime scene. From this point forward, no one will have access to this office without the permission of the RCSO. Understood?"

Adjakian nodded.

Keller looked at Mia. Both knew it was a stretch claiming the office as a crime scene, as there was no evidence that Tolken had been killed there. But they also both knew that neither Adjakian nor the spunky Catalina would know any better. They needed to get their forensic computer team there as soon as possible. They couldn't risk someone trying to delete anything or tampering in any way with Timbers' computer.

"Of course," replied Adjakian. "I'll let Mr. Crombach know. I'm sure he'll want our legal department informed of what's transpiring here."

Keller used his cell phone to call into RCSO dispatch and requested a half-dozen uniforms to respond to their location. They would need them to stand guard while he and Mia took the next step of interviewing Tolken's co-workers.

Keller motioned for Mia to follow him into the hall, out of earshot of Adjakian and Catalina. They stood just a few feet outside the doorway where they could keep an eye on the two. Keller spoke in a low voice.

"We've got a bunch of stuff we need to move forward on. First, we need to call Commander Espy and let him know what we've got going here. Tell him we need a warrant, pronto. We also need to contact Denver PD, as a courtesy, to let them know we're in their jurisdiction. We'll need to get our forensic people down here right away to do their thing with the computer. And another thing—we need to have a couple investigators go out to the Centennial Airport and find the place that rents planes. See if Timbers has rented a plane in the past few hours. Timbers could very well be on his way to God-knows-where right now. I can send a photo of Timbers to whoever goes to the airport so they can show it to the rental people."

"I'll call Espy and get things rolling."

"I'll stand guard in Timbers' office while you make the calls. I don't want anybody screwing around in there before we can get the place secured," Keller said looking back through the open door. Adjakian and Catalina were standing there silently, both looking a little spooked.

"Once the uniforms arrive we can begin our interviews of the co-workers. We'll need another team of investigators to help with that. I'm not sure who's up in the rotation, but whoever it is, we need them down here ASAP. This is going to take some time. Make that request of Espy as well."

"Got it," Mia replied, taking her cell phone from her pocket.

Keller walked back into the office.

"Mr. Adjakian, can we get that headshot of Timbers? If it could be sent to my cell, that would be best."

"Yes, I can have that for you shortly. Just write down your number."

Keller turned to Catalina.

"Oh, and thanks for the heads up about your boss renting planes out of Centennial. That saves us a lot of time. Who knows—maybe he's out there right now and we can scoop him up real quick like."

It was an obvious dig at the young woman, but Keller felt she had it coming.

Catalina glared at him, turned, and marched out of the office.

"One other thing," Keller said turning back toward Adjakian. "I don't want her trying to contact her boss and tipping him off to anything going on here. I'm going to ask that she be placed somewhere where she has no access to a phone. Maybe a conference room? I'll have one of our deputies monitor her."

"Oh, I'm sure she wouldn't try anything like that."

"Just the same, until we really know what we've got going on here, I want her monitored. At least until her shift is over."

CHAPTER 13

"Can I bring you another drink, sir?"

Christopher Houston was on his third Grey Goose and was, in fact, feeling loose as a goose.

"No, that'll be it for now,' he replied to the young flight attendant.

"Okay, I'll check back with you in a little bit," she said with a flirtatious smile.

"Please do."

His mind flashed to his wife and two children left behind in Littleton. It was only two in the afternoon; they were not yet aware they had seen the last of him. A few hours from now, Diane and the kids would be home, expecting him to be there by six. Only he wouldn't be there at six, and he'd never be there again.

"I think I will have another, actually," he said to the cute attendant as she walked by.

"Coming right up."

Houston quickly twisted the wedding ring off his finger and slid it into his suit pocket.

RCSO Investigators Bob Clemmons and Thomas Kilbride arrived at Freedom Flight Rental at the Centennial Airport fewer than thirty minutes after being assigned the task by Commander Espy. The commander had given them a quick briefing on what needed to be done and Mia gave them more detail about the case via cell phone while they were en route to the airport.

As they pulled into the small parking lot of the rental facility, it quickly became apparent they were the only ones there. The lot was empty but the sign on the door said OPEN, so they quickly parked and went inside. They were met by a young woman at the counter.

"Welcome to Freedom Flight Rental. Can I help you?"

Kilbride responded, "We're from the Rocklin County Sheriff's Department and we need some information. We're hoping you can help us."

The clerk looked at the two plainclothes investigators as they displayed their badges.

"Sure, I'll do what I can. What do you need to know?"

Clemmons showed the clerk the photo of Timbers that Keller had sent to his cell phone.

"We need to know if this man has come into your shop today?"

"Sure, that's Jonathan Timbers. He's a regular customer here. But no, I haven't seen him today."

"Have you been here all day?" asked Kilbride.

"Yes, since we opened at nine. I'm the only one working today. Weekdays are kinda slow in the plane rental business."

"So you're positive he hasn't been in today?"

"Yes, I'm sure. Like I said, I'm the only one here today."

Clemmons continued, "You say he's a regular customer of yours?"

"Yeah, he probably rents from us three or four times a month. He got his pilot's license a few years ago. Caught the flying bug and so I think he goes up about as often as he can afford it."

"Can you tell us the last time he rented from you?"

"Sure, I can do that. It's all tracked in the computer. Give me just a second."

Clemmons and Kilbride stood at the counter and waited while the clerk queried the computer.

"Yep, he was in last week. Rented a Cessna one-eighty-two from us."

"What day would that have been?"

He looked back at the computer screen.

"That was last Friday. Checked the plane out at six forty-five that evening and returned it at eight ten. We only charged him for an hour. He's a really good customer and we give guys like him our best rates."

The two investigators gave each other a quick sidelong glance.

"Were you working that night?"

"Yeah, Fridays are a regular work day for me."

"Do you remember if he was alone when he rented the plane that night?"

She shrugged, adding "I don't really recall but he usually flies by himself."

"Think back—it's important."

The clerk folded her arms and replied, "I really don't remember. I'm sorry."

"The Cessna one-eighty-two he rented last Friday—is it here now?"

"Yes, it's parked right over there. Like I said, it's been slow and we really haven't—"

Clemmons interrupted the young woman.

"Okay, we need to speak to your boss right away."

"I'm sorry, have I upset you somehow? I didn't mean to . . . "

"No, we just need to speak to someone in authority right away."

The woman looked a bit shaken.

She picked up the phone and dialed a number from memory.

"Yeah, Jane, this is Leah down at the shop. There are a couple of cops here and they said they need to speak with you. I don't know . . . all they said was—"

"Give me the phone."

The clerk handed the phone to Kilbride.

"This is Investigator Thomas Kilbride with the Rocklin County Sheriff's Office. Who am I speaking to?

"I'm Jane Waters, the owner of Freedom Flight Rental. Is there some kind of problem?"

"We need to secure one of your planes. It could be part of a criminal investigation we're handling. I'm not sure how long we will need it, but I really need your cooperation on this."

"Well, okay, I guess. Which plane is it?"

"A Cessna one-eighty-two—your employee says it's on the ground here."

"Okay, so what's next? I mean, what happens now, exactly?"

"We'll get a search warrant for the plane and then have a CSI team come out to the airport and do what they need to do. I don't think there's any reason we'll need to take the plane from the tarmac; we should be able to do everything we need to right here. And I'm guessing that by tomorrow it should be back in your fleet and available for rental service. But I can't guarantee that; it depends on what our CSI people find."

"Well, I hope it doesn't take too long. That plane is one of my more popular rentals. It's a big moneymaker for me."

"I understand, and we won't keep it a second longer than we need to. I really do appreciate your cooperation on this."

"All right. Put Leah back on the phone and I'll give her the okay."

A few minutes later, Kilbride called Commander Espy and filled him in on what they had found. A search warrant would be written and, before long, a CSI team from RCSO would be dispatched to the Centennial Airport. The Cessna 182 parked on the tarmac would be getting their full attention.

It didn't take long for the forty-sixth floor of the Tower Bank building to become a hub of activity. The six deputies Keller requested were busy handling their respective assignments. The forensic guys had to wait for a search warrant, but once it was in place they got to work on the computer in Timber's office. Catalina sat in a conference room watching television while a deputy stood at the door. She had protested loudly to anyone and everyone that she was being held against her will, but Adjakian had explained to her that as long as she was on the clock, Tower management could assign her to any task necessary. And that task, at least for the rest of her work day, was to sit in the conference room and watch television.

Mia and Keller began interviewing Vanessa Tolken's co-workers. There were more than thirty employees in the unit who processed payments and came into the center each day. Anyone who knew Vanessa was questioned. The interviews typically lasted only a few minutes as it quickly became clear that the relationship most of them had with Vanessa was really nothing beyond seeing her each day at work. After three hours Keller and Mia had spoken to everyone and the interviews yielded nothing useful.

At five o'clock, the employees began to clear out and Catalina asked if she was free to go. Keller said she could leave but gave her a stern warning about what could happen if it was discovered that she had made contact with Timbers to tip him off. Being an accessory after the fact, he explained, was not something that she'd want to be accused of; a conviction carried a prison sentence. She seemed to get the message and left the office quietly.

After the interviews with co-workers were completed, Keller and Mia huddled and discussed their next steps. Mia suggested they get a warrant and search Timber's home. Keller agreed, so Mia placed a call to the RCSO warrant team and got them started. This case was keeping the team busy. Having a specialized group who wrote virtually all the search warrants for the RCSO was something that had been hugely beneficial in many critical investigations. Warrants weren't overly difficult to put together, but investigators had more pressing things to do in the critical early hours of an investigation. Having a team put them together saved valuable time and because they did it with regularity they were able to hone their skills to the point of getting most warrants written in less than an hour.

CHAPTER 14

"God, I'm exhausted. Do you mind if I sit for a few minutes?"

Christopher Houston smiled up at the flight attendant. "Of course not. Have a seat."

She smiled and lowered herself into the comfortable first-class seat, kicked off her shoes, and leaned in toward Houston. She was just coming out of a serious relationship and had certainly noticed this young, well-dressed man sitting in first class. He was cute, and what the hell, she thought, there was no harm in a little flirting.

"Don't tell anyone I took my shoes off. It's a big no-no with the FAA. Something about safety . . . "

"So, I shouldn't get up and make an announcement on the PA system over there?"

"I'd kill you if you did!" she responded, laughing as she grabbed his arm and shook it playfully.

"So, where are you based?"

"Miami. The whole crew is based there. We work together most of the time."

"You're headed home, then?"

"Yep. In the last three days I've been to LA, Denver—of course, Minneapolis, Chicago, and now Miami. I'll have two days off and then I do it all again. Ah, yes . . . the glamorous life of a United Airlines flight attendant."

"Well, let's face it—you do it for the big bucks, right?"

She laughed at the joke. "Yeah, it works out to about fifteen bucks an hour. I'm another Warren Buffett."

"How long have you been a flight attendant?"

"Three years. I graduated from Florida State with a degree in finance a few years ago but couldn't find a job—the recession killed everything for people like me, especially in banking and finance. So, when a girlfriend told me she could get me on with United, I figured why not? And so, here I am."

"Nice. You might as well see the world. There'll be plenty of time for career and the other serious stuff that life brings your way. Might as well have some fun."

"That's what I figure. Hey, here we are chatting away and I don't even know your name!"

He extended his hand. "Christopher Houston, but I go by Chris. And I see from your name tag that your name is Gina."

"Nice to meet you, Chris Houston," she replied, shaking his hand.

"So, now you know my life story—tell me yours."

"Me? There's not much to tell . . . "

"No fair! You gotta share, Chris."

"Okay, I graduated from Florida State with a degree in finance, and—"

"You are such a tease! Knock it off, Mr. Houston, or I'm going to tell the pilot on you."

He looked at the beautiful young woman sitting just inches from him and realized he wasn't sure what to do. It was obvious that she was interested in him, but was it really a good idea to be going down this path? He was a man on the run . . . did he really need the baggage of a woman, even a beautiful one like Gina?

"I'm in real estate. Buying and selling—commercial mostly."

"So, what brings you to Miami?"

"I'm here to look at some property. I have a client with more money than God who asked me to go and check out a couple of buildings in the Fort Lauderdale area. He's looking to invest and so I'll see if there's anything worth investing in."

"Now that wasn't so hard was it, Mr. Houston?"

"Nope. Hell, you should be a cop. You'd have the bad guys confessing to you as soon as you smiled at them."

"Oh, aren't you sweet."

Just then an announcement came over the PA system, "Flight attendants, please prepare for landing."

"Oops, that's me. Duty calls."

Chris Houston watched as Gina slipped back into her shoes and made her way to the front of the first-class section. She took a seat, buckled herself in, and looked back at him.

He smiled at her and she gave him a little wink.

God, he thought. What the hell am I doing?

"Can I have a word with you, investigator?"

Keller was looking over the notes he had taken during the interviews with Tolken's co-workers. He looked up and saw an older gentleman, in his early sixties, standing before him.

"And you would be . . . ?"

The man extended his hand. "I'm John Crombach. I run this processing center."

Keller shook the man's hand.

"Sure, we can talk."

"Perhaps we can go over to my office. I'm around the other side of the elevator."

"Okay, lead the way."

The two walked to an office much larger than those of Timbers and Adjakian. Rank had its privilege, Keller thought, as he went in and took a seat next to an oversized mahogany desk. Crombach took his seat behind the desk and began to speak.

“This has been a very difficult day for us. I didn’t know the young lady, but from what I’ve heard from my staff today, she was hardworking and a popular member of the Tower Bank team.”

Keller nodded but didn’t speak. There must be more this guy wanted to say beyond some benign accolades for the dead woman. And then it came.

“An hour ago I was made aware of a possible situation involving Mr. Timber’s division. His area of responsibility is the collection of credit card and loan payments made by our customers each month. The checks they send to us all come through this center—in fact, anyone in the country making payments on a Tower Bank account sends those payments to us here in Denver. We process the checks and post them to the proper account. Of course, there is an elaborate system of checks and balances in place to avoid any impropriety by our employees.”

“Go on,” Keller answered, anxious to hear the next part of the man’s story.

“I was contacted by Martin Lynch—he’s our head of security—who told me there appeared to be some discrepancies in some of our account receivables balances. He was going to look deeper into it and bring in several people from our fraud unit, all trained to detect cybercrime. At this point Lynch is about ninety-nine percent certain that there is money missing. He needs to check a few more things before he’s absolutely sure, but it looks highly probable.”

”And how much money are we talking about?”

“Seven-point-two million, give or take a little bit. We’ll know the exact amount down to the penny shortly. It appears that the money was wired from one of our collection points to several offshore bank accounts a few hours ago.”

“Who else knows about this?”

“Just Lynch, members of his fraud team, and John Chancer—he’s the president of Tower Bank—back in New York. I called him to let him know what was going on. That was before we knew anything about Ms. Tolken or that Jonathan Timbers would suddenly go missing."

"Well, that gives us a lot more to go on. Money is always a great motive for murder. Are your fraud people looking forensically at everything Timbers and Tolken have done in recent weeks or months?"

"They are now. Obviously with today's developments we have a good starting point."

Keller sat quietly for a few moments, pondering what Crombach had just told him. He was concerned that having the Tower Bank fraud people doing their own investigation could create some difficult problems for him and Mia as they conducted their investigation.

"Look, Mr. Crombach—I appreciate you sharing all this with me and it certainly gives us a very solid direction with respect to where we go next in this investigation, but I need to tell you that before your fraud people go any further, we need to bring in our own people. We need to protect the integrity of a murder investigation. And while I can appreciate the concern you have over the bank missing more than seven million dollars, finding Vanessa Tolken's killer takes priority. I'm sure you understand."

"Yes, of course. I didn't mean to imply otherwise. I just wanted to make you aware of this situation. But at the same time I have a duty to my stockholders to get to the bottom of this. Seven million dollars is not a small amount of money. And, if the media gets wind of this, it won't look very good for the bank."

So there it was—Crombach's real concern. The bank could absorb a loss of a measly seven million bucks. It was the bad publicity he was more concerned about. Gotta protect the stockholders, Keller thought to himself.

"I'll contact my superiors right away, and it might be a good idea if your security guy Lynch talks with our computer forensic guy so they work things out—set the ground rules, that sort of thing."

"I think that's a good approach. I'll let Lynch know he can expect a call from the RCSO. What's the name of your forensic person?"

"Jameson Hayes."

"I appreciate your time, investigator, and I'll have Martin Lynch contact him." Crombach stood up, signaling the meeting was over.

Keller walked out of the office and briefed Mia on what he had just learned.

Rocklin County Superior Court Judge Stanton Myers signed off on the collection of search warrants brought to him by the warrants team and soon all systems were go. As a courtesy, Keller called Littleton PD to let them know they would be searching the home of Jonathan Timbers, and inquired if there had been any calls for service from the residence in the past. Only one, he was told—a Ms. Diane Timbers had reported a prowler two years earlier.

Most importantly he learned there was no history of any guns in the home—something deputies always liked to know when they were going to carry out a warrant.

Mia and Keller arrived in the Timbers' neighborhood shortly before seven that evening and waited for the warrant team to arrive. They parked around the block from the residence at a location from which the team had agreed to deploy. They weren't expecting any kind of resistance at the house, and they certainly didn't expect to find Jonathan Timbers sitting in his dining room having dinner. But this was a fluid situation and the team had to be ready for any possible scenario.

Once the team was in place, they formulated their plan to hit the house. It would start with a knock on the door, and, assuming someone was home to let them in, the team would enter. They would give a copy of the warrant to Timber's wife, or whoever opened the door, and proceed from there. One deputy would be assigned to stay with that individual during the search in the event they attempted to interfere with the deputies, or hide or destroy evidence. It was the belief of the warrant team, Mia and Keller included, that Mrs. Timbers would be stunned at what was about to transpire, and that she most likely had no idea her husband was missing at this point, much less being looked at for the murder of a co-worker.

If no one answered their knock, they'd enter using force, as allowed under the law.

Once the team had its plan in place they moved quickly to the house. It was a large home in an upscale neighborhood with a Subaru SUV parked in the driveway.

The team of six, including Keller and Mia, approached the door. Sergeant Chavez, the leader of the team, knocked firmly on the door, shouting "Police! Open up!"

A few seconds later a woman opened the door and gasped at what she saw.

CHAPTER 15

Jameson Hayes was impressed with the speed of the elevator in the Tower Bank building. He had a habit of counting off, in his head, the number of seconds it took the various elevators he rode each day to reach their destinations. The Tower Bank elevator climbed the forty-six floors in less than a minute—fifty-two seconds, to be precise. It wasn't the fastest he had ridden, but it was close. Then there was the elevator at RCSO headquarters—it climbed only three floors but was painfully slow. Even when it didn't stop at the second floor, which was a rarity, it often took more than twenty seconds to go from the first floor to the third floor. All that time to climb a lousy thirty feet. Pathetic, he thought. He had places to go and work to do. How much time did he waste in elevators?

When the doors opened at the forty-sixth floor, Hayes rolled out of the elevator and into the reception area. He took a quick look around and saw several RCSO deputies along with what he assumed were Tower Bank employees.

One of the deputies heard the elevator doors open and glanced over.

"Hey, Jameson."

Hayes recognized the deputy and returned the greeting with a nod.

"Keller is in one of those offices over there," continued the deputy, motioning toward the other side of the reception area.

"Thanks."

The deputy watched as Hayes made his way toward the offices. He knew better than to ask Hayes if he needed any assistance. That was a good way to get your head bitten off.

Jameson Hayes had been to the brink and back. He was a star baseball player in high school and college—so talented, in fact, he had been drafted by the Cincinnati Reds after graduating with highest honors from Clemson University. Back then he had his whole life mapped out—first, a career in pro baseball and then a move into the broadcasting booth. He had the looks, often being told he bore a striking resemblance to the actor Denzel Washington, and he certainly had the brains. But as often happens, life didn't turn out the way he had planned. Getting hit by a drunk driver seven years earlier and living life in a wheelchair wasn't something he had ever envisioned.

Keller saw Hayes as he approached.

Keller spoke first. "You need to get with Martin Lynch—he's the Tower Bank fraud guy."

"We've already spoken by phone. We're meeting here shortly."

Keller nodded. "Let me show you the office. We've got a team in there already."

"Sure. Let's go."

At Centennial Airport, the CSI team got busy going over the Cessna 182 parked on the tarmac behind Freedom Flight Rentals. The team did some initial checks for fingerprints, and, as expected, they found several different prints within the cockpit area and the small back seat. It was a rental, after all, used by different people every day. The odds of finding a usable fingerprint that could be matched to Vanessa Tolken were relatively slim, but they did their best just the same. They managed to lift several prints from the passenger side of the cockpit, where their victim likely sat if she had indeed been up in the plane with Jonathan Timbers the previous Friday night. Those prints would have to be compared to Tolken's once the CSI fingerprint tech got back to the station. If there was a match, the case against Timbers would grow much stronger.

"So, good luck looking at those properties in Fort Lauderdale."

The plane had taxied to the gate and most of the passengers had disembarked.

Chris Houston found himself lingering, taking his time gathering up his stuff. It was just him and Gina left in the first-class section of the plane.

"Thanks. I'm sure I'll find something my client can throw his money at."

Gina looked at him and smiled. "Look, I've got the next couple of days off. If you need anyone to help you find Fort Lauderdale, well—I can help you with that."

Houston's spirits lifted immediately and he felt a surge go through him.

"Yeah, I hear it can be hard to find. Maybe I will need a little help," he replied with a smile.

"Here, I'll give you my number. If you decide you want some company, just give me a call."

Houston took the number, placed it in his pocket, and happily made his way to the terminal.

CHAPTER 16

"Are you Diane Timbers?" Sergeant Chavez demanded.

The woman covered her mouth and staggered backward a few feet, not understanding what was unfolding before her. Fearful that she was going to faint, two members of the warrant team rushed in and grabbed her by the arms. They held her up and led her to a sofa in a sitting room just off the foyer.

"Yes, I'm Diane Timbers. What's going on? I—I don't understand," she stammered.

"My name is Sergeant Chavez and we're with the Rocklin County Sheriff's Department. We have a warrant to search your home."

Diane Timbers sat on her sofa, too stunned to respond.

Chavez handed her the warrant. She took it but didn't look at it. She suddenly jumped up and began running for the stairs.

One of the warrant team members grabbed her before she got very far. "I'm sorry, ma'am, but you need to stay down here."

A tearful, panicked Diane Timbers answered, "I don't understand—what are you doing here? Why are you doing this?"

"It's all explained in the warrant, ma'am."

"My children . . . they're upstairs in their rooms. I need to get them."

Chavez looked at her and responded, "Okay, we'll go up with you and you can bring them downstairs. We need to clear their rooms anyway. Mia—would you mind escorting Ms. Timbers up to get her kids?"

Mia nodded, feeling true empathy for this poor woman whose life was in the process of being turned upside down. She reached out for the woman and put her hand on her arm.

"Come with me; let's go get your kids. We can bring them downstairs and they can be with you."

Mia began walking her up the stairs. The poor woman was trembling.

She turned again to Mia. "I don't understand. Why are you here? What have I done?"

"You need to read the warrant; it's all explained in there," replied Mia.

They gathered up the two kids from their bedrooms and went downstairs into the sitting room. The kids, a girl who looked about eight and a boy who appeared a few years younger, had not heard what was going on downstairs. They were wide-eyed as they descended the stairs and took in the scene playing out before them.

"Can I call my husband?"

Mia looked at the woman and paused before speaking. She considered whether or not to tell her that her husband was the reason for their visit. It was all clearly outlined in the warrant, but despite Mia's suggestions, Diane had not looked at the document. So, Mia figured, why not let her call him? You never know, she thought. He might answer a call from his wife. It was a bit of a long shot but she didn't see any downside to it.

"Sure. Do you have a cell phone with you or do you have a land line here?"

"I don't know where my cell is. I'm not thinking straight. I can use the phone in the family room."

"Okay, I'll need to go with you. Show me the way," Mia replied.

"Kids—stay on the sofa. I'll be right back."

The two walked through the house until they reached the family room. Mia turned to her. "I'm sorry, but I'll need to dial the number for you. Can you write it down for me?"

"Okay."

She scribbled the number for Mia on paper she tore from her notepad. Mia dialed the number and handed the phone to Diane. Mia stuck the paper in her pocket. She had fibbed to Diane Timbers—there was no reason for her to dial the number, but her motive was simple—she now had a phone number that certainly belonged to Jonathan Timbers. She would check to see if the number matched the cell number given to her by Adjakian. If he was smart he'd dump his cell, but Mia had seen criminals do dumber things.

"He's not answering. What am I going to do?" Tears were running down her cheeks.

"You need to read the warrant. Let's go back to the sitting room and you can read it there."

Mia led her back through the house and returned her to the sofa where her children were sitting.

Diane Timbers began looking at the warrant. Mia took the opportunity to compare the cell number Adjakian had given her for Timbers to the number his wife had called. Unfortunately they matched, so it was a dead end. Mia looked over at Diane and it was becoming clear that the woman had figured out what was going on.

"My husband? You think that he . . . "

She stopped mid-sentence, realizing that her children were sitting just a few feet away.

"What about daddy?" asked the daughter, looking confused and worried.

"It's nothing, Alex. Don't worry—these officers will be leaving soon."

"What are they doing here?"

"They're looking for something they think they lost. It's all a big mistake."

"But why are they—"

"That's enough, Alex. We'll talk about it later."

The warrant team was going through everything, from the drawers in the kitchen to every closet, looking for anything that could shed light on the murder of Vanessa Tolken. The home was large and it took the team more than two hours to complete the search. They found no obvious signs that the murder had taken place inside the home; investigators had no reason to believe that it had. But they were able to gather up two desktop computers, a laptop, and an iPad. They found a Nikon camera and a desk calendar in the study of the home. All were collected and tagged. It was too early to tell what these items might yield, but the deputies gathered everything and placed the items in the RCSO van parked on the street in front of the house.

"I think the team has things under control here. Let's run out to the airport and see how the CSI team is doing with the plane," Keller said to Mia as they stood outside on the driveway of the home.

"It's a little after nine right now," Keller added, looking at his watch. "When I talked with Debra Schambra earlier she indicated the team would likely be out there till early morning."

Mia was exhausted but the adrenalin from the day's activities were keeping her going.

"Yeah, that sounds good. I'll let Chavez know we're going to head out."

"I'll meet you at the car."

Christopher Houston stood at the foot of his bed staring at the contents of his suitcase. There were his clothes, an untraceable burner phone, his fake Christopher Houston passport, a stack of twenty dollar bills and the piece of paper with Gina's phone number scrawled across it.

He realized he hadn't eaten since breakfast some nine hours and two thousand miles ago. He was hungry and decided he'd go out and grab a bite. He had no transportation so he'd need to find something close by the hotel or grab a taxi. There was no shortage of places to eat in South Beach—the place was crawling with restaurants, bars, and clubs. He could also eat at the hotel, but he was feeling like getting out for a bit.

He grabbed the paper with Gina's number and considered calling her. After a few seconds he decided to leave her be. It had only been a couple hours since they had parted ways; he didn't want to seem too eager. And besides, he thought, he wasn't sure he wanted to be encumbered with someone, given his situation. He wasn't going to be in Miami very long and keeping it complication-free was probably for the best. But damn, he thought, she was cute and certainly seemed interested.

He quickly changed into board shorts and a Tommy Bahama shirt he had packed. He grabbed a few twenties from his money supply and slipped them into his front pocket. He scooped up his passport and his room key and headed out to explore South Beach.

It was a short drive from the Timbers' home in Littleton to the airport in Centennial.

The small airport was nearly deserted at the late hour, but as they drove through the entrance they could see bright lights coming from one area of the tarmac. They drove toward the lights and saw the building that housed Freedom Flight Rentals. The lights were coming from behind the building, so they parked in the lot and walked out onto the tarmac.

It was an eerie scene. The lights shining on the plane in what was an otherwise dark environment gave it a look one might see on a movie set. Keller and Mia approached the plane and saw Debra Schambra offering direction to two other techs. Keller and Mia paused momentarily, not wanting to disrupt things. Schambra looked up and gave them a wave, indicating they should approach.

Mia spoke, "We don't want to get in the way. We just wanted to see how things were going out here."

"Good, I guess. It's a challenge processing something that so many people have had access to. I mean, who knows how many different people have been in this plane in the past few weeks . . . "

"Well, the folks at Freedom Flights Rentals can tell us that, so if we need to start eliminating fingerprints we could go that route," replied Mia.

Schambra answered, "Yeah, but what a hassle. We could be chasing that down for weeks."

"Any signs of blood or anything that would give you reason to believe there could have been some sort of struggle on board?" asked Keller."

"No obvious signs, but we're about to go in with the luminol, so that should answer the blood question."

CHAPTER 17

Jack Keller got to his office early the next morning. There was a lot to do. First, he sent a quick email to Mark Archer asking him to come by his office as soon as possible. He wanted to get Jonathan Timbers' photo out to the media and he needed Archer's help to make that happen. He had given serious thought to putting out Timbers' photo the night before but knew that doing so would cause a drain on RCSO resources. He also believed there was little chance Timbers was still in the greater Denver area. With his resources and a pilot's license, Keller knew Timbers could be virtually anywhere in the world by now.

He called Mia and suggested that they set up a meeting later that morning with all those who played a role in the investigation the day before. There were so many moving parts to the case, and with so much having transpired in the past twenty-four hours, he didn't want anything to slip through the cracks.

As he hung up the phone, he saw Mark Archer standing in his doorway.

"Come on in."

"What's up? Something to do with the one-eighty-seven from the other day?"

"Yep, we caught a break and I need your help. Thanks to the composite you put out for us, we've identified the victim. We have a suspect and we need to get his photo out. He's on the loose and the sooner we get it circulated the better, although I suspect he's long gone by now."

"Sure, I can do that. Send me his photo and I can get it out pronto."

"I've got it in my cell phone—it was sent to me by his employer. I'll just forward it to you."

"Sure, that'll work. What do you want me to say?"

Back at his office, Mark Archer typed out the media alert outlining the search for Jonathan Timbers. He attached the photo and with the push of a button sent it electronically to "All Media." Within three minutes, his phone began to ring. Reporters were eager to cover the story and wanted to arrange interviews with him. He was able to group all the interviews within a two-hour window: six in total—four TV news stations plus the *Denver Post* and KDEN news radio.

He closed his office door and sat at his desk formulating the questions he anticipated getting and the responses he would give. This was always the challenge of the job—reporters feeling he was being too tight-lipped while the investigators believed he had said too much. He looked at his notepad where he had scribbled down the details for the six interviews he had committed to doing. He looked at the interview he had set for 11:30, the one with Channel Eight, and wondered if Angela Bell would be the one doing the story.

Jack and Mia were the first to arrive in the upstairs conference room. Coffee and pastries were brought in for the dozen or so personnel expected to attend. Mia had sprung for the goodies; there was no budget for that.

Shortly after ten, everyone was present and Jack started the briefing.

"Let's get started. We have a lot to cover today. We had a very busy day yesterday with lots of different scenes going down simultaneously. Let me start with what Mia and I handled and then we can move on from there."

Keller handed out an outline of his abbreviated notes on the case, then moved to the front of the room. He referred to the notes as he discussed the case.

Tower Bank: Timbers Office—found photo of him with rented Cessna. Confiscated his computer and asked for all his phone records. Was told there is likely $7.2 million missing. Interviewed three dozen employees. Made contact with the bank's head of security.

Victim's home: Contacted neighbors. Served search warrant and found no obvious evidence the homicide had occurred there. Confiscated victims computers, camera.

Timbers' house: Served search warrant. Told wife Diane about the investigation. Confiscated computers, camera.

Centennial Airport: Found plane rented by Timbers last Friday. Secured plane at airport, CSI team combed for evidence.

Things to do: Follow up with Tower Bank regarding the missing money. Put out photo of Timbers.

Once Jack had completed his comments, he asked Debra Schambra to tell the group what she had found at the airport.

Schambra stood up and walked to the front of the room.

"We did a very thorough examination of the plane, but were hindered by the fact that the plane is a rental and there have likely been dozens of people in the plane in recent weeks. We found twenty-two distinctive latent prints, and we will do our best to match them to our victim. Because the prints are of relatively poor quality, I would say that a conclusive match is unlikely. However, one very interesting thing that we found during our sweep of the plane was glitter in and around the passenger seat. Not something you would normally expect to find, but Jack and Mia had mentioned that Dr. Mora discovered glitter on our victim during the autopsy. I did some research and found that glitter has unique manufacturing qualities which may allow us to determine if the glitter on our vic matches the glitter in the plane. That's probably our best investigative lead at this point. Jack, if I could get the glitter from the cut I can start to look at possible matches."

Jack responded, "We can do that. Did you find any evidence of blood in the plane?"

"No blood at all, so our victim was not bleeding while in the plane."

Keller continued, "That likely rules out any kind of significant struggle in the plane. And if she was killed elsewhere, transported in the plane and ultimately dumped while in flight, there would almost certainly have been blood present inside. Then you factor in the autopsy findings where Dr. Mora said there were no obvious wounds aside from the scratches from tree branches and the ruptured femoral artery. He also said there was nothing under the victim's fingernails. So what all this means is that she was likely pushed out of the plane while still alive."

There was silence for several seconds while Jack's comments sunk in.

Keller continued, "Jameson, can you give us a quick briefing on what you found yesterday at the bank?"

Jameson Hayes wheeled easily to the front of the room.

"I did a cursory review of the records provided by the head of security for Tower Bank, and it's pretty clear that our guy not only whacked our victim, but managed to sneak more than seven million dollars by his employer while doing so."

"How in the hell can someone pull that off?" asked Mia.

"He had access, and very likely had an accomplice—someone who worked under him in the accounts receivable department at Tower Bank. And, lo and behold, our victim, Vanessa Tolken, worked in that very role. I know it's preliminary, but I think it's pretty likely these two were working together to pull off this heist. And I suspect they were more than just partners in crime. I'm willing to bet there was a relationship. Now why that plan went south is anybody's guess, but I'd bet the plan, at least initially, was to rip off the bank and then split together."

Mia interjected, "So, what went wrong? Did she get cold feet? She get pissed off at him? Did Timbers decide that he wasn't going to leave his wife and kids and when she threatened to expose the plan to rip off the bank he had no choice but to kill her?"

Jack responded, "We may never know the answer to that question, but it does shed some light on what likely happened here."

The meeting lasted another hour and culminated with a plan for how investigators would move forward with the investigation into the murder of Vanessa Tolken.

CHAPTER 18

"You'll like my dad. Stop worrying."

Gina looked over at Chris and took his hand.

It had been two weeks since the they had met on the flight from Denver to Miami. At first, Chris had fought the urge to call her, not entirely sure he wanted to get involved with someone, given his situation. But after a few days in South Beach he had given in and made the call. The chemistry they experienced on the flight had continued and the two had been spending all her days off together. She was on a three-day layover, and the two were in Chris's rental car en route to Gina's father's place in Key Largo.

"I'm sure I will, Gina."

Chris looked at the beautiful young woman sitting next to him. He squeezed her hand as he continued down the Overseas Highway toward the Florida Keys.

"What have you told him about us?"

"Just that we met on one of my flights, you work in commercial real estate, and that you're a serial killer," Gina said with a giggle.

"Just what every father wants to hear," Chris responded nervously.

"God, would you lighten up! He's going to love you. And his place down in the Keys is fabulous. It's right on the beach and he's got a pool and there's great fishing and diving. We're going to have fun—you'll see."

Chris smiled at Gina. "Okay, I believe you."

"Oh, one other thing. Did I tell you my dad's a cop?"

"Let's get together today. I need to get an update from you and Jack on the Tolken homicide."

Mick McCallister was facing the biggest challenge of his short time in office. The Tolken killing had received extensive news coverage, not just from the Denver press, but many of the tabloid shows as well. Once reporters learned that the nude body of the beautiful Ms. Tolken had been found suspended forty feet high in a pine tree, they couldn't get enough of the story.

Mia replied, "I'm pretty open. Want me to check with Jack?"

"Yeah, and tell him it's a priority. I need to know where we are with the case."

More than two weeks into the investigation and they were at a standstill.

"It's great to meet you, Chris. I'm Tom Barone. Gina's told me a lot about you."

Chris shook the man's hand and managed a "nice to meet you" in response. Barone was tall and tan, and looked like someone who enjoyed the beach life.

Chris was still mulling over Gina's little announcement about her dad being a cop. How had that not come up before?

"I hope you enjoy fishing and diving because I've got a few things planned during your stay down here."

Chris nodded and managed a smile. "Sure, that sounds great."

"Dad has a little boat docked out back. The water here is so warm and clear—it's amazing."

"Gina tells me you're from Denver. Got to be a lot of outdoor stuff you can do there. Not much in the way of diving I would guess, though, huh?"

"No, but the skiing is great and I manage to get out and do a little hunting during deer season. And I'm a pilot, so I fly every chance I get."

"A pilot, huh? I'm guessing that can run you some big bank. There's no skiing here, unless it's the water kind. Ever do any water skiing?"

"No, I never have. I'd love to try it sometime, though."

"Gina, remind me to drag Chris behind the boat during your visit. We have to get him a taste of life here in the Keys."

Gina laughed at her dad's comment. "Don't worry, Chris—Dad doesn't mean that literally."

"No worries," replied Chris, "I assumed he wasn't planning on drowning me. He hasn't even gotten to know me yet."

Barone looked at Chris and smiled. "I like this one, Gina. Not all of your boyfriends have appreciated my humor."

"Geez, Dad. Thanks for bringing that up!"

"A father can't be too protective of his little girl. In my business we see a lot of horrible stuff, so forgive me, Chris, if I come off a bit strong."

"No problem at all. I'd be the same way if I had kids."

Chris was surprised at how easily he claimed to have no children.

Barone continued, "We live in a violent world, Chris. And I know my perspective of things is a bit jaded, but I'd rather be that way than going through life with a blind naivety. You know what I mean?"

"Of course. Gina told me you're a police officer. I can imagine that worldview comes with the territory. Where do you work?"

"I'm with the Miami-Dade PD. Been there almost twenty-five years now. I work in the Special Enforcement Bureau."

"Wow, that's impressive. What kinds of things do you do working special enforcement?"

"Well, I can't share too much with you. Let's just say a lot of shit goes down in South Florida and I have my fingers in a lot of it. Never a dull moment, you know?"

"So, you're like Don Johnson in Miami Vice?" Chris asked with a smile, trying to make inroads.

"Oh, hell no. What a piece of crap that show was. It's nothing like that, really. And I've never owned a god-damned pink sports jacket."

Gina stepped in. "Relax, Dad, Chris didn't mean anything by it. Dad's a bit sensitive about how law enforcement is portrayed on TV."

"Yeah, I can see that. No offense, Tom."

Gina quickly changed the subject. "So what do we want to do for dinner tonight, gentlemen?"

"I picked up some stone crabs at Havana's this morning. Does that sound good to everyone?"

"Sounds great to me. Chris, have you ever had stone crabs?" Gina asked.

"No, can't say that I have."

"You'll love it. It's a lot like lobster. Served up with a little butter or mustard sauce, it's a Keys favorite."

CHAPTER 19

It was late afternoon when Mick, Mia, and Jack gathered in the executive conference room just outside Mick's office. Jack brought the murder book and placed it on the table.

Mick looked at Jack and Mia. "I need a quick rundown on the case. Mark Archer tells me he's still getting a ton of media calls. We need some good news to give reporters. "

Jack started in. "At this point the motive for the one-eighty-seven isn't totally clear, but it looks like Timbers and Tolken were conspiring together to rip off the bank. Something definitely went south between them. We know seven-point-two million is missing and Jameson is working with their security director on that part of the investigation."

Mia added, "I spoke with our CSI people and the glitter found in the plane does match the glitter found on Tolken's body. So there's our link between her and Timbers. It puts her in the plane with him and explains how she ended up in that tree. The asshole pushed her out. And we think she was alive when he did it because there's nothing to suggest she was killed in the plane. If he killed her prior to going up in the plane and his plan was to dump the body in some remote area, we'd have trace evidence in the plane. We've got nothing."

Mick responded, "Does Jameson have any idea how they managed the caper? I mean, that's a ton of dough, even for an outfit as large as Tower Bank."

Mia responded, "I spoke with him this morning. It's a pretty sophisticated scam, but both Jameson and the bank security guy said there was no way to cover up the crime. It was a wham-bam kind of thing, something that would be discovered pretty quickly. And now we have a dead woman and a missing bank executive."

Mick continued, "Any luck with tracking Timbers' cell? I can't believe he'd be stupid enough to hold on to it, but you never know."

Jack answered, "Yeah, we pinged it early on and it came back to a homeless guy not far from the airport. He was more than a little surprised when our undercover guys grabbed him. He said, 'Whoa, not me, bro, I didn't do nuthin'.' When they questioned him he said a well-dressed guy in a nice car gave it to him. Our guys showed him Timber's picture and the homeless guy confirmed it. We also found his car parked at DIA in the long-term lot. Our boy had swapped out the plates with a car in a shopping center, not far from where we found the homeless guy. Timbers is no dummy."

Mia jumped in. "The other interesting thing was that we had an airline security guy in Toronto contact us reporting that a passenger found Timber's ID in a seat on a flight that had originated in Denver. The security guy checked the manifest for that flight and found no one named Jonathan Timbers on the flight. He got a little suspicious and googled Timber's name. He found the story in the Denver papers about him missing and our interest in finding him, so he gave us a call."

"I can't believe a guy like Timbers would be dumb enough to lose his ID while on the run. I'm guessing that was a decoy?" Mick responded.

"Yeah, the security guy in Toronto pulled the videotape from the terminal. No one resembling Timbers got off that flight," answered Mia.

"He's a clever bastard, that's for sure."

"One thing we are fairly confident about is that he left Denver via DIA. His car was found there, the ID left behind on the plane, et cetera, all point to it. It also means he didn't fly out of here in a Cessna or some other private aircraft. That's not to say he hasn't done that since his escape from Denver; he could really be anywhere," offered Jack.

Mia responded, "We could check airport videotape, but—geez—how many people fly out of DIA? Probably a quarter million a day?"

"True, but we should at least check the tape from the terminal where the flight to Toronto originated. Maybe we can get him walking through the terminal. And if we get really lucky we might get a look at what plane he got on," answered Jack.

"Why don't you guys pursue that. And I need you to give Mark Archer a call and let him know where we are with the case. Poor guy is getting bombarded by reporters. Obviously we can't give the press any of the things we spoke about today, but there's gotta be some tidbits we can offer that will get them off our backs for awhile."

"Sure, I can do that," Mia replied.

"On another subject, how are things coming along with the preparation for the Lennox trial?"

Jack jumped in. "We still need to sit down with Luke Dominic and go over some of our testimony. It should be a slam dunk. We've got Lennox for the Lombard killing and the attempted murder of Lisa Sullivan."

Mia didn't say anything, but shot Keller a look. Mick didn't notice.

Mick continued, "As you guys both know, it's the biggest case in the history of the county. I talked to the DA the other day and he told me there will be gavel-to-gavel TV coverage. Live in the courthouse stuff. We gotta make sure it comes off perfectly. Scott Lennox has to pay for his crimes."

While the case against Scott Lennox looked very solid, Mia was consumed with the secret she was hiding about her partner, Jack Keller—a secret she knew could blow the entire case and allow a murderer to go free.

Mia walked down the hall to media relations and tapped on Mark Archer's office door. He was on the phone, but motioned for her to come in and take a seat. She glanced around the office and saw photos of Archer with more than a dozen nationally-known reporters and news anchors. While Rocklin County wasn't the largest police agency in Colorado, it had its share of sensational cases. Archer had been the media guy for RCSO for longer than Mia had been with the department, handling virtually every major case that came through the RCSO.

Archer hung up his call. "Hey, Mia. What's up?"

"The sheriff wanted me to come over and give you a rundown on the Tolken homicide. He said you were getting a lot of calls on it."

"Yeah, and the reporters are getting tired of hearing the same old information from me. If you have anything new, maybe I could keep them at arm's length for a while."

Archer scribbled notes on a pad on his desk as Mia ran down the case. As he listened to Mia recite the facts, he carefully considered things he could tell reporters without compromising the integrity of the investigation. Mia was giving him enough new information that Mark was confident he could satisfy the reporters, or at least keep them at bay until something else caught their attention. Reporters were like kids at times—if you could show them a new shiny object, they often forgot about the subject at hand. After Mia was finished, he changed subjects.

"So, what's going on with the Lennox trial? It's scheduled to go next week, isn't it?"

Mia shifted uncomfortably in her chair. "Yeah, Keller and I still need to get with the DA to work out the final details of our testimony, but it should be ready to proceed on schedule."

"Who's handling the prosecution?"

"Luke Dominic. He's handled some big cases before, but none as big as this."

"No doubt. The Lennox case is the biggest murder case I've been involved with in all my years at RCSO. But it's a rock-solid case; he should be going away for life."

Mia didn't respond. Archer picked up on it.

"You seem a bit preoccupied, Mia. Are there problems with the case?"

Mia turned and looked out the window of Archer's office. She didn't speak.

Archer grew concerned. "Mia, if there are issues, I need to know about it now. If this trial is going to be a difficult one, I'll need to prepare for the fallout from the media. The last thing I need is to be surprised."

"I know that, Mark. And the last thing Mick needs is to be embroiled in a controversy concerning the biggest case in the history of the county."

Mia was trying to keep her emotions in check. But, after keeping a secret for nearly nine months, she found it very difficult to continue to do so. She trusted Archer; everybody at RCSO did. He was certainly a guy who knew how to keep a secret.

Chris Houston was on his fourth beer and finally starting to relax around Gina's dad. The stone crabs were delicious and the three of them were sitting around the firepit in the backyard enjoying the evening. The moonlight glistened on the water and the temperature had cooled a bit. Chris had only been to Florida once before, on a Disney cruise with his wife and kids two years earlier. That was before his big promotion, meeting Vanessa Tolken, and absconding with seven million dollars from his employer.

"Another beer, Chris?"

"Sure, why not? I'm not going anywhere."

Tom Barone ambled off to the kitchen, leaving Chris and Gina alone in the backyard.

"How're you holding up, big boy?"

Chris looked at Gina. The moonlight reflecting on her face made her more beautiful than ever.

"I'm doing great. Seems like your dad's interrogation of me is over and I have to say, I love his place. It is so cool down here. I could see myself living in a place like this."

"Yeah, I love it here, too. I try to visit whenever I get a three-day layover. It's hard to beat the relaxing pace of the town."

Tom reappeared holding three beers, and handed one each to Gina and Chris. He popped the top off his and offered a toast.

"Here's to my new friend, Chris. May he treat my daughter well, because if he doesn't, I will hunt him down and hurt him. Cheers."

"*Dad!*"

"What's going on, Mia? We've been friends a long time. Tell me what's on your mind."

Mia looked at Archer. For more than nine months she had been living with the burden of keeping a monumental secret from Mick and she didn't know what to do. Her dilemma was simple: if she did the right thing and told the truth, it would blow the lid off the case against Scott Lennox and he'd very likely walk free. If she kept her mouth shut and proceeded, she would essentially guarantee a guilty verdict in the case, and justice would be served. The truth or justice? They shouldn't be mutually exclusive, Mia thought.

"If I tell you what's going on you have to promise me that you won't share it with anyone—not even Mick."

Archer looked at Mia. He didn't like making promises to people before he knew what he was promising. And he certainly didn't like keeping secrets from his boss. It was one of his golden rules—share everything with the boss, even if it was really bad news. Better the sheriff learn it from Archer than some reporter or member of the community. So, while he was very reluctant to make such a promise to Mia, he realized that if Mia wasn't telling Mick, then he probably would be better off if he knew what was going on. It could put him in a better position to protect his boss.

"Geez, Mia. I don't like the sound of this. You've got a secret that you can't share with Mick?"

"I haven't shared it with him at this point, but I'm not sure if I should continue to keep it from him. But if I tell him, it will put him in an awful position, and sometimes I think it's better if he doesn't know. It's an ignorance is bliss kind of thing."

Archer contemplated what Mia was saying. His personal philosophy throughout his career was he always wanted to know the truth: the good, bad, and ugly. It wasn't always pleasant and he had more than a few sleepless nights, but, for the most part, the strategy had served him well.

"What is it, Mia? Go ahead and tell me. Maybe it'll help you sort things out."

Mia took a deep breath and started in. "When Lisa Sullivan turned herself in last year we struck a deal with her—she'd serve no jail time in exchange for turning state's evidence against her former lover, Scott Lennox. As you probably remember, the two had conspired to kill Lennox's business partner. Initially, we had arrested Lennox but she dodged us and was nowhere to be found. Almost a year later she turned herself in, and we agreed to the deal provided she wore a wire and got Lennox to confess to the crime."

"Yeah, I remember all that. So what's the problem?"

"Lennox caught onto her wearing the wire and realized she was working with us to get him nailed down on murder charges. That's when he ran her over with his car in the parking lot of his business. She spent a couple weeks in the hospital recuperating and while she was there Jack and I paid her a visit."

"Okay, and then . . . ?"

"I never trusted Lisa Sullivan. There was just something about her. And I had a funny feeling about Jack as well, like he was protecting her while we were doing the investigation. My concern was that he was having an inappropriate relationship with her. I even confronted him at one point, but he denied it."

"Wow, Mia. I didn't know any of that."

"Well, Jack's reputation was at stake and I wasn't a hundred percent sure of my suspicions. I had no proof, so aside from Mick I didn't tell anyone."

"So, was Jack having an affair with Sullivan?" Archer asked, almost afraid to hear Mia's response.

"No, he wasn't. So he was truthful about that. But when we visited her at the hospital, Jack excused himself to take a phone call and I took the opportunity to talk to Sullivan, one-on-one. She was pretty heavily drugged, but she was talkative."

"And?"

"She blurted out that Jack was her father."

There, she'd said it. It was out there and immediately Mia felt a huge burden lifted from her shoulders.

That burden quickly fell onto Mark Archer.

"Oh, my God. Jack is Lisa Sullivan's father? And he was protecting her during an active, ongoing murder investigation?"

"Yep, pretty much. And Jack knows I know. Jack had come back in the room when it came out. And there was no denial from Jack."

"Did you say anything to him later?"

"Nope, not a word. Neither of us has brought it up. I've been living with this for nine months."

"And Mick has no idea?"

"None. And I kept it from him on purpose. This all happened the day before the election and I didn't want to lay this on him—imagine the burden on him if he knew the truth. And now with the trial just a week or so from opening arguments, I just can't imagine telling him. I can't do that to him."

"But, Mia, do you realize what will happen if this somehow gets out during the trial? My God, the media will be descending on Rocklin

County soon to cover this thing. If this gets out, it'll be national news, maybe even international news. It'll ruin Mick. And Scott Lennox will walk; no jury would ever convict him knowing the lead investigator was protecting the prosecution's prime witness in the case."

Both sat quietly for several seconds, contemplating the horrific mess they found themselves in.

Archer broke the silence. "All right, so let's think this thing through. First off, we need to keep in mind that Scott Lennox did, in fact, kill George Lombard and that he is going to trial for that crime. Lisa Sullivan conspired with him on the one-eighty-seven, but the deal we made allowed her to avoid jail time if she wore the wire and testified at trial against Lennox. She lived up to her end of that bargain. None of that changes with what we know about Keller and Sullivan. And while there was an obvious close relationship between them, she's no longer on the run. It's possible Keller may have convinced her to turn herself in—who knows?"

"Yeah, maybe . . . but come on—Jack almost certainly helped her escape. We were running around trying to find her and that asshole knew all along where she was? And that, at the very least, is obstruction of justice. There's no getting around that."

"True, but we need to look at the bigger picture here. Okay, Keller did some stuff that was totally unethical and almost certainly illegal, but the bottom line is that the right guy is in custody and the woman that played a relatively minor role in the crime will walk free in exchange for her testimony. We make these kind of deals all the time, and it's really the only way we could make the case against Lennox. That's the bottom line."

"I don't know, Mark."

"Look, Mia, I'm just trying to figure out the best course of action—a way to bring Lennox to justice and protect Mick at the same time."

"Yeah, but that means we need to stay quiet about all this and Keller gets a free pass. It's not right. The guy needs to pay."

"But are you willing to tell the truth about what you know even it means allowing Lennox to get away with murder, and at the same time costing Mick his job? The voters of Rocklin County will not be very understanding if all this comes out."

"But Mick didn't know any of this—it's not his fault! Only Keller, Sullivan, and I know the truth. And those two aren't about to spill the beans."

"True, but the public will still hold Mick responsible. It happened on his watch. And he'd never throw you under the bus; he'd accept the responsibility. So, if we just keep quiet about it, we really get everything we need—justice for Lennox's victim and no problems for Mick. Granted, Keller skates, but we can deal with him later if need be. And Mick will never need to know about any of this."

CHAPTER 20

Mia went to work early the next morning, hoping to catch up on some paperwork. She was exhausted, having spent a restless night thinking about the conversation she'd had with Mark Archer. On one hand, she was relieved to talk to someone about it, but at the same time she felt a great foreboding. More than anything, she felt a growing anger toward her partner. Keller had put everyone in this predicament and was now likely to walk away unscathed. It wasn't fair and it wasn't right, but the cost of bringing him down was simply too high. She felt like beating Keller to a pulp. But she knew that when he came in that morning she'd have to once again put it all aside and work with him on the Tolken case like nothing was wrong. They were scheduled to go to DIA and check for videotape of Timbers in the terminal where the Toronto flight had originated the day of his escape.

On the ride out to the airport, Jack filled Mia in on the research he had done the day before in anticipation of their trip to DIA. He had called the airport police and let them know what they needed. The supervisor he had spoken to said she'd pull the videotape and have it ready for them when they arrived.

They pulled up in front of the terminal, parked their unmarked unit, and headed for the door. But before they reached the entrance, security personnel were shouting for them to stop. Jack looked over his shoulder at the officer and quickly waved his RCSO badge at the guy. It didn't work.

"Hold on—you can't park there. I'm sorry, but you'll need to use one of the parking lots."

"Look, Officer . . . " Jack looked quickly at the name on the officer's shirt, " . . . Hines, is it?"

"Yes, sir."

"I'm Jack Keller and this is my partner, Mia Serrano. We're investigating a homicide and we need to speak with your security personnel inside. They're expecting us. Now, if you'll excuse—"

"Not so fast, investigator. We have rules and those rules say you have to use one of the parking lots. No exceptions."

"You've got to be kidding me. Look, I'm heading inside and I'm not moving the car. It's a god-damned police unit. Deal with it."

"Then I'll have it towed, sir."

Mia stepped forward. "That's fine, we'll move the car. Jack, it'll only take a minute. Sorry for the confusion, officer."

"No problem, ma'am. Thanks for your understanding."

Mia walked back to the car and motioned for Keller to get in.

"Can you believe this shit?"

"Jack, it's no big deal. Let's just move the car and get inside the terminal."

A few minutes later the two were sitting with Sergeant Sunie Dahl inside the DIA police storefront office in terminal B.

"I've pulled the tape from the day you mentioned. The flight to Toronto left DIA at ten after twelve, so I thought we'd go through the tape from around eleven o'clock till the flight finished boarding at approximately eleven fifty-five. The quality of the tape is quite good and if your guy was in the terminal during that time we should be able to spot him."

Jack and Mia gathered around the computer screen as the video began to play.

The screen depicted a busy hub of activity, with hundreds of people walking through the terminal on their way to catch their flights. After ten minutes or so Mia said, "Hold it, I think I spotted him."

Sergeant Dahl stopped the tape and rewound the video for a few seconds. She replayed the footage in slow motion and the three watched the screen closely.

"There, in the shirt and tie, with a suit coat over his arm. That looks like our guy," Mia said excitedly.

Dahl stopped the tape and zoomed in on the man Mia had spotted.

"Yeah, that's him," Jack confirmed. "Great picture quality, sergeant . . . you should see most of the video we have to work with—you wouldn't recognize your own mother."

"Can we follow him and see where he goes?" asked Mia.

"Sure, no problem. But if he goes out of frame we'll need to look at the video from other cameras in the terminal. All doable, though."

"I can't believe the guy didn't try to disguise himself or stay clear of the cameras. He's walking through the terminal like he owns the place," Mia commented, shaking her head.

"I'm not surprised at all. Guys like this think they're smarter than anyone else. Stupid cops will never catch me is the common mindset. Their arrogance works to our advantage," responded Jack.

The video continued in slow motion, with the man taking a seat near one of the gates. After a minute or so the man started a conversation with someone in a nearby seat. Something changed hands between them and Jack asked the sergeant to freeze the frame. Zooming in, they could make out a driver license with cash attached by a rubber band.

"That son of a bitch. That's him giving his ID to that guy with the ponytail so he could leave it on the plane to Toronto," Jack said.

"Let's see where he goes next," replied Mia.

They followed Timbers as he left the man with the ponytail and approached another gate. He took a seat and appeared to wait.

"Can we figure out what gate he's waiting at?" asked Mia.

"Maybe. Let's see if we can see anything."

All three peered at the screen for some evidence of a gate number.

"There, in the upper left corner. Gate twelve," Jack pointed.

"Can we can find out what flight left gate twelve that day at around this time?" Mia asked.

"Sure, no problem . . . give me a minute."

Sergeant Dahl accessed an airline database and soon had the information.

"Looks like there was a United flight to Miami leaving gate twelve shortly after the other flight left for Toronto. I can access the flight manifest if you'd like."

"That would be great," replied Mia.

Jack spoke next. "There is virtually no chance that Timbers used his real name for that flight, but the manifest will be a good starting point."

A few seconds later the manifest was printing out.

"Is there a way to find out how many United flights to Miami there are each day from this terminal?" asked Mia.

Sergeant Dahl nodded, and soon handed them that information.

"You've been a huge help to us today. Can't thank you enough."

"Any time. It was my pleasure. Hope you bag the guy."

Mark Archer closed his office door and began to return the media calls he had received regarding the Tolken homicide. Most of the reporters just wanted to know if there were any updates on the case so Mark gave each a quick rundown, offering nothing new, but couching it in such a way that made the reporters feel they were getting something they could report. It was a useful skill he had developed over the years. He often joked with people that he had the ability to talk a lot without really saying anything.

It was a little after noon and he was halfway through the calls when he flipped on the TV, tuning in to the Channel Eight news program. There she was, Angela Bell, anchoring the newscast. He watched her for several seconds reporting on a story about global warming and the effect it had on the Rocky Mountain snow cap. God, she was gorgeous, he thought to himself, as his mind drifted back to when they were a couple.

"Luke Dominic is here. He says you wanted to see him?"

"Send him in," responded Rocklin County District Attorney Dave Baxter.

Dominic walked in, shook hands with his boss, and took a seat.

"Tell me how things are going with the Scott Lennox case. We're close to jury selection, and I want to make sure we're good to go."

"Yes, we're in great shape. I still need to tie up a few loose ends but everything is in place. I'm ready to roll."

"Good, glad to hear it. I don't have to tell you how big this case is. Probably the biggest trial in the history of Rocklin County. We can't afford to have anything go wrong. The world will be watching."

"I understand. Once we get Lisa Sullivan on the stand and she explains to the jury how she and Lennox pulled off the murder . . . that should be enough to convict right there. Plus we have all the other evidence against him—the financial gain he'd receive from the life insurance policy on the victim and the medical examiner's report. We've got a great case."

"How has the RCSO been with the preparation for trial? The new sheriff was not happy with the plea deal we offered Lisa Sullivan in exchange for her testimony. Any residual heartburn from anyone over there?"

"Yeah, maybe a little bit. I've been working with Jack Keller and Mia Serrano, the two lead investigators on the case. Serrano seems more perturbed about the plea deal than Keller. I think Keller has been through it all before, just par for the course for him."

"Good to hear. I spoke with Judge O'Brien the other day. He's pretty open to allowing the media access and is going to allow cameras in the courtroom. So that'll bring a bit of a circus environment to things. Are you ready for that?"

"I'm ready. I handled the Vargas murder trial two years ago and that received a lot of media coverage as well. Nothing like this case, but it gave me a taste of what to expect. I'm fine with it."

"Okay, just let me know if you need anything. We need to win this case, Luke. I'm counting on you."

"Of course, and I have every confidence that we will get a conviction for Scott Lennox."

"Once the trial begins, I want daily updates from you on how things are progressing. I need to monitor this very closely."

"No problem, sir. I will keep you posted every step of the way."

Back at the station, Jack and Mia began reviewing the manifest for the flight from Denver to Miami. There were more than two hundred passengers on board, along with twelve crew members. A quick perusal of the list of passenger names yielded nothing, which was not surprising, given Timbers would certainly have used a false name.

"How many passengers were there in first class?" Mia asked Jack.

He looked down the list. "Looks like there were eleven flying first."

"How about business?"

"Sixteen."

"Well, that may be a good starting point. If I'd just ripped off my employer for seven million I don't think I'd be sitting with all the riffraff back in coach. I'd be living large, thinking about how many piña coladas I'd be having in Miami Beach."

"Or maybe he doesn't want to draw any attention to himself so he sucks it up and goes coach. I'm not sure we can assume anything about first class or coach, we just know he was on that plane. We have to figure out what name he used to board the flight. If he's using that same name down in Florida we could be onto something. Although there's a very good chance he didn't stay in Florida—he just used Miami as his jumping point to somewhere else. He may have caught another flight when he landed in Miami. And then we have the private pilot factor which adds a nightmare component. He could have rented a plane and flown off to anywhere, really."

Mia responded, "Yeah, I think we need to focus on what name he used. There's no guarantee he's still using it but it's really all we've got right now. Let's contact United Airlines and see if we can circulate a photo of Timbers to whatever crew members worked that flight."

"That works. I just hope the son of a bitch stayed in Florida. I don't even want to think about how many places there are in the Caribbean he could have escaped to. And a lot of them don't have extradition agreements with the US. If he reached one of those countries, it's going to be almost impossible to get him back, that is, if we ever find him in the first place."

"I'll call the airline."

CHAPTER 21

Chris Houston and Gina Barone were spending most of the last day of her three-day layover in bed. After leaving her father's place in Key Largo, the two had made their way down the Overseas Highway to the town of Key West. They had found a great little hotel right on the water, complete with french doors that led directly out to their own private beach. Two empty wine bottles sat on the table.

"Are you sure you need to go back to work? We could go flying tomorrow. Rent a plane and take it out over the Keys. God, I'll bet it's gorgeous from the air. Come on, can't you call in sick?"

"Oh, yeah, and come back with this tan?"

"Yeah, I guess they'd catch on. I wonder what the rest of your crew would think if they could see that you don't have any tan lines?" Chris asked, laughing.

"God, you are terrible, Mr. Houston. Can't a girl lay topless on her own private beach?"

"Personally, I've got no problem with it. In fact, I encourage it."

"Yeah, I'll bet you do," Gina added playfully, reaching under the covers.

"Again? Really? Oh . . . all right . . . "

Later, with Gina sleeping, Chris left the bed and went out to the beach. He sat on the sand and considered his situation. He had developed feelings for Gina, but he was a man on the run and wasn't sure how long he could safely stay in South Florida. To continue his cover as a commercial real estate agent, Chris had told Gina he traveled up to Fort Lauderdale to look at properties, always scheduling those trips during her work days. In reality, he had never left Miami.

With Gina's dad being a Miami-Dade cop things quickly got complicated. Chris had tracked the media coverage of his disappearance and knew that RCSO had launched a considerable manhunt for him. His photo had been widely circulated in the Denver area, so would the police now be putting his photo out nationwide? They sure as hell would be doing something to find him, that much was sure. The media coverage offered no motive for the murder, and didn't talk at all about the missing money. The RCSO was playing it close to the vest, but there was no doubt in his mind that investigators had a very good idea of what had transpired. The bank would discover the missing money and share that with the RCSO. The discovery of Vanessa's body connected all the dots and everything would be pinned on him.

At some point he needed to make a decision—either leave Gina behind and start his new life in the Caribbean or make up some story and see if she would go with him. He could tell her that he was tired of selling commercial real estate and wanted to start a new life in the Caribbean. He could say the commission from the non-existent deals in Fort Lauderdale afforded him the ability to live for a few carefree years. Would Gina consider coming with him?

But all this didn't take into account the wildcard in the equation. Her dad was a Miami-Dade cop and at some point he could learn the truth. By that time he and Gina would be in an extradition-free country in the Caribbean but what would Gina do if she learned the truth about what went down in Colorado? Essentially he'd be forcing her to make a choice between him and her father. He believed she loved him, but was forcing her to make such a decision asking too much?

His mind wandered to the beautiful Vanessa. If only she hadn't wanted to back out of the embezzlement scheme they'd be together in the Cayman Islands by now. Stupid bitch, he thought. They could have had a great life together. He had assured her over and over that the plan was solid, and that they would live the rest of their lives together in luxury. But when she said she was having doubts about going through with it he knew he had to do something. Bank security required two sets of passwords to move money—essentially a dual-control system—but she had stupidly shared her passwords with him so he didn't need her to carry out the crime. So on that fateful Friday night he slipped her a roofie while the two were enjoying a drink at a Denver bar. He took her up in the Cessna he often rented at Centennial Airport, waited until they were over a heavily forested area, and pushed her out. In his mind he could still hear the blood-curdling screams as she fell from the plane.

CHAPTER 22

"So, why did you call me?"

Mark Archer looked across the table at Angela Bell and smiled.

"What, a police spokesman can't have a conversation with a TV reporter?"

"Yes, that can happen. It just doesn't usually happen in the penthouse bar at the Ritz Carlton in downtown Denver. Or is this where you do all your press briefings?"

"Yes, I do a lot of my interviews here. In fact, I'm considering moving my office to this exact location. What do you think?"

"I think you have a little too much freedom with your expense account."

Both chuckled at the comment, but Angela got serious again.

"So, why did you call me, Mark?"

"I wanted to give you an update on the Tolken homicide. Your station called and it's my duty and responsibility to respond to all media inquiries. You know, part of the job."

"Okay . . . I'm not sure I'm buying any of that, but what can you tell me about the investigation?"

"We're still looking for Jonathan Timbers, that's the key thing right now. We know the cause of death, and we have a pretty good timeline for how things went down. He's in the wind and we need to find him."

"So, is he your primary suspect at this time?"

"Are we speaking on the record or off the record?"

"Let's do on the record first. Then we can delve into more details off the record."

Archer knew how to play this game; he'd been doing it for years. With reporters he trusted he would provide some off-the-record information about a case with the understanding they couldn't make that information known. It could be a risky thing on his part, and the chance a reporter would burn him and release that information was always there, but he'd only been double crossed a few times. If a reporter didn't live up to their end of the agreement in an off-the-record conversation, then that breach of trust was certainly noted. People in law enforcement talk to each other and any spokesperson burned by a reporter would let all his counterparts know about it. Those reporters would never get anything except the basic facts of that case or any other case from that point forward. Mark certainly trusted Angela.

"On the record, Mr. Timbers is a person of interest and someone we would like to talk to."

"Can you tell me, on the record, why he's a person of interest?"

"Nope. He's just someone we think may have knowledge about the crime. We have been unable to talk with Mr. Timbers and we are anxious to do so."

"So, all the efforts of the RCSO to find Mr. Timbers have been unsuccessful?"

"Geez, Angela—that's kind of a harsh way to put it. You make it sound like we're incompetent."

"I'll soften it a bit for the story, but I'm guessing it's accurate?"

"Yeah, pretty much. But investigators are confident they will locate Mr. Timbers and have the necessary conversation with him, blah, blah, blah . . . you know what to say . . . "

"So, let's shift gears and go off the record."

"Okay, what do you want to know?"

"Did Timbers kill Vanessa Tolken?"

"It's all circumstantial at this point, but almost certainly, yes."

"Motive?"

"That we're not totally sure of, but it looks like he and the victim were involved in a relationship and things went south."

Archer intentionally left out the part about the missing money.

Angela nodded. No big surprise, she thought. Young women who are murdered were usually killed by someone they knew. There were relatively few random killings of young females.

"Was she sexually assaulted?"

"There was evidence of recent intercourse, but there was no trauma, no obvious signs of rape. But as you know, that's not conclusive, just the opinion of the medical examiner."

"So you have semen, then? DNA?"

"I didn't say that. I said there was evidence of recent intercourse, but no obvious signs of trauma that are often found in a sexual assault."

"So whoever had sex with her used a condom . . . "

"Angela—you're killing me. I don't know that for sure."

Angela moved on. "What exactly was the cause of death? The autopsy report didn't shed much light on that."

"That was purposely left a bit vague. It's an important facet of the investigation and we can't really comment on that right now."

"Even off the record?"

"I'd rather not go there."

"You know, Mark—saying that is like waving a big red cape at a bull. Reporters don't like being told no, especially on stuff that is routinely released by the medical examiner. Why is the cause of death such a secret?"

"I just can't go there yet. When we can release it, we will. For now, I've just got to go with the 'we can't compromise the investigation' response those in law enforcement are fond of using."

Angela wasn't happy with that answer, but she switched topics.

"Does Timbers have any history of violence?"

"No."

"Is he married?"

"Yes."

Angela looked at Mark.

"Love the one word answers. I'd hate to think what I'd be getting from you on the record."

"Sorry, but that's the best I can do right now."

"You know I can have one of our reporters find out a lot of this stuff pretty easily. Do you really want us knocking on doors and investigating Mr. Timbers ourselves?"

"No, I'd prefer it if you didn't. Just give me some time, Angela. Once I have something of interest I'll personally call you with the story. I'm just asking for your patience for a little while longer."

Angela considered what Archer was saying, running it down in her head. No other media outlets were hot on the story at this point, so she could afford to be patient, especially if it meant getting a little inside scoop when the time came.

"All right, have it your way. For now, at least."

"Thanks, Angela. I appreciate it."

"So, getting back to my original question . . . why did you invite me to have drinks?"

Jack and Mia arrived at DIA and drove straight to the passenger parking area.

"Good boy, Jack. That wasn't so hard, was it?" Mia teased as Keller pulled up and grabbed the ticket that opened the gate to the parking lot.

"Whatever happened to a little professional courtesy? It's degrading having to park out here. We ain't no friggin' terrorists."

"Well, I don't think they were worried about me. But you, on the other hand—you've got that look. Like you might go off at any time.

Gotta learn to relax, big fella."

"I suppose if you were working alone and wanted to park in front of the terminal, you'd just give the guy a little wink and a smile and they'd park your damn car for you."

"Oh, yeah—piece of cake."

With no shuttle bus nearby they walked the half mile to the terminal and found the UAL offices. They knocked on the door and a woman appeared.

"I'm Jack Keller and this is my partner, Mia Serrano, from the Rocklin County Sheriff's Office. We're looking for Brandon Samson, head of security. He's expecting us."

"Sure, hold on."

A few minutes later Mr. Samson appeared and showed them to his office.

Mia started in, "As we discussed on the phone, I brought the picture of the man we are looking for. If you could just get this to the crew that worked the flight to Miami a couple weeks back we'd greatly appreciate it."

"Well, actually your timing is quite good. I just checked to see which crew worked that particular flight and saw they're scheduled for that same twelve forty-five flight to Miami today. They should be checking in here around eleven thirty or so. But as I said on the phone, this might be like trying to find the proverbial needle in the haystack. Our flight crews encounter hundreds and hundreds of passengers, and the fact the flight was a couple weeks back . . . I'm not sure how much luck you'll have."

Keller glanced at his watch. It was ten forty-five.

"Maybe my partner and I can grab a cup of coffee and catch the crew when they get here at eleven thirty."

"Meet me back here then and I'll put you in touch with everyone."

Jack and Mia found a Bean Crazy coffee kiosk not far from the security office and took a seat.

"Nice timing with the same crew working today. It's much better if we can show the picture ourselves. Folks tend to take things more seriously if they are being talked to by an investigator."

Mia nodded in agreement. "Yeah, we caught a break."

Both sat quietly sipping their coffee. After a few minutes, Mia broke the silence.

"So we've got the Lennox trial coming up in a few days. I got a message from Luke Dominic the other day, saying he wanted to get with us to go over our testimony in the case. I've been so busy with this case I haven't had a chance to call him back. I'll have to do that when we get back to the office later."

"Yeah, I'll do the same. I'm not too worried, the case should go smoothly. We've got the prick dead to rights."

"Yeah, it seems so. But this case is going to get so much attention we've got to make sure we get the conviction. Mark Archer told me he's been bombarded with media inquiries about it. Says the thing will get huge coverage."

"Great, that's all we need. A bunch of media whores standing outside the courtroom reporting on all the 'breaking news.' All of whom are clueless about how the criminal justice system works."

"Geez, Jack . . . you're in a good mood."

"Don't have much need for reporters. I don't know how Archer doesn't put a bullet in his skull, or at least take out a reporter every once in awhile. The guy has the patience of Job."

"At least he keeps the reporters from hassling investigators. Can you imagine if we didn't have a media guy? Think of all the calls we'd be getting."

"If that was the case I would never have come out of retirement to take the RCSO job. Life's too short to deal with all those dumbasses."

Mia looked at Jack and hoped she would never become that cynical. She was often frustrated by the media coverage of some of the cases she worked, but she knew the media had a job to do and they played an important role in the system.

Jack looked at his watch.

"Come on, it's almost eleven thirty. It's showtime."

The two walked back to the security office and reconnected with Mr. Samson. He led them to the employee lounge where he introduced them to Mary Hakes, the shift supervisor. He explained that they needed to have a few minutes with the crew working the Miami flight.

"Most of them are here already, getting ready in the back. We have a total of twelve crew working that flight. Want to start with the captain?" Hakes asked.

"Sure, that would be great," Mia answered.

The supervisor led them to a small locker room and introduced them to Captain Pam Valovcin.

"These investigators are with the Rocklin County Sheriff's Department and they're looking for a person of interest in a recent homicide. I'll let them explain more about what they need."

The captain, a tall woman in her early forties, looked at them. "That sounds ominous. You think a killer flew on one of our flights?"

"It's quite possible," responded Mia.

"Got a photo of the guy?"

Mia produced Timber's photo from her coat pocket and showed the captain.

"He doesn't look familiar to me, but keep in mind the co-pilot and I have very little contact with the passengers. You'll probably have more luck talking to our flight attendants. They're in the employee lounge. I can take you in there if you'd like."

Jack replied, "Yeah, we'd appreciate that."

The three walked to an adjacent room where there were a half dozen women and two men. The captain made the introductions and explained what the investigators were after.

Mia held up the photo of Jonathan Timbers, but each shook their heads as they studied the photo.

One of the attendants, an older woman, said "I'm sorry, but do you have any idea how many people we encounter on our flights each week? We've probably served Diet Cokes and peanuts to five thousand passengers over the past two weeks. And, frankly, we don't pay them much attention, unless the person is a jerk."

Mia nodded at the woman, "We understand. We knew it was a long shot, but thought maybe someone might remember him."

Keller spoke up, "Is this the entire crew? Is there anybody not here that normally works this flight to Miami?"

The attendants looked around, and the older woman spoke up again, "Yes, we're missing Lance and Gina. Lance must be running a little late this morning and Gina is on her days off."

Jack answered, "Okay, we'll leave this photo with you then. Could you check with them and anyone else who might recognize this man? Maybe post the photo to a bulletin board with our contact information? It's really important we find him."

The woman reached over and took the photo from Mia.

"Sure, we can do that."

"Great. Thank you for your time, everyone."

Jack and Mia left the terminal and headed back to RCSO headquarters.

Mia peeked into Mick's office on the top floor of the justice center.

"Hey. Thought I'd drop in and say hello. Is this a good time?"

"Of course, come on in. Close the door behind you."

Mia walked across the large office and approached Mick.

"Is it okay if I kiss the sheriff?"

"Of course. That's why I told you to shut the door."

Mia wrapped her arms around Mick's neck and gave him a kiss, then wiped her lipstick from his mouth.

"I can't be leaving any evidence. The voters might not like that."

"To hell with the voters. I don't have to worry about them for another three years. Hey, I bumped into Commander Espy earlier and he said you and Jack were out at DIA checking on that Miami flight."

"Yeah, we showed a photo of Timbers to the crew that worked the flight he took. Got a big fat nothing for our efforts. No one remembered him."

"So, what's next?"

"We are going to intensify our efforts in South Florida. We're confident he flew to Miami, but there's no way of knowing if he's still there, or if he proceeded on to another destination. He could really be anywhere, but we thought there's no harm in putting out the APB again to Miami and the surrounding jurisdictions."

"Sounds reasonable."

"It's really frustrating. This guy has so many tools at his disposal. He's a pilot, has a fake ID, and seven million bucks in his back pocket. It's the damn trifecta."

"I don't want to further dampen your spirits, but there's another factor working against us. There are a lot of small Caribbean nations a short flight from Miami, many of which do not have extradition agreements with the US. This could prove very problematic if we do find him and he's in one of these places."

Mia jumped in, "And he's certainly no dummy. It could be the reason he chose Miami as his first escape point."

"Got any dinner plans tonight?" Mick asked, changing subjects.

"Just dinner with you, I hope."

"I can make that happen. How about someplace special? We haven't been out in a while."

"Pick you up around six?"

"You got it, boss."

Before Mia headed home, she and Jack put out an APB on Timbers to every agency in the state of Florida. Now they just needed to wait and see.

Jack left the office a few minutes early and headed south on I-25. Thirty minutes later he was in a café in the small town of Monument. He took a seat at a table near the back and surveyed the place. It was nearly deserted, just a handful of regulars ordering from the early dinner menu and sharing the town's gossip. The waitress brought Jack a glass of water and offered him a menu.

"There'll be someone joining me in a few minutes. Leave me a couple menus."

"No problem."

Jack hadn't seen his daughter in several weeks. Since she had turned herself in to authorities some ten months earlier, they had communicated only by burner phones and an occasional stolen visit. The extensive news coverage had given her a high profile in the Denver area and her testimony was to be the cornerstone to the prosecution's case against Lennox. The fact that she was Jack Keller's daughter was something that could never come out.

Lisa walked into the café wearing oversize sunglasses and a dark wig over her blonde hair. It was a disguise she wore on those rare occasions she was able to see her father, and the getup worked. Even Jack did a double take when he saw her; she looked like a totally different person.

"Hey, it's great to see you. How have you been?" Jack asked, pulling out her chair.

"I'm okay. I just want to get past this trial and I'll feel a lot better."

"That's totally understandable. In a few weeks this should all be in your rearview mirror and you can get on with your life."

"I hope so. What's your take on things?"

"The case looks very solid. Once you testify about how the crime went down, Scott Lennox will be toast."

"God, I hope so. I still have nightmares about him running me down in his car that night."

"I know, sweetie, I know."

Jack thought back to the night she was injured. Part of the plea deal she struck with the DA's office was that she would serve no jail time for her part in the murder if she agreed to wear a wire and get Lennox to admit to killing George Lombard. The plan worked and she got everything on tape, but once Lennox figured out what was going on, he ran her down with his car. She had spent two weeks in the hospital recovering from her injuries.

"I hope the judge throws the book at him. Life in prison isn't long enough if you ask me."

"He'll do at least twenty years, probably more."

"Good."

"But you need to be ready—Branch Kramer is going to make you look like the brains behind the plot to kill Lombard, and like you turned state's evidence to save your own bacon. He's going to paint you as someone who can't be trusted—a snitch and a complete liar. Has Luke Dominic prepped you for that?"

"Geez, Dad—stop sugarcoating it. Don't worry, that's how we spend most of our time. He pretends he's Branch Kramer and gets really nasty with me. He's coached me on how to answer those questions."

Rocklin County had gotten their first taste of famed Texas attorney Branch Kramer nearly a year earlier when he arrived via Learjet from his offices in Dallas to represent Scott Lennox following his arrest in the case. Kramer was a larger-than-life figure, famous for his late-night ads on cable TV. Lennox's wife, Laura, had sprung for the high-priced mouthpiece using her family money. It was not an easy decision for her; she had seriously considered letting her husband rot in jail for his crime. Her decision to stand by her man was one of self interest; she had a certain standing in the Castle Springs community and she wasn't willing to let it all go. And weirdly, she somehow enjoyed the spotlight she found herself in. She was married to a man standing trial for murder and she relished the drama of it all.

Jack changed subjects. "Have you given any thought to what you want to do once the trial is over? What you want to do with the next stage of your life?"

Lisa knew what Jack was really asking. After fleeing Colorado as a wanted woman, she spent nine months hidden away at her father's beach condo in Mexico. There she met and fell in love with Peter Donnelly, a wealthy businessman in the port town of Puerto Peñasco. Ultimately, she returned to the US and surrendered to authorities, leaving behind the man she loved.

"I don't really know, Dad. I've had no contact with Peter, if that's what you're getting at. He hasn't made any effort to contact me and I don't even know if he knows what happened after I left him that night in Mexico. It all happened so fast. For all I know he put it all in the past once I walked off that beach."

Jack had never told Lisa that Peter had been planning to propose to her that night and that everything had blown up before he could ask her for her hand. She was also unaware that Jack had contacted Peter when Lisa was run down by Scott Lennox. Peter had said he would come immediately to Colorado to be with Lisa, but Jack advised against it. No one knew that Lisa had been hiding out in Mexico and they didn't need anyone or anything surfacing in Colorado that could make that fact known.

Following dinner with her father, Lisa returned to her apartment in Rosebud. There, she decided that she would write Peter a letter, hoping that it might give her the closure she needed. She loved Peter, but couldn't really see a future with him after things had ended so horribly on the beach that night.

She took out a pen and paper and began writing.

My dearest Peter—I have been wanting to write this letter to you for a long time. Things ended so abruptly in Mexico—it took me a very long time to process things in my mind. I needed to work through my feelings and now I hope to can convey my thoughts to you in this letter. I considered calling you or even visiting you in Puerto Penasco, but I just wasn't sure how you'd feel about that.

So, please accept my deepest apologies for what I've done. I wasn't truthful with you and this is my biggest regret. As you told me on the beach that day a relationship not built on trust isn't worth having. I should have told you what was happening, who knows—maybe we could have worked through it. But I got caught up in the relationship and I was just so afraid I'd lose you if I told you the truth. I went to Mexico to escape my problems, but instead I fell in love with you the very first night we met. I hoped and prayed everyday for a resolution to my situation, but the bottom line is—I should have told you. And for this I am truly, truly sorry.

I know that I can't expect you to forgive me, but I hope you can find it in your heart to at least understand a little bit about why I did what I did.

I hope you are well and I miss you.

~Lisa~

She addressed the envelope and slipped the letter inside with the plan to mail it the next morning.

CHAPTER 23

Mark Archer felt like a high school kid as he drove to Angela Bell's high-rise apartment in Denver. He was both nervous and excited at the prospect of starting things up again with her. Meeting for drinks the night before had brought back the chemistry between them and the decision to have dinner the next night seemed like a good idea. The relationship, which had lasted for nearly a year, had ended six months earlier. Mark wanted to marry her, but Angela wasn't ready to make that commitment. Eventually, the issue became a major point of contention between the two and the relationship ended.

"Dad, I'm home."

"Hey, Mia. I'm in the basement."

Mia made her way down the stairs to find Chuck hanging out with the dog.

"How was your day, Dad?"

"Good, pretty quiet. Just me and Sasha. Nice to see you home at a reasonable hour."

"Yeah, I know. It's been crazy at work. Mick should be here shortly. We're headed out to dinner. Can I make you something before we leave?"

"No, I'll be fine. I'll just make myself a sandwich and watch a little TV tonight. Glad to hear you two are heading out for the evening. You guys don't do that enough."

"Okay, that sounds good. I'm going to go up and get ready."

Mick arrived at the house a few minutes later and Chuck offered him a vodka. Mick accepted the offer on the condition that Chuck join him. Chuck grabbed a beer from the refrigerator.

"Word on the street is you and Mia are headed out to dinner."

"Yep, I made a reservation at a new Italian place on the Sixteenth Street Mall up in Denver. I've heard great things about it, and you know how much she loves Italian food. And I've got a little surprise planned for her."

Chuck looked at Mick, but decided not to ask about the surprise.

Mick looked at Chuck and smiled. "And . . . I've got a question for you."

Chuck didn't respond, but turned his full attention toward Mick.

"You know how I feel about Mia and I've been thinking a lot about the future."

"Okay, go on . . . " Chuck prompted, his eyes starting to tear up.

Seeing Chuck get emotional, Mick smiled and put his hand on Chuck's shoulder.

"I want to ask Mia to marry me, but it's really important that before I do that, I make sure I have your blessing."

"My God, Mick, of course you have my blessing. You two are great together and I can't think of anyone I'd rather have for a son-in-law than you."

"I feel the same way about you as a father-in-law. You know I think of you as my real dad."

Chuck broke down and wrapped his arms around Mick.

"And please know I will take care of your daughter forever."

"I know, Mick . . . I know."

"Okay, we better get our act together before she comes downstairs.

I want this to be a surprise for her tonight, so no letting on. Agreed?"

Both men laughed and did their best to gather themselves.

A few minutes later Mia came downstairs to find the two in the kitchen enjoying a drink and talking about the prospects of a good upcoming Broncos season.

As Mick and Mia excused themselves, Chuck made himself a turkey sandwich, grabbed another beer, and headed back to the basement to watch television, happy as could be.

Mark and Angela walked the two blocks from her apartment to the restaurant on the 16th Street Mall. It was a beautiful late September night with temperatures in the mid seventies.

"Welcome to Di Amore. Will you be joining us for dinner this evening?" the host asked as Angela and Mark entered.

"Yes, we have a reservation for seven o'clock. Archer is the name."

The host looked at the reservation list and nodded.

"Right this way."

They were given a table with a window view. Foot traffic was heavy along the mall and it was fun to people watch.

"Have you been here before, Angela?"

"No, it's my first time. I've heard great things about the place. It's supposed to have the best Italian food in Denver."

"I'm glad you suggested it."

The conversation was briefly interrupted as a waiter approached the table, offered them menus, and took their drink orders.

"So, where are we going?" asked Mia, as they headed north on I-25 toward Denver.

"You'll see. I think you'll like it."

Mia looked out the window at the Denver skyline off in the distance. Wherever they were going, it was nice to get out.

Mick continued, "You know, our lives are way too busy. Once we get past the Lennox trial things should calm down. We'll put Scott Lennox away for good and the media coverage will show the department in a really good light. It's our chance to shine and I'm excited about it."

Mia felt her stomach churn at the mention of the Lennox trial. While talking about the situation with Mark Archer had helped by lifting the burden somewhat from her shoulders, she was still very worried about the fallout if the relationship between Keller and Lisa Sullivan was somehow discovered. She forced the thought from her mind and tried to focus on dinner with Mick.

Gina arrived at the United Airlines terminal at DIA after working the flight from Miami. She made her way to the employee lounge and put her things in her locker. She had just come off her three days with Chris and was feeling great about the relationship. Chris was smart, handsome, successful, and very sweet. He had gotten along well with her dad despite the good-natured teasing he'd been put through. She and Chris were totally compatible, she thought, starting to allow herself to fantasize about a future with him.

"Hey, Gina. How were your days off?"

She looked up and saw Jeannette, the crew supervisor.

"Oh, it was great. Went down to the Keys with my boyfriend. Got way too much sun," she responded with a laugh.

"Sounds nice . . . I'm jealous."

Gina walked over to the small kitchen in the lounge, poured herself a cup of coffee, and took a seat at a table. A minute later Jeannette left the area and Gina was alone with her thoughts. As she was reflecting back on the three days she had spent with Chris, her eye wandered to the bulletin board on the wall nearby. A photo posted there caught her attention and she quickly got up and walked over for a closer look. Her knees buckled and she braced herself from falling.

"Oh, my God."

Gina grabbed the photo down from the bulletin board and fell into a seat in the breakroom. She was close to hyperventilating as she read the words written at the bottom of the flyer.

Please contact Investigator Jack Keller or Mia Serrano at the Rocklin County Sheriff's Department at (303) 555-6085 if you have seen this man. It is believed he was a passenger on a recent UAL Denver-Miami flight. He is wanted for questioning by authorities.

It must be some kind of mistake, she thought. There was no way the man she loved was wanted by police. She kept staring at the flyer, wishing his photo would disappear from the page. She fought the impulse to call him; she needed to think before she did that. She considered calling her father to see what he could tell her about it, but she decided she'd hold off on that as well, at least for the time being. She folded the flyer and put it in her purse. There would be time to sort all this out once she returned to Miami where she could talk to Chris.

CHAPTER 24

"I have a reservation for two, under McCallister," Mick said to the host at Di Amore.

"Yes, of course. Right this way."

Mick took Mia's hand as the host led them to a table near the back of the restaurant.

"Wow, this place is so beautiful. I've never even heard of it."

"It's new—only been open a few months. It got rave reviews in *Denver Today*."

They took their seats and looked around the place.

"So elegant. I'm guessing it's Italian with a name like Di Amore?" Mia asked.

"Yes, it is. And the wine list is supposed to be incredible."

"Well, let's get ourselves a nice bottle."

"We can do that."

The waiter came over offering menus and Mick asked for a wine list. After looking over the extensive list of selections, he chose a California pinot noir.

"Wonderful choice, sir. I will be back shortly with your wine."

At their table by the window, Mark and Angela were enjoying their cocktails and an appetizer while making small talk. The parade of people going by on the mall provided entertainment and gave the two plenty to chat about. Occasionally someone passing by would stop and wave at Angela, recognizing her from her newscasts. She always smiled and waved back.

"Do you ever get tired of being recognized in public?"

"Not really. Every so often I get some weirdo and that can be disconcerting, but for the most part I don't mind it. It's part of the job, really. How about you? You have your share of TV time—you must get recognized."

"Nothing like you. I'm on TV when something big happens, but I think mostly people are focused on what I'm saying about the crime, not so much on me."

"That's because you're very good at what you do."

"Thanks, Angela. I appreciate that."

"So, these people are waving at me then I guess, huh?" she replied, waving back at a couple who were peering in through the window.

"Yeah, that's a pretty safe bet," chuckled Mark. "I do get recognized a lot around Castle Springs, but not so much in Denver. I'd be pretty surprised if someone walking by our window starting smiling and waving at me. Although I remember a few years back being in some big box electronics store looking to buy a TV. I was standing there and all the TVs were tuned to the same channel. All of a sudden my face was on the screen for some news story I had been interviewed for. Anyway, there I was, like on thirty TVs all in a row. It was pretty surreal. There were a few other customers in the store standing nearby and the double takes I got from them were priceless."

Angela burst out laughing. "Oh, my God—what did you say?"

"What could I say? I just kind of smiled and waved at the other customers. Kinda like you're doing tonight."

"Such a grounded man," Angela said with a smile. "You never get caught up with the craziness that's going on around you."

"Well, thanks for that."

"You're welcome."

Angela looked across the table and realized how much she missed being with Mark. We shouldn't have broken up, she thought.

"So, I spoke with the DA today."

"What about?" Mia asked, hoping it would be something other than the Lennox trial. No such luck.

"We went over the trial stuff, just making sure everybody is ready to go. I told him that you and Jack still needed to have one last meeting with Luke Dominic but otherwise we were ready."

Mia nodded, but didn't respond.

"Baxter is planning to make himself available for media interviews during the trial. It's pretty obvious he wants to have the world take notice of him and his office. Personally, I think it's a bit too much grandstanding, but he seems determined to do it."

"Seems a little over the top to me, too. He's such a politician."

"He's always running scared. When he came close to losing his office a few years back, I think he made the decision that he would do everything in his power to stay in the job. So, essentially, he's in a non-stop campaigning mode. God, I couldn't do that. Remember how draining the whole experience was last year?"

Mia didn't hear anything Mick was saying, her mind racing with thoughts about Keller and the trial and the horrible predicament he had put them all in.

"Mia, are you listening to me? Are you okay?"

"Yes, of course. I'm sorry, Mick."

"You look like you've seen a ghost."

"No, I'm fine. I was just remembering something back at the office."

"Okay, let's make a pact—no more talk about work tonight. Deal?"

"Deal."

After two cocktails, Angela excused herself, asked the waiter for directions to the restroom, and headed toward the back of Di Amore.

As she passed through the restaurant, she heard a voice call out to her.

"Angela! Over here . . . how are you doing?"

Angela walked over to the table. "Well, hello, sheriff! Good to see you get up to the big city on occasion."

"Yeah, every once in awhile. Angela, this is Mia Serrano. I don't think you two have ever met."

Angela reached out and shook Mia's hand. "Great to meet you, Mia."

"My pleasure, Angela. I recognize you from your newscasts."

"Thanks, Mia. I appreciate you watching Channel Eight."

"Is this your first time here?" asked Mick.

"Yes, it is. I live just a couple blocks away, so I really have no excuse. I've heard so many good things about it. We're just through our appetizer, but so far it's been wonderful."

"Well, you're a little ahead of us, then. I hope you enjoy your evening."

"Thanks, sheriff. And it was nice to meet you, Mia."

"You'll never guess who I just bumped into on my way to the ladies' room."

"Another one of your many fans?"

"Um, no . . . your boss and his girlfriend are back there."

"Mick and Mia?"

"None other. She's really beautiful."

Mark quickly considered the situation. There was nothing illicit about having dinner with Angela. Both were single and they were doing nothing wrong. Mick knew about the previous relationship. In fact, Mark had asked Mick for his opinion about it when they first began dating. Mick didn't see anything wrong with Mark dating a member of the media, just so long as there was never a conflict of interest. He couldn't be giving Angela inside information, so to speak.

Angela could see the concern on Mark's face. "It's not a problem, is it?"

"No, not at all. In fact, Mick knew about our relationship from before. He was fine with it."

"Good. I don't want to cause any problems for you."

"Did you tell them you were here with me?"

"No, we only talked for a half a minute. Just a quick hello."

"I should probably go say hello, then. It would be weird if they see us together when they leave."

"Okay, do you want me to go with you?"

"No, it's fine. I'll just be a minute."

Mark made his way toward Mick and Mia's table.

Before they looked up and saw him, Mark said in a loud voice, "Geez, you guys don't get enough of me at the office?"

"Oh, wow. Everyone's here tonight!" said Mia, laughing.

Mick added, "This place is like Grand Central Station."

"Look, I don't want to interrupt your dinner, but Angela told me she bumped into you and so I just wanted to say hi."

Mick looked up at Mark. "You're here with Angela?"

"Yes, we decided to try this place out. She lives close by."

"Yeah, she mentioned that."

Mia jumped in, "That's great, Mark. She seems really nice. Hope you guys have a great time tonight."

"Thanks, Mia. I'll let you guys get back to your dinner. I just wanted to say hello."

"Okay, see you tomorrow."

Mia looked at Mick, "I think it's great Mark has found someone he cares about. Angela seems really nice, and from what I've heard she's a really fair reporter."

"Yeah, she's been great. Unlike the *Denver Post,* Channel Eight has treated us pretty well."

Mick looked around nervously and it didn't go unnoticed by Mia.

"You okay? Now *you* seem a bit distracted."

"Yeah, I'm fine. Couldn't be better."

Mia didn't buy it but decided to let it go. Just then the waiter came over with the menus. He handed Mia a menu and then gave the other to Mick. Mick quickly opened his and took a look inside, then eyed Mia as she held her menu. But Mia didn't open it, and placed it on the table instead.

"You sure you're okay? You're acting kinda weird."

"I'm fine, really. Let's make our dinner choices, and pour ourselves another glass of wine."

Mia picked up her menu and opened it. Inside the menu were the words . . .

Mia, I love you with all my heart. Will you marry me?

Mick looked for her reaction. Her eyes got large as she stammered "Oh my God, Mick!"

Mick quickly left his seat and knelt down next to her. Several other patrons in the restaurant began to take notice. All eyes were on them.

"Mia, you are my whole life and I love you with all my heart and soul. I want to spend the rest of my life with you. Will you marry me?"

Mia looked at Mick kneeling in front of her and tears began to flow. She nodded yes, but was so overcome with emotion no words came out.

Mick smiled and said, "I'll take that as a yes."

Mia laughed and wrapped her arms around Mick, burying her head in his neck. She was shaking with emotion, and after several seconds got the words out.

"Yes, of course I'll marry you. I love you, too."

Mick reached into his pocket, pulled out a small box and opened it. He held it out for Mia to see and she put her hand to her mouth. "Oh, Mick. It's beautiful!"

He took the ring from the box and gently placed it on Mia's finger. The diners around them began to applaud.

"It can be returned if necessary. I want you to have the perfect ring. You won't hurt my feelings if you want to exchange it for something else. I was just guessing as far as the style goes."

The ring was a classic halo style two-and-a-half carat princess-cut diamond with a platinum band.

"Mick, I love it. And it's never coming off this finger again!"

Mick leaned in and gave her a gentle kiss on the lips.

"Good."

A few seconds later the waiter appeared with a bottle of champagne and two flutes and quickly popped the cork. Mick looked at the waiter and said, "Please provide glasses to the other patrons around us that are sharing our big moment. Open another bottle if necessary."

The waiter nodded and filled the flutes for Mick and Mia. A few minutes later a dozen strangers were busy toasting the happy couple.

"I'm in shock, Mick. You planned all this out? The menu, the champagne, the ring?"

"Yep. I called the manager here earlier today and asked him to help me with my big plan. They were great, got the proposal inserted in the menu for me and everything. I was so afraid they were going to hand me the menu with the proposal in it, and then I'd have to go to plan B."

"And what was plan B?"

"I didn't have one . . . that's why I was was so nervous about all this!"

Mia laughed and replied, "Thank God they got it right. Otherwise our fellow diners wouldn't be enjoying free champagne tonight!"

"That's true."

"I can't wait until I tell Dad. He'll be thrilled."

"Oh, he already knows. I asked him earlier tonight for permission to ask you to marry me."

Mia smiled, "That was so sweet of you, Mick. I'm sure he was ecstatic."

"Yeah, he was pretty happy about it. I wasn't sure he could keep the secret when you came downstairs. I warned him to put on his best poker face."

"I didn't notice a thing. You boys are pretty sneaky."

Mick nodded, and replied, "Hey, we should have the waiter take a glass of champagne over to Mark and Angela."

"Perfect, and he could suggest they wander over our way."

Mick nodded and called the waiter over, asking him to do the favor.

A few minutes later Mark and Angela appeared at their table, champagne flutes in hand.

"So, what's the occasion?" Mark asked.

After a passionate night of lovemaking, Mark Archer woke up feeling like a new man. He and Angela were picking up right where they left off before the breakup six months earlier. The feelings he had for her came flooding back, but he knew he had to be careful not to push her about marriage. He would play it slow this time and see where things went. Being with her is better than being without her, he thought to himself, so he would just let her call the shots about any marriage plans.

He reached over and took Angela in his arms. She was just starting to wake up and he pulled her close. She didn't seem to mind, putting her head on his chest.

Mark glanced over at the clock on the nightstand. It was a few minutes before six, so he had some time before he'd need to run off to work. He thought about starting things up with her, but decided to just enjoy the closeness they were sharing.

After a few minutes, Angela looked up at him. "Hey, there . . . how'd you sleep?"

"Like a million bucks. You?"

"The same."

"What time do you have to go to the station today?"

"I need to get there around eight thirty. I've got a little time still. Why, what do you have in mind?"

Archer laughed. "Actually, I'm just enjoying lying here with you. No ulterior motives on my part."

Angela gave him a little hug and kissed his chest.

"Me, too."

After a celebration with Chuck and more champagne, it was well past midnight by the time Mia got to bed, and she had not slept well. It was morning and she had just a few minutes before she would have to start her day. As she laid in bed her thoughts kept racing between Mick's wonderful proposal and worrying about the Lennox case. What Mick had said to her about the DA making a big deal out of the case raised her level of anxiety tenfold. With Baxter grandstanding, even more attention would be focused on the courtroom, and if things went south, it would be devastating for everyone. And she couldn't allow that happen to her future husband.

She grabbed her cell phone, typed a text message, and sent it.

"You want to shower first or you want me to go?"

"I've got to get out of here before you, so maybe I'll go now," replied Mark.

"Okay, take your time."

Mark headed for the shower and Angela decided to get up and have a cup of coffee. She started a pot and grabbed the newspaper on her doorstep.

With coffee in hand, she decided to return to bed and read the paper.

Once she settled back into bed she heard a familiar chirp coming from Mark's phone on the nightstand. Sounds like a text message, she thought. She ignored it at first, but then her curiosity got the best of her. She put her coffee down and reached across the bed for his cell. There on the display screen was a text message from Mia. Her first reaction was to wonder why Mia was texting Mark at such an early hour. Then she read the text.

> I'm afraid the truth about Keller is going to come out and Lennox is going to walk. Can't let it ruin Mick's career. Be in around 8, need to talk

She put the phone back on the nightstand and sat on the edge of the bed, her mind racing.

CHAPTER 25

Mark dressed quickly and left Angela's apartment, headed for work. He wanted to allow for a few extra minutes so he could swing by his place for a change of clothes. He didn't need people drawing any conclusions about why he was wearing the same clothes as the day before.

Once he arrived at his office, Mark saw Mia's text. He quickly texted her back, telling her to come by at her convenience. He was growing more and more concerned about her, worried about how rattled she seemed about the Lennox case. He knew that the only way Keller would be exposed was if someone within the department went public with the facts, and that wasn't going to happen. There were only three people who knew the truth and nobody wanted it disclosed. He needed to calm Mia down and give her the reassurance she needed.

"Hey, Mark. Got a few minutes now?" Mia asked, peeking her head inside his office.

"Yeah, come on in. Close the door."

Mia took a seat and started right in.

"Mick told me last night at dinner that the Dave Baxter was planning on making a huge deal about the Lennox case. He even plans on holding daily briefings during the trial. He wants this case to be as big as possible. He's so confident in a conviction, and he sees it as a way to make a name for himself."

"Geez, what a politician."

"That's what I said . . . but Mark, what if this doesn't go well? What if the truth comes out? Then Lennox walks and Mick's career as sheriff gets derailed before he really had a chance to be the great sheriff we know he'll be."

"Whoa, Mia. You're getting way ahead of yourself. What makes you think the truth will come out? If you think about it, the only people who know about Keller sure as hell don't want it coming out, so I think we'll be fine."

"I don't know, Mark. I've just got a bad feeling about things. And my intuition is right more often than it's wrong. I can't explain it . . . it's just this sense I have."

Mia paused, hoping that Mark wasn't looking at her as some crazy, emotionally-overwrought woman.

Sensing Mia's concern about how she might be perceived, he responded, "I totally understand your concerns, but let's not overthink this. Like I said, I really believe things will turn out fine for all of us."

Mia seemed to calm down a bit and allowed herself to breathe.

Mark saw an opportunity to change the subject, so he did.

"So, did you have any idea a marriage proposal was coming last night?"

"No, he really surprised me. I mean, we've been getting really close and all, but I didn't see it coming," she responded.

"I'm really happy for you guys—you make a great couple. And I know how much Mick loves you."

"Thanks, Mark. That's really sweet of you to say. And Angela seems really nice. Mick tells me you guys had a past relationship?"

"Yes, it ended about six months ago. But last night went really well, and I think we're back on track. I guess we'll see how things go this time."

"That's wonderful, Mark. You deserve it."

"Thanks, Mia. She's really special to me. Just hope we can work it out this time."

Mia stood to leave.

"It'll be fine, Mia. Stop worrying."

Mia nodded and headed back to her office. While she appreciated Mark's reassurances, the anxiety remained. She could feel it in her gut.

Gina could hardly think straight on the flight back to Miami. The flyer with the photo of Chris was lurking in her mind and she was unable to shake the image. There must be some kind of mistake, she kept telling herself. There was no way Chris had done anything wrong. She was falling in love with him and he was the nicest, sweetest man she knew. This would all get sorted out once she returned to Miami and talked to him about it. If need be, she would get her father involved to help get things resolved.

"Hey, I missed you. How were your flights?"

Gina mustered a smile. "Okay, I guess."

"What's wrong? You get some jerk on your flight?"

Gina didn't respond. She wasn't sure how to start the conversation with Chris about the flyer.

"No, the passengers were okay."

"What is it, Gina? You look upset."

Gina opened her purse, took out the flyer, and handed it to Chris.

He looked at it, and hiding any emotion or concern, asked, "Where did you get this?"

"At work, in Denver. It was on the bulletin board in the UAL employee lounge. It says the police want to talk to you."

There was no use denying it. "Yeah, I can explain."

"Please do, Chris. This is freaking me out."

"It's nothing to worry about. Look, before I met you I was a witness to a crime. I was showing a property in Denver and it wasn't in a great neighborhood. As I was leaving and getting in my car I heard gunshots and saw three guys running away. I looked over to where they were running from and there was a guy on the ground. I ran over to him, offered first aid, and called nine-one-one. The police told me that it looked gang related and that I might be called on to identify the shooters if and when they made an arrest. Sounds like they may have caught the guys and need me to do that."

"Oh my God, Chris . . . that's scary. Sometimes there's retribution in cases like that. I've heard plenty of stories from my dad."

"Well, to be truthful, I am a bit worried about it. I guess I don't have to testify but it's really my duty as a good citizen to do that, isn't it?"

Gina thought about it and responded, "Yeah, but I don't want you to be in any danger. Those gang members are bad dudes. Look at it this way, if you don't testify, it'll just be a matter of time before they do another crime and get caught. Let the next guy do the testifying in court."

She couldn't believe what she was saying. It went against everything her father taught her growing up. But now the reality was setting in and someone she loved could be in danger. It changed things considerably, and she felt a pang of guilt about all the times she had judged people who refused to cooperate with police.

"I don't know, Gina. I think it's my duty to testify. I mean, what if everyone shirked their duties? No one would ever get prosecuted for their crimes. I can't worry about what might happen to me. I think I'll contact the police back in Colorado."

Chris hoped he wasn't overplaying his hand. He saw an opening with Gina and was about to make it her idea for him not to contact the authorities.

"No, let's hold off for now. See how things play out."

"All right. I guess we can do that."

Chris took Gina in his arms and hugged her gently.

"What did I ever do to deserve you? I love you, Gina."

He had said the magic words, and in doing so he sealed the deal.

"I love you, too, Chris. And I just want you to be safe."

Angela Bell closed the door to her office and got busy searching the Internet for stories about the Scott Lennox case. She couldn't get Mia's text message out of her mind. What did it mean that the truth about Jack Keller was about to come out? He and Mia were the lead investigators on the case, and by all accounts it was a slam dunk. The evidence against Lennox in the killing of his former business partner was overwhelming, and police had him on an additional charge of attempting to kill Lisa Sullivan, his former lover. Even with Branch Kramer as his lawyer, the best Lennox could hope for was twenty years to life in prison.

So how in the world could Lennox walk? Angela wondered. And why was the new sheriff's job at risk? She pieced her thoughts together as best she could. If something the RCSO had done caused the case against Lennox to fall apart, then she could see where that could be devastating to McCallister. Did Keller cut some corners in the investigation? She knew he had a reputation for being an outstanding homicide investigator, but did he do something so egregious that the judge or jury would have no choice but to free Lennox?

God, that would be a huge story, she thought. A story she would love to break.

The meeting between Luke Dominic, Mia, and Jack took place at the DA's office at the Rocklin County Justice Center. The three spent more than two hours going over their testimony, not leaving anything to chance. Once Dominic finished going over the questions he was planning to ask, he shifted gears. He went into attack mode, firing questions at both Mia and Jack that would likely come their way from Branch Kramer during cross examination.

Jack had been through the routine hundreds of times in his career, so there was very little that could rattle him. Mia, on the other hand, had testified only during traffic fatality cases. Going toe to toe with a snake like Branch Kramer in a homicide case was an entirely different animal. Much of the time spent in Dominic's office was focused on her testimony.

She was struggling with the questions Luke was firing at her, and seemed unable to find her focus, so he suggested they take a break.

"You okay, Mia? You seemed distracted today," he asked as the two sat with their coffee in the breakroom.

"Yeah, I'm fine. Just a little tired. No worries."

"Okay, I want to get you ready for anything in there. Branch Kramer is known for his antics in the courtroom and so the more I grill you with these questions now, the better you'll be prepared to answer."

"I understand. I'll be fine. Let's get back to it."

The three returned to the conference room and Mia did her best to free her mind of her concerns about the case and refocus her attention on the DA's questions.

CHAPTER 26

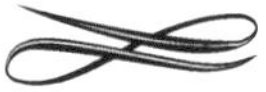

A week later the trial of Scott Lennox began in courtroom ten at the Rocklin County Justice Center.

"All rise. This court is now in session, the Honorable Richard O'Brien presiding."

All present rose and watched the judge take his seat on the bench.

"Good morning, everyone. Today we will begin jury selection in the case of the State of Colorado versus Mr. Scott Lennox. Mr. Dominic, are the People ready to go?"

"Yes, Your Honor."

"Mr. Kramer, are you ready to proceed with the defense of Mr. Lennox?"

"Yes, sir, we certainly are. And it is my great honor to be—"

"Save it for the jury, counselor. There will be plenty of time for your theatrics, no doubt."

At the end of the day, Mick, Jack, and Mia sat in Mick's office going over the jury pool.

Jack filled Mick in: "Luke seems pleased so far. He had several jurors he could live with and only one he definitely wanted bounced. He'll use one of his peremptory challenges to dump that one. On the other hand, he thought Kramer would be unhappy with three or four jurors interviewed today. So all in all, a good first day for the prosecution."

"How long does he expect jury selection to take?" asked Mick.

"Couple more days. Opening arguments could begin as early as Thursday and he expects the trial to run about two weeks."

"How was Kramer today?"

Mia responded, "Judge O'Brien set the tone early with Kramer. He started off with some grandstanding at the start of jury selection and O'Brien came down on him. He was well behaved the rest of the day."

Mick answered, "Good, but I'm sure it won't keep him down for long. His style is creating lots of drama in the courtroom, and juries can be either drawn in by that or turned off by it. Let's hope Colorado juries see through the blowhard."

The start of the Lennox trial was the big story of the day, not only in Rocklin County, but throughout the state of Colorado.

Like the other news agencies, Channel Eight led with the story, showing video footage of jury selection. It wasn't particularly compelling television, but the media was getting their audiences geared up for the coverage that would be coming their way each day. Angela Bell read from her teleprompter, explaining to viewers what happens during the jury selection process.

Once she finished the newscast, she quickly headed home. She had to get ready for her date with Mark Archer. She was determined to uncover the big mystery with Jack Keller and the Lennox trial.

It took two more days to get through jury selection and by Thursday they were ready for opening statements. Jack and Mia weren't needed to testify until day three or four at the earliest, as Luke Dominic wanted to lay out the physical evidence against Lennox before calling his main witnesses. After Jack and Mia were through with their testimony, he would bring out the prosecution's star witness, Lisa Sullivan. Sullivan, who was Scott Lennox's lover at the time of the killing, would testify against Lennox, telling the court how he planned to commit the crime. She had received immunity in exchange for her testimony, something Branch Kramer would exploit, no doubt. But her testimony would put Lennox away, and the fact that he had attempted to kill Sullivan by running her down with his car once he realized she was working with police would be the icing on the cake.

Branch Kramer held court at the end of each day on the steps of the courthouse, offering his insights into the case. The media loved it and covered every minute of his grandstanding. His antics were largely for personal publicity, as the jury was in place and had been ordered by the judge not to look at any media coverage of the trial. But no one really knew what the jury would do in the privacy of their homes; there was a decent chance one of two would catch Kramer's diatribe against the prosecution and their "weak" case against his client.

Some fifty feet away DA Dave Baxter stood on the same courthouse steps and pontificated about the fine job his office was doing in bringing a coldblooded killer to justice. Scott Lennox would pay for his crimes—Dave Baxter essentially guaranteed it. Clearly, Baxter's performance was solely for the voters of Rocklin County. He had come within a hair of losing his office a few years earlier and he was damned if he'd let that happen again.

CHAPTER 27

"Yes, I'm trying to reach either Jack Keller or Mia Serrano."

"What is this concerning?" asked Janet, the secretary in the Investigations Bureau.

"I'm calling about a flyer that was posted at DIA. I think I recognize the person on the flyer and this was the number listed to call."

"Okay. One moment, please."

Janet put the call through to Keller.

"Keller. Can I help you?"

"Yes, my name is Lance Palazzo and I'm a flight attendant for United Airlines. I'm calling about the flyer that was posted in our employee lounge. I think I recognize the person in the photo."

"Thanks for calling. What can you tell me about it?"

"I think the guy was on a flight I worked a couple weeks back. I'm not one hundred percent sure, but it does look a lot like the guy."

"Was it the flight from Denver to Miami?"

"I think so; it's one of my regular routes."

"Did you happen to catch his name?"

"No, I don't have that information but the flight manifest should have it."

Jack knew that was a dead end.

"Do you remember where on the plane he was sitting?"

"Yes, he was in first class. I remember that because he got pretty chummy with one of the gals I work with."

"And what is her name?"

"I'm not going to get her in any trouble, am I? I don't want that."

"No, not at all. But she may know his name, especially if she seemed to know him," Jack responded, immediately wondering why a UAL employee who seemingly knew Timbers wouldn't have called it in after seeing the flyer.

"Her name is Gina Barone. She works the same schedule as me."

"Okay, I appreciate that, Mr. Palazzo. Are you working today?"

"Yes, I just got into work after a layover. I meant to call you sooner. I saw the flyer a few days ago and copied down your number, but it just slipped my mind. I noticed that the flyer was gone from the bulletin board so I thought maybe you had found the person."

"No, we're still interested in talking to him. Is Gina working today?"

"Yes, like I said, we work the same schedule."

"Is she there now?"

"No, but I expect her any minute. We have a flight in ninety minutes."

Jack ended the call and texted Mia. The two were soon headed to DIA to talk with Gina Barone.

Jack and Mia made their way through the terminal to the UAL lounge. Mia had called ahead and let the security personnel know they were en route. When they arrived they were let right in and found the supervisor they had spoken to before.

"We're looking for Gina Barone. Can you make the introduction?"

"Sure, I believe she's in the back. I'll get her."

The woman left and Jack and Mia took a seat in the lounge.

"Gina, there are two detectives here that want to see you. I believe it's about that flyer they posted last week about the guy they were looking for."

Fear gripped Gina. She looked at her supervisor, but didn't speak.

"Gina, are you okay?

"Oh, I'm fine. I just don't have time right now to talk with them. Could you make an excuse for me, tell them I'm not here?"

"Gina, what's going on?"

"Nothing, I just can't speak to them right now. Can you please do this for me?"

The woman stood there, looking at the young flight attendant. She thought about the flyer; the investigators weren't looking for Gina per se, it was the man on the flyer they wanted to question.

"Sure, I can tell them that, but I don't think they're going to give up. If you don't talk to them today I'm sure they'll be back."

"I know, but if you could do that for me I'd really appreciate it."

"Okay."

The woman returned to the lounge and told Jack and Mia that Gina wasn't there and they'd have to try to reach her another time.

"Are you sure she's not here? Is there a reason you'd lie to us about this?"

"She's not available. I'm sorry, but that's all I can tell you."

"So, which is it? Is she 'not here' or is she 'not available?'" Jack pushed.

He said it with an edge to his voice, and Mia reached over and grabbed his arm.

"Come on Jack, we can do this later. Let's go."

Jack looked at his partner and nodded. They walked back into the terminal.

Mia spoke first, "The flight to Miami leaves in ninety minutes. The crew goes onboard ahead of the passengers, so I'm guessing Barone will be walking to the gate before too long. Maybe we should park ourselves where we can see the crew as they come by, and see if we can catch a name tag with the name Gina on it."

Jack replied, "I like it."

A half hour later Mia nudged Jack's arm as the crew began to come by. They walked toward the Miami flight's departure gate in small groups, and both Jack and Mia were able to see the name tags on the uniforms.

They spotted her in the middle of the second group. They quickly stood up and flashed their badges.

"Ms. Barone, we need a few minutes of your time."

Gina blanched, stopping dead in her tracks.

"Who, me?"

"Yes, are you Gina Barone?"

"Yes, but I don't have anything to say. I have a flight to work, I'm sorry."

Gina started toward the gate, but Jack stepped in front of her, his arm blocking her way.

"We just need a few minutes of your time."

Seeing no choice, Gina nodded. "Okay, I'll give you two minutes. Let's go over there," pointing to an area of the terminal where no one was sitting.

The three took a seat and Mia began with the questions.

"We have reason to believe you may know this man," Mia said, producing a photo of Timbers from her coat pocket and showing it to Gina.

"Um, no . . . I don't know him. Sorry."

"One of your co-workers said you were pretty chummy with him on a flight to Miami a few weeks ago. It's pretty clear that you know the guy," stated Jack.

"I meet a lot of passengers, but he doesn't look familiar to me."

"Is there some reason you're protecting him? We don't want to cause you any trouble, but if you're protecting him from us you could find yourself in a lot of trouble," Mia offered, trying to scare the woman into telling what she knew.

"No, I'm sorry, but I don't know him. Now, I need to get back to work."

Jack and Mia looked at each other. They didn't have enough to hold her so they stepped aside and let her board the plane.

"She's really spooked. Which means she knows a lot more about Timbers than she's letting on."

Jack looked at Mia, "Yeah, but we'll get her to talk. We'll call the president of fucking UAL if we have to."

CHAPTER 28

"Angela, you're an even better cook than I remember."

"Well, aren't you sweet for saying that, Mark."

The two were sitting in Angela's apartment sipping a cognac and watching the fire dance in the fireplace. It was nearly ten and they were enjoying a relaxing evening together. Neither had mentioned their respective jobs and they somehow got to discussing some of the trips they had taken together while dating previously.

"I think our trip to Italy was my favorite," Angela offered. "It's hard to beat the romantic nature of the people, the food, and the wine."

"Yeah, that was my favorite, too . . . although I didn't mind Hawaii at all."

Angela smiled, "Yeah, I think I know what you liked about Hawaii . . . "

Mark looked at her, "Yeah? And what's that?"

"The bathing-suits-optional beach that we went to on Kauai."

"Oh, yeah, I had totally forgotten about that. Was that with you?"

Angela threw a pillow from the sofa, hitting Mark on the side of the head.

"Ouch . . . watch yourself, young lady."

"Yeah, what are you going to do about it, big boy?"

Mark shifted over toward Angela and grabbed her. He kissed her for several seconds, then moved his lips to her neck.

"I should throw stuff at you more often."

The two made their way to the bedroom.

Gina arrived home just after nine and found Chris asleep on her sofa. The two had made the decision a week earlier that he should forgo his hotel room in South Beach and stay with her. They were together whenever Gina wasn't working, so it just seemed like a logical step. Save him some money, they both reasoned. Their relationship was growing more serious each day. He was amazed by how well he could lie, making stuff up on the fly. He was careful not to say anything that would trip up his story, but it was clear she was in love with him and would believe almost anything he said.

Chris didn't hear her come in, so she slipped into the bedroom and changed out of her work clothes. She poured herself a glass of wine and sat on the loveseat next to the sofa where Chris was asleep. She badly needed the wine—something to calm her nerves after the confrontation with the investigators from Rocklin County. She sipped from her glass, thinking about her situation. Clearly, the police weren't going to let things go. They needed Chris to testify about what he had seen that day while showing property in Denver. If they were that determined to find him and get him to testify, these gang members must really be bad news. They were trying very hard to get them off the street, and Chris was evidently the key to doing this. This realization made her even more determined not to do anything that would lead them to Chris. They didn't care if it put Chris in danger. Let them figure it out on their own, she thought.

As she sat thinking things through, Chris slowly opened his eyes and was startled to seeing her sitting there.

"Oh, hey, when did you get home?"

"Just a little while ago. Decided to have a little something to drink and watch you sleep. You looked very peaceful."

"Just catching a little nap. How was your flight?"

Gina thought about telling Chris what happened, but decided not to burden him with it.

"Fine . . . uneventful. What did you do today?"

"I ran up to Fort Lauderdale, checked on some more properties. Called my client, gave him the rundown."

"Is he getting closer to making a decision on what to buy? I mean, you've been looking at stuff for almost a month. I'm not complaining, of course—I love having you here. But at some point are you going to have to go back to Denver and meet with him?"

"That's a really good question. I will likely have to do that, but I don't know when that might be. He's kinda unpredictable. He's cool with everything, then suddenly he'll say that he wants to meet with me tomorrow. When that happens, I'll have to jump on the very next flight and go back, at least for a short time. But, the bottom line is I'm really liking South Florida."

"And I love having you here, Chris. I just worry if you go back to Colorado the police will still be looking for you in connection to that shooting. And what if you get pulled over for speeding or something? I'm guessing you're in their system."

"I promise to obey all traffic laws while driving in the state of Colorado."

"Chris, I'm serious. I'm really worried about this."

I'm one hell of an actor, he thought to himself. She really bought the story about the gang members.

"I know, Gina. Look, I'll be careful when I'm back there, and I'll get the first flight back here once I'm done with my client. With the way he operates, that could mean I'm flying back here the same day. Spend an hour with him going over the info on the properties then run back to DIA to catch a return flight. You won't even know I'm gone, and there's a decent chance you'll be working the flights I'm on."

"Okay, and you'll promise me to be super careful?"

"Of course. There's nothing to worry about."

CHAPTER 29

It didn't take long for Branch Kramer to get theatrical in Judge O'Brien's courtroom. Luke Dominic hadn't yet reached his seat after delivering his opening statement when Kramer leapt to his feet claiming there was no evidence against his client and that the judge should set him free.

"Really, Mr. Kramer?" Judge O'Brien responded.

"Yes, Your Honor. If that's the best the state has, then I move for a directed verdict."

"Sit down, Mr. Kramer. Your courtroom antics may play well in Texas, but here in Colorado we like to actually hear the evidence before a decision is made by the judge or jury. Motion denied."

Kramer looked at the judge a good long time; something that didn't go unnoticed by O'Brien.

The rest of the day consisted of a lengthy presentation outlining all the physical evidence uncovered at the location where Lennox's body was found. Dr. Mora, who had performed the autopsy on George Lombard, testified to his findings. Luke Dominic timed it so the last thing the jury heard about was the inconsistencies Dr. Mora found in the examination of George Lombard's body. All his findings pointed to murder, not a random accident on a deserted Colorado highway. His testimony was finished a few minutes before five, and while Kramer immediately jumped up for cross examination, Judge O'Brien said that they were done for the day. It was a nice end to a very good day for the prosecution.

Mark and Angela were lounging in bed, neither one anxious to get up and start the day. Angela's head rested on Mark's chest and he lightly stroked her back. The snooze button on the alarm was allowing them some quiet, ten minutes at a time.

"So, what's your day look like?" asked Angela.

"Nothing out of the ordinary. But you never know what the day will bring."

"I can relate to that," she responded.

Both Angela and Mark worked in a world where things could change very quickly. A slow news day could turn very busy when something significant happened.

"So, what's happening in the Lennox trial? How's that been going?"

"Good, so far. I get daily briefings on the trial proceedings and the prosecution is very pleased. Jury selection went well, and the opening arguments seemed to resonate with the jury, at least that's Jack and Mia's take on things so far."

"The evidence is pretty overwhelming against Lennox, huh?"

"Yeah, we've got him dead to rights. Stuff with the autopsy, a financial motive, a lover Lennox was hiding from his wife, the same lover who will deliver the death blow with her testimony. Not to mention we've got him on a wire admitting to the killing. You can stick a fork in him—he's done."

"What about Branch Kramer? I mean, the guy comes up here from Texas to handle the case. Is that just about money, or publicity, or does he think he's got a legitimate chance to get Lennox off?"

"Probably a little of all those things, but I can't really see where he could think Lennox is going to be acquitted. This is a really solid case."

"What if something goes wrong?"

"What do you mean?"

"What if something unexpected pops up in the trial?"

"Like what?"

"I don't know, but sometimes that happens. Trials can take unexpected turns, especially with a guy like Kramer."

"I don't see that happening in this case. Lennox will go down for his crime."

"You seem pretty confident."

Mark was agitated by Angela's line of questions. He climbed from the bed and stood facing Angela, wondering where these questions were coming from.

"I am confident. And I think it's time for me to take a shower. Duty calls."

Angela didn't respond. She could sense Mark's frustration. She'd brought up the subject of the trial and he hadn't bitten. Not that she expected him to, but at least she had started a dialogue. He hadn't shared anything with her yet, but she knew she could be very persuasive, and she would get to the bottom of Mia's text.

Prosecutor Luke Dominic felt it best that Mia be the first investigator on the stand. Both she and Jack had played major roles in the investigation but she had been first on the scene. Jack hadn't been called in until it was apparent that it was indeed a homicide and not a routine fatal traffic collision.

With Luke Dominic calmly leading her through her role in the case, Mia performed well on the stand. She was able to outline the discovery of the insurance policy on the victim that listed Lennox as the beneficiary. She explained that the married Lennox was having an affair with Lisa Sullivan, and that Sullivan played a rather minor role in the planning of the crime. Mia stated they had arrested Lennox initially, but his accomplice, Sullivan, had eluded capture. Sullivan ultimately turned herself in and agreed to wear a wire to capture a confession from Lennox on tape. She explained that in his anger upon discovering what Sullivan was doing, he ran her over, nearly killing her. After nearly two hours on the stand, Dominic finished up his questions for Mia.

"Your witness, Mr. Kramer," announced the judge.

Kramer stood up and walked toward the witness stand.

"Good afternoon, Ms. Serrano."

"Good afternoon."

"Ms. Serrano, how long have you been a homicide investigator?"

"Almost two years."

"And what did you do before becoming a homicide investigator?"

"I worked in the traffic unit. I investigated traffic accidents, some of which were fatalities."

"So, I'm confused. How in the world did you end up investigating this case? I mean, there's a huge leap going from traffic cop to suddenly being an investigator on a murder case, isn't there?"

"I was assigned to the Lombard death because at first it appeared to be a traffic fatality. Once we determined that it was not an accident and it was, in fact, a murder, I was asked to partner on the case with Investigator Keller."

"Wow, baptism by fire."

Luke Dominic stood up. "Objection, Your Honor. Is there a question there, or is it just more color commentary by Mr. Kramer?"

"Sustained. Mr. Kramer, please keep things in the form of a question."

"Yes, Your Honor. So twenty months ago you found yourself as co-lead in your first murder investigation, is that correct?"

"Yes, that's correct."

"Who assigned you to the case?"

"My boss, the commander of the Investigations Bureau."

"And who might that be?"

"Mick McCallister was the commander of the bureau at that time."

"Isn't it true that Commander McCallister is now the sheriff of Rocklin County?"

Luke Dominic stood up. "Objection, Your Honor. Relevance?"

"Overruled. I'll allow the question, but Mr. Kramer—I assume this is leading somewhere?"

"It is, indeed. It is my intention to show the court that a completely unqualified investigator was put in charge of this murder investigation, and that—"

"Mr. Kramer, that's enough," O'Brien said sternly. "Proceed with your questioning, but again, I am going to ask you to refrain from giving a speech."

It was a crafty move by Kramer. He had made his point to the jury about Mia's inexperience. But it also tipped off the prosecution as to his strategy. He was going to go after the integrity of the investigation and try to show sloppy police work. Dominic quickly realized he would need to shift gears in his trial strategy and lean heavily on Keller's role in the investigation, highlighting his vast experience. Show the jury that Keller really called the shots, and that Mia played a much smaller role.

"Very well, Your Honor."

Kramer approached the witness stand, standing no more than a few feet from Mia. He took on an almost paternal role, talking to Mia like she had something to confess.

"Ms. Serrano, what kind of relationship did you and your boss, Commander McCallister, have at the time of Mr. Lombard's death some twenty months ago?"

Luke Dominic jumped to his feet. "Objection, Your Honor! Again, relevance?"

Judge O'Brien looked at Kramer. "Mr. Kramer, Ms. Serrano's personal life is not on trial today. Move it along."

"Of course, Your Honor. I was merely trying to—"

"Go no further, Mr. Kramer. Making your point to the jury in comments to me won't work in my courtroom. Move on and let's keep the questioning focused on the matter at hand."

"Your honor, I am simply trying to show that Ms. Serrano was essentially put in charge of a homicide case by her boyfriend, who happened to be the commander of the Investigations Bureau at that time."

"Move it along, Mr. Kramer," he replied angrily.

Again, the crafty defense attorney had managed to make his point to the jury, essentially putting an element of doubt in their minds as to Mia's competence in handling a murder investigation.

"Ms. Serrano, is it true that you were the first investigator on scene the morning of the accident?"

"Yes, that's correct."

"And what did you do when you first arrived?"

"I surveyed the scene and talked to the deputy who was with Ms. Sullivan. She was the person who had called nine-one-one reporting she'd struck and killed a man on the highway."

"And what did you talk about with the deputy?"

"About what he had observed when arriving on scene. What steps he had taken, that sort of thing."

"Yes, well, that sounds like real good police work."

Dominic stood again, "Your Honor, he's badgering Ms. Serrano, and once again, there was no question for the witness."

"Sustained on both points."

"Did you spent a lot of time out at the crime scene that morning?"

"Several hours."

"And you supervised everything? Telling your personnel what to do, what evidence to collect, et cetera . . . ?"

"Yes, I had responsibility for the scene. Our traffic team is very knowledgeable, so they know what to do."

"Is the traffic team the same group of personnel that typically respond to murder scenes?"

"No, that would be our CSI personnel. They're trained to process crime scenes. The traffic team is focused on accident reconstruction, that sort of thing."

"Would you say your traffic investigations team is qualified to process a homicide scene?"

"Objection! Your Honor, I don't see where this is going."

"Overruled. The witness will answer."

"They are a highly-trained, very professional group of technicians who have worked together for years. They have an exemplary record."

"Ms. Serrano, you didn't answer the question. Is your traffic team qualified to process a homicide scene?"

"The morning of the accident we weren't aware that we had a homicide. It appeared, by all accounts, to be a fatal traffic accident and so the team that handles those kinds of investigations was called out. It wouldn't have made any sense to have our CSI team respond."

"So you had an inexperienced team of technicians process the scene that morning?"

Mia glared at Kramer. "I strongly object to your insinuation."

"Well, sure . . . I'm sure you'll do anything to protect your team. Nothing further at this time, Your Honor. But I'd certainly like the opportunity to call on this witness at a later time."

Mick heard about Mia's testimony and decided to drop by the Serrano home after leaving his office. He found her sitting with Chuck and Sasha in the living room.

"Can I get you a glass of wine?" Mick asked.

"Sure, but only if you and Dad join me."

Mick brought in a bottle and three glasses, placed them on the coffee table, and slipped Sasha a treat he had brought from the kitchen. He opened the bottle, poured three generous glasses, and handed one each to Chuck and Mia.

Mia held her glass in the air. "Here's to getting crucified on the stand."

Mick responded, "Don't beat yourself up over it, Mia. It was bound to happen. Look, it's the guy's job. He's a scumbag, but it's what he's paid to do."

Chuck jumped in. "I don't care if it's his job, I think he took some cheap shots at Mia. It's not right, Mick."

"Luke will get you back on the stand later in the trial and the stuff about your team, the CSI folks, et cetera, will all get worked out. I'm not worried about it. It's just part of the trial process and we'll get our chance to set the record straight. And besides, I just don't think our juries are impressed by people like Kramer. They'll see right through him. If anything, they probably felt some sympathy for you, Mia."

"I don't care about me, what bothers me is he went after my team. Making it sound like they're incompetent. No one knew that morning that we were looking at a one-eighty-seven. But they did nothing out there that would compromise the investigation."

"Of course not, and the jury is smart enough to know that. And a guy like Kramer can sometimes push his antics too far and lose the jury. It's my bet Colorado juries have less tolerance for people like him than Texas juries do. Who knows, today he may have caused more damage to himself than to you."

"Nice of you to say that, but I'm not so sure. The jury looked like they were hanging on his every word."

"That's because this was really the first time they saw him being Branch Kramer. If he's not careful, he'll have jurors rolling their eyes at him soon."

"If I was on that jury, I would have told him to knock that shit off. The guy is all hat, no cattle," offered Chuck.

Mia smiled, "Thanks, Dad. But then I'm sure he would have pointed out to everyone that I'm your daughter. He sure wanted everyone to know I was involved with the sheriff and that you assigned me to the case."

"Mia, it's all subterfuge. He has to resort to this because he's got nothing else. His case is weak and he's just throwing mud on the wall to see what sticks."

Mia knew he was right, but it still stung. Being on the stand in the biggest murder case in the history of the county and being made to look like a fool was hardly pleasant.

Chuck jumped in. "Hey, I know . . . let's all go out and grab a nice dinner tonight—on me."

"No thanks, Dad. I think I'm just going to turn in early."

Mick looked at Mia. "Okay, I think you'll feel better in the morning. You just gotta hang in there. The trial has a ways to go and remember the evidence against Lennox is overwhelming. We're gonna be just fine."

Mia looked at her fiancé and felt sick to her stomach.

CHAPTER 30

"The People call Investigator Jack Keller to the stand."

All eyes were on Jack as he walked confidently to the witness stand, took the oath, and settled in for Luke Dominic's line of questions. Luke wasn't overly concerned about Mia's testimony the day before but thought putting Jack on the stand immediately afterward would right the ship, so to speak.

"Please state your name and occupation, sir."

"My name is Jack Keller. I'm a homicide investigator with the Rocklin County Sheriff's Department."

"And how long have you held that position?"

"I've been with the RCSO for twelve years. I've been a homicide investigator for all twelve of those years."

"Typically, investigators don't start their careers in that position. How did you come to be assigned to that role from your very first day with RCSO?"

"Previous to my appointment to the RCSO I was a homicide investigator for the St. Louis Metro Police Department. I held that position for more than twenty years. I retired in 2003 but after a year or so I got bored and missed the job. I applied for the position with RCSO and they hired me. That was in late 2004."

"So, all told, you have more than thirty years under your belt investigating homicides?"

"Yes, sir."

"How many homicides have you investigated during your career?"

"I'd say three hundred, give or take."

"And what's your clearance rate for those cases? How many did you solve?"

"My clearance rate in St. Louis was nearly seventy-five percent; it's been a bit higher here in Colorado."

"Nationally, the average clearance rate is only fifty percent. A seventy-five percent rate is quite—"

Branch Kramer interrupted, "Your Honor, we all get it, the guy is good at his job. Can we move this along?"

Judge O'Brien responded, "Mr. Kramer, he's only been on the stand for ninety seconds. I think we can allow a few minutes outlining his experience at investigating homicides. Mr. Dominic, you may continue."

"Thank you, Your Honor. As I was saying, a seventy-five percent clearance rate is quite remarkable. Let me ask you this—was the murder of George Lombard a challenging case for you?"

"Not really, it came together quite quickly. The defendant made some critical mistakes and those mistakes led to his arrest for murder."

"Take us through the case, starting with your first involvement."

"This case was a little different in that it was believed, at first, to be a fatal car accident. Our traffic division handled the investigation initially, but through some excellent police work they quickly determined that this was not an accident at all, but rather a murder staged to look like a car accident. That's when I was asked to get involved."

"How much time had passed by the time you got involved in the investigation?"

"The day after the murder. Investigator Serrano, our traffic investigator, quickly surmised that this was no accident. She told our boss, Commander McCallister, and he asked me to take the lead on the investigation. I immediately took over the case, with Ms. Serrano assisting me. She's a very talented investigator, and together we determined rather quickly that Scott Lennox had committed this crime."

"What made this look like a murder to your highly-experienced eye?"

"There were many things. The body temperature of our victim didn't match the time of the accident, the injuries found on Mr. Lombard didn't match the damage to the car that supposedly struck him, the autopsy results didn't match what you'd expect with a traffic accident death, the victim wasn't properly dressed to be out hunting on such a cold morning, the rifle and ammunition he was found with didn't match up . . . and then there was the money."

"What money are you referring too?"

"A two-million dollar life insurance policy the defendant had taken out on our victim."

"Payable to Mr. Lennox in the event of Mr. Lombard's death?"

"Yes, that's correct."

Luke took a quick look over at the jury. The insurance policy issue had their full attention.

"Did the policy get paid out?"

"No, the insurance company got suspicious and held up the claim."

Luke waited several seconds to let that sink in to the jury. Then he shifted gears.

"So, the RCSO quickly became concerned that the 'accident' that killed Mr. Lombard was, in fact, no accident and that it had been staged?"

"Yes, that's correct. They did a rather poor job of staging the accident."

"You say 'they' . . . so Mr. Lennox didn't act alone?"

"That's correct. In order for Mr. Lennox to pull off this murder he needed someone to assist him."

"And who might that have been?"

"Lisa Sullivan, a woman he had become romantically involved with."

"Mr. Lennox was a married man. You're saying he was having an affair?"

"Yes, he was. And the woman he was involved with did play a small role in the crime, essentially posing, after the fact, as the person that had struck and killed Mr. Lombard out on the highway that morning."

"Was she arrested for her role in this crime?"

Luke had decided to bring this out into the open before Branch Kramer had the chance. He knew it would be a significant part of the defense strategy—to pin the crime largely on Sullivan.

"No."

"What? Why in the world wasn't she arrested?"

"We arrested Lennox pretty quickly but Sullivan eluded us. Finally, after nine months she had a change of heart and turned herself in. She fully cooperated with us, telling us exactly how the crime went down."

"And the district attorney offered her a deal in exchange for her testimony?"

"Yes. Without her testimony we would have a difficult time convicting Lennox for his crime. It was critical we had her testify so we could learn the exact truth about what happened that morning."

"Objection, your honor. It would appear that we are getting into testimony that should come from Ms. Sullivan, not Mr. Keller."

"Sustained. I agree with Mr. Kramer on this one."

"No problem, your honor. Ms. Sullivan will soon be testifying in these proceedings. At this time I have nothing further for Investigator Keller."

Branch Kramer made the decision not to cross examine Keller. It was obvious that he was a highly skilled investigator and he didn't see any value to having him on the stand any longer than necessary. If he needed to he could cross examine later in the proceedings.

Keller climbed down from the stand and walked confidently back to his seat in the courtroom, pausing ever so slightly in front of the jury and nodding toward them. They were clearly impressed with the veteran investigator.

Luke waited several seconds before speaking, letting the full effect of Keller's testimony sink in for the jury.

"The People call Lisa Sullivan."

Sullivan, dressed very conservatively in slacks, a pale blue blouse, and a blazer, walked to the stand. Luke Dominic walked her through her testimony, carefully outlining her involvement in the case. Given Lisa was the State's star witness the line of questioning was friendly and without drama. Luke just needed to lay the groundwork—something he and Lisa had rehearsed several times. After forty-five minutes Luke was finished with Lisa and he took a seat back at the prosecution's table. Lisa stayed on the stand, ready for Branch Kramer's cross examination. It was what she and Luke had spent weeks preparing for.

Kramer approached the witness stand and stood just a few feet from Lisa. It was a common ploy used by attorneys—get inside the witness's personal space to try to intimidate. Luke had warned her about this. Lisa leaned in toward Kramer, and for a split second he looked surprised. He took a half step backward and then began.

"Ms. Sullivan, are you married?"

"Relevance, Your Honor?"

It was a new personal record for Luke—making an objection three seconds into cross.

"Overruled, I'll allow it. The witness may answer."

"No, I'm not."

"Were you married when you met Scott Lennox?"

"No."

"When you met Mr. Lennox, were you aware that he was married, and, in fact, had been married nearly twenty years?"

"No. He told me he was single."

"A smart, young, beautiful woman like yourself must have no shortage of interested men. Do you consider yourself a good judge of character?"

"I think so."

"And yet you believed Mr. Lennox when he said he was unattached?"

"I had no reason to believe he wasn't being truthful with me."

"Well, I can certainly think of a few reasons . . . "

"Objection. Your Honor, counsel is badgering the witness."

"Sustained. Counselor, Ms. Sullivan's marital status has been established. Move it along."

"Very well. At what point did you realize that Mr. Lennox was married?"

"A few months into the relationship."

"And how did you feel about that?"

"I was furious with him. He'd lied to me."

"But not so furious that you ended things with him, correct? The relationship continued, did it not?"

"It was a huge mistake on my part not to end it right then. I deeply regret that decision."

"Yes, I can imagine you do. Did you love him?"

"At the time I thought so, but in retrospect, I know now I never loved him. And I know now he was just using me, and—"

"Move to strike, non-responsive."

"Sustained. Ms. Sullivan, just answer the questions you are asked."

"Sorry, Your Honor."

"So there you were, having an illicit affair with a married man, and you decided that he should divorce his wife and marry you?"

"No, that's not what happened. Scott decided to kill his business partner. He said the money from the insurance policy would allow him to leave his wife and that we could be together. And like a total fool, I believed him."

Lisa took a quick look at Scott sitting at the defense table. He had a smug look on his face. She wanted to walk over and smack him.

Scott's wife, Laura, was at her usual place in the courtroom, third row behind the defense table. Lisa gave her a quick glance. She was busy filing her nails.

Kramer continued, "So the defendant cooked up this whole big scheme?"

"Yes, sir. And that's the absolute truth."

"So when you called nine-one-one the morning you struck and killed George Lombard—"

Dominic lept to his feet. "Objection, Your Honor! My client did not strike and kill George Lombard that morning. He was already dead, murdered in cold blood by Scott Lennox. Those facts are not in question. This is ridiculous and I request the court sanction Mr. Kramer for this outrageous display!"

Kramer moved toward the jury box, and with great flair, shouted, "It is the truth! And I will prove that in this courtroom!"

"Gentlemen, both of you, approach!"

As the attorneys walked to the bench, Judge O'Brien announced, "Ladies and gentlemen, we will recess for the day. I have two hearings this afternoon that can't be rescheduled. We will resume tomorrow morning at nine."

Lisa left the stand visibly upset, and with Luke being asked by the judge to stay behind, Jack motioned for her to follow him. He led her from the courtroom to a private conference room down the hall. The room was small, but provided a private place for attorneys to meet with their clients. A phalanx of reporters followed the two as they made their way down the corridor. Jack pushed their way through, trying his best to use his body to shield Lisa from the cameras. The reporters were shouting over each other, but he and Lisa kept moving. After making their way through the chaotic scene, they were able to get into the conference room and secure the door behind them.

Once inside, Lisa buried her face in her hands and let the tears flow. Jack tried his best to comfort her, but couldn't do much as he leaned against the conference room door, blocking the reporters from looking through the window.

"It'll be okay. You're doing great, you just need to be strong."

"That attorney is making things up. He's lying to everyone!"

"That's what assholes like him do."

Lisa looked up at Jack and tried her best to calm herself.

"When will this all be over?"

"You're almost there, sweetie."

"Dad, I don't know if I can handle any more of this. Scott keeps trying to make eye contact with me when I'm testifying, like that's going to win me over. God, what an ass! And the attorney is trying to make it look like killing Lombard was all my idea!"

Jack looked at his daughter, and realized there wasn't much he could say to make things better. She just needed to buckle down and get through her testimony.

CHAPTER 31

Kit and Ralph Bumgartner arrived home after a week-long trip in their tent trailer. The couple had visited relatives in Kansas and Nebraska and managed a little sightseeing along the way. Ralph had done all of the driving and was looking forward to a little downtime now that they were back at their apartment in Golden. Ralph parked himself in front of the big screen and got busy channel surfing. As Kit came in with an armful of gear from the trailer, she immediately got after him.

"Geez, Ralphie—could you give me a little help?"

"Aw man, Kit . . . I'm tired. You know all that driving wears me out. I'll help you later; just leave the stuff for now."

"No, I'm not going to leave it for later, 'cause I know it'll be dang near Christmas by the time you get around to it. Let's do it now—come on, Ralphie!"

"In a minute, Kit . . . for chrissakes, a man can't even—"

"Whoa, turn it up!"

Kit had stopped dead in her tracks when she saw what was unfolding on the television in front of her.

"What is it, Kit? You wanna watch the news? I thought you wanted to unpack the trailer."

"*Shhhhh*. I gotta watch this."

Kit Bumgartner stood fascinated, listening to Angela Bell on Channel Eight report on the Scott Lennox trial. On the screen was video footage showing Jack Keller leading Lisa Sullivan down the hallway of the courthouse.

"Oh . . . my . . . God."

"What's going on, Kit?"

"Remember last year when I called the sheriff's department telling them I seen the woman they were looking for? I told them I'd seen her and an older guy out at the café. I waited on them and I remember it 'cause she threw a glass of iced tea in his face."

"Sure, I remember. You called it in for the reward."

"Yeah, a reward I never got. I talked to a detective and he said he'd personally check on it. He never called me back and then she turned herself in later, so I forgot about the whole dang thing."

"Yeah, so what's got your panties in a twist?"

"That was the guy."

"Who was the guy? You ain't making any sense, Kit. What're you talking about?"

"That guy they just showed with that pretty girl. You know, the lady in the trial . . . what's her name? Lisa something or other? She was the one I seen that day in the café and the old guy she was with—that's him! The guy walking her down the hallway!"

"That was some police guy, Kit. Why would a police guy be with her in the café?"

"I don't know, but something ain't right. You know me, Ralphie—I can smell a rat a mile away!"

Kit racked her brain the rest of the evening trying to remember the name of the investigator who blew her off when she called about her sighting of Lisa Sullivan. She remembered writing his name down at the time, but that piece of paper could be anywhere.

Frustrated, she fired up the computer in the den. A few minutes later she was googling different combinations that included *Rocklin County sheriff*, *investigator*, *homicide*, *reward*, and other related terms. It didn't take long for her to hit pay dirt.

"Keller, that's his name—Jack Keller! He's the guy I spoke with on the reward line. I'm going to call him and give him a piece of my mind!"

Kit dialed the number for the Investigations Bureau she found listed on the RCSO website. She asked for Jack Keller and waited while the call rang through. Getting no answer, Kit decided not to leave a message. She wanted to speak directly to Keller, not leave a voicemail so he could blow her off again.

Ralph looked over at his wife, but didn't say anything. He knew when she got worked up about something there was no calming her down.

I feel for you, Jack Keller, he thought to himself. I feel for you.

Kit didn't sleep much; she couldn't get Jack Keller out of her mind. She tossed and turned, eventually moving to the sofa in the den so she wouldn't bother Ralph. She kept going over things in her mind. It made no sense that Keller and the woman on trial would be together at the café. She was a wanted woman, so why didn't he arrest her then? She thought long and hard about it, and then it clicked—maybe the woman wasn't wanted until after she saw them together. The news story had come out days later; that's how she remembered seeing the two of them together. The day they were in the café, the woman wasn't wanted by police, so then she must have done something soon after that caused her to be wanted. But then, if she was some awful, evil woman, what was an investigator doing with her? And why did she throw a drink in his face? They must have been romantically involved, Kit surmised. The woman was clearly upset, the kind of upset you get when you've been screwed over by a man.

Her head was spinning. It was no use trying to sleep, so she got up and made herself some coffee. The clock on the microwave showed it was five thirty, too early to call Keller again. She'd wait until eight to do that.

CHAPTER 32

Lisa had a rough night—one filled with dreams about the night of George Lombard's murder. The dream was so real it was as though she was experiencing it for the first time.

She pulled up the collar of her coat in an attempt to fend off at least some of the bitter cold of the November Colorado morning. The sun was still hidden from view but judging from the sliver of orange on the eastern horizon she knew sunrise was just minutes away. For the time being she could see only what was illuminated in the headlights of her car. She shifted nervously in her seat and lowered the window an inch or two. She put her ear to the opening, listening for sirens of the emergency vehicles headed her way. There was nothing but silence—the 9-1-1 dispatcher said it would take several minutes for help to arrive at such a remote location. Her heart was pounding like a drum.

She glanced in the rearview mirror to see what, if anything, she might see in the roadway behind her. Nothing—it was too dark. She moved her foot to the brake pedal and pressed down; the area behind her vehicle lit up red. She looked back to the mirror and could see the bloody, lifeless body of George Lombard lying in the roadway. Quickly, she removed her foot from the brake and Lombard disappeared from view. Dark again.

Tears began to stream down her cheeks. She thought back to a few hours earlier and watched in her mind's eye as Scott Lennox ran Lombard down in the parking lot of their shared business. It was the only way, Scott had told her—the insurance money on Lombard's life would give them what they needed to start their life together. He would divorce his wife and they could be together forever.

Her foot slipped back to the brake pedal, and Lombard was once again visible. He had to go, Scott said—it was the only way. As she waited for the sheriff's department to respond to the staged accident scene, she wished she could take everything back. But it was too late.

A tired Lisa Sullivan arrived at the courthouse a few minutes before eight so she and Luke Dominic could go over the testimony she'd likely be giving when the cross examination resumed. She knew Kramer would continue his efforts to make her look like the mastermind behind the murder, but she kept reminding herself that the trial would soon be over and the whole thing would be behind her. She thought about the letter she had written Peter just days before. It brought her a sense of relief, but at the same time, a great deal of sadness as well.

Keller was in the second-floor breakroom grabbing coffee when the phone in his office rang. With no one there to answer, it kicked to voicemail. Kit Bumgartner cursed at the phone and hung up again without leaving a message. Lisa was scheduled to take the stand at nine, so Jack left to walk over to the courtroom.

Just before nine Lisa and Luke entered and took their seats at the prosecution's table. She took a quick glance toward the back of the room and saw her father was there. Both were careful not to acknowledge each other. A few minutes later things were underway.

"Mr. Kramer, are you ready to continue with your cross examination of Ms. Sullivan?"

Kramer stood, “I certainly am, Your Honor.”

“Then proceed.”

Lisa took the stand, gave the jury a small nod, and turned and faced Kramer.

“Ms. Sullivan, I remind you that you are still under oath,” said the judge.

“Yes, your honor.”

Kramer began, “Good morning, Ms. Sullivan.”

“Good morning.”

“Yesterday, we left off with you claiming you were not the mastermind behind the murder of George Lombard, so we’ll pick up there.”

Kramer looked down at his notes, taking several seconds before continuing. The move was a deliberate one, calculated to give the jury time to think about what he had just said.

“Tell us what happened the night George Lombard died.”

“Scott knew that Mr. Lombard came to the office every Tuesday and Thursday night, when no one was there. He said he liked to do his work then, when it was quiet. Scott hid in the building one night and waited for Lombard to leave, then he ran him over in the parking lot with his car.”

“Wow, that’s quite a story. What happened next?”

“It’s not a story, it’s the truth.”

“And where were you when all this happened?”

“I was in an upstairs office, hiding.”

“And why is that?”

“Because Scott wanted to stage the murder to look like an accident and he needed me to help him do that.”

“Okay, let’s hear the rest of your story.”

Luke Dominic stood, “Your Honor, argumentative.”

“Sustained.”

Kramer continued, unaffected.

“So, what happened next, Ms. Sullivan?”

"After Scott killed him, he asked me to help him move the body into a refrigeration truck."

"And why was that?"

"Scott said he didn't want the body to decompose. He said it would be several hours before he staged the accident and he was concerned that the time of death wouldn't look right to investigators. I didn't really understand all that, but he had obviously thought a great deal about it and had done a lot of planning."

Nicely put, thought Jack, sitting in the back of the courtroom. She was gaining some confidence up there on the stand.

"So, what did you do next?"

"After Scott ran him down we moved the body into the truck and then waited in the office until it was almost morning. An hour or so before sunrise we put everything in place on the highway so we could stage the accident."

"I see, and then?" asked Kramer with just a hint of a smirk on his face.

"Once Scott had everything exactly the way he planned it, he left and I called nine-one-one."

"And what did you tell the deputies who responded?"

Lisa looked down for a moment in embarrassment.

In a voice that was barely audible, she replied, "I lied to the deputy and told him I had accidentally killed Mr. Lombard as he was crossing the road."

As Lisa was saying this, Jack felt his cell vibrate. He grabbed the phone and checked the screen. It was a text message from Heidi Eng, the admin secretary in the Investigations Bureau.

Someone keeps calling saying it's urgent they speak to u.

Jack quietly stood, slipped out the courtroom door, and walked back to RCSO.

Back at the office, Jack tracked down Heidi and asked her for the contact number for the caller. She jotted it down and handed it to him.

He walked back to his office and looked at the number. He didn't recognize it. He sat and thought about what might be so important that the caller said it was urgent they speak to him. Always leery of calls from people he didn't know, he googled the number.

Ralph and Katherine Bumgartner popped up on the screen. The names sounded familiar, he thought, but he couldn't exactly place them. He googled both names and looked at the search field. An address in Golden appeared, but that was it. He queried the RCSO database and found a crime report that had been filed two years earlier. Looked like the Bumgartners had been victims of a residential burglary. He opened the file. It was a pretty routine burglary—nothing out of the ordinary. He wouldn't have been involved in a burglary investigation, so that couldn't have been it.

Then he saw it. Under the occupation heading in the victim's section of the report, it listed Katherine Bumgartner, waitress at the Mountain View Café.

Jack closed his eyes as it all came flooding back.

Jack sat in his office, thinking back to Katherine Bumgartner. He was starting to remember the details about his conversation with the woman some eighteen months earlier. He recalled that she was very persistent, and she wanted the reward the department was offering for the capture of Lisa Sullivan. She reported that she had seen Lisa at the café out on I-70, saying she was with some "old guy," as she put it. Bumgartner had no way of knowing that "old guy" was him; there was no reason for her to put those pieces of the puzzle together. Her tip had not led to the arrest; Lisa had ultimately turned herself in after returning to Colorado from Mexico. To make sure she didn't tell anyone else at RCSO about what she had seen at the café, he had given her his private number, instructing her not to call the publicized reward line. Don't want your tip to get lost, he'd said. He remembered she continued to call him after the arrest, but he didn't return any of her calls. He had assumed she'd finally gotten the message and stopped calling.

And now she was back, probably because of the publicity on the case. He needed to get rid of her. He grabbed his office phone and started to dial the number. Just then his cell vibrated, a text from Lisa.

On a break . . . are you coming over?

Without completing the call to Kit, he returned to the courthouse. He found Luke and Lisa in the conference room down the hall from courtroom ten.

"I had to step out for a few minutes. How's it going?"

"She's doing really well. Kramer keeps trying to break her down, but she's having none of it."

Keller looked at Lisa. "Keep it up and we'll have a conviction on Lennox. Well done, Ms. Sullivan."

"Thanks."

Once court resumed, Branch Kramer wasted no time zeroing in on Lisa during more cross examination.

"So, after the accident, you avoided arrest and just disappeared. Where did you go, Ms. Sullivan?"

Luke Dominic interrupted, "Your Honor, may I approach?"

"Yes, and Mr. Kramer, please join us."

The two approached the bench and pleaded their cases about this part of the testimony. Judge O'Brien issued a quick decision.

"Ladies and gentlemen of the jury, the question asked by Mr. Kramer as to the whereabouts of Ms. Sullivan during her time as a fugitive is not relevant to this case. It doesn't matter where she was; that's not what's at issue here today. So, I've instructed both attorneys to move along. You are to ignore Mr. Kramer's question and not give it another thought. It's immaterial to the State's case."

Both men walked back to their positions.

"You may continue, Mr. Kramer."

"Why did you turn yourself in to authorities?"

"I was tired of running, and I felt it was the right thing to do."

"And the first thing you did was secure an attorney?"

"I'm not sure it was the first thing I did, but I did hire an attorney. I wanted to make sure that I had the representation I was entitled to under the law."

"And this attorney, a Mr. Danny Velasco, met with the district attorney so he could work a deal, so to speak, is this correct?"

"I'm not sure of the terminology, but Mr. Velasco said if I turned myself in and testified truthfully to what happened to Mr. Lombard, there was a good chance I would receive a lesser sentence."

"No jail time in exchange for your testimony, isn't that what Mr. Velasco was able to work out for you?"

"The district attorney felt it was a fair arrangement. Mr. Velasco advised me to agree to it and so I did."

Jack was proud of his daughter. This was one of the sticky parts of her testimony. Kramer wanted the jury to believe Lisa acted only to save herself, not because it was the right thing to do. So far, she was handling the questions perfectly. Luke had prepared her well.

Just then his cell phone vibrated. He glanced down and saw another text from Heidi Eng.

she's baaaaack......

He cursed under his breath and put the phone away.

"Ms. Sullivan, a reasonable person might think you might lie on the stand in order to save your own bacon . . . "

"Your Honor! This is ridiculous. Move to strike."

"Sustained. Mr. Kramer, I'm getting tired of your antics. The next time you go off the rails, it's going to cost you a thousand bucks. Got it?"

"Your Honor, this is a critically important part of the testimony. Ms. Sullivan sold her soul to the devil and I think the jury should—"

"That's it. One thousand dollars, Mr. Kramer . . . care to make it five grand?"

Kramer didn't respond, and turned his attention back to Lisa.

"Ms. Sullivan, I want to ask you about a life insurance policy taken out on Mr. Lombard by Mr. Lennox. Were you aware of such a policy?"

"Scott told me about it, yes."

"It was for two million dollars. Were you aware of that?"

"Actually, no. Scott lied about that, too. He told me the policy was for half a million dollars."

For a split second Kramer looked surprised. It was evident that Scott Lennox hadn't shared the little fib he had told Lisa. Laura Lennox, sitting in her usual place in the courtroom, let out an audible laugh. Judge O'Brien gave her a look and she sat back quietly in her seat.

Kramer, realizing he might be able to use this new information to his advantage, asked "So, you were willing to participate in this murder for just a half million dollars?"

"The money wasn't the reason I went along with Scott's plan. It was because I loved him—well, I thought I loved him."

Jack felt his phone vibrate. He snuck the phone out of his pocket and took a peek.

Another call...I put her off, you owe me.

He quietly typed a response.

Ignore her. She's a nut job. I'll call her back later.

The rest of the day's testimony went well, with Lisa handling the cross examination from Kramer with no major hiccups.

CHAPTER 33

Jack Keller arrived at his office early the next morning and slowly reviewed the murder book on the Tolken homicide. He was hoping it might trigger something and lead him down a new path that hadn't considered previously. It was something Keller had done countless times before—sometimes taking a fresh look at a case from the very beginning would prompt a new thought or direction for the investigation. At this point they had a victim and a very strong suspect. The APB they had put out on Timbers hadn't triggered any calls, and efforts to trace the missing $7.2 million were fruitless. Jonathan Timbers was a very smart guy—nothing had popped up as far as credit card use or cell phone calls.

For the time being he had put Kit Baumgartner on the back burner. Maybe she would go away, he thought . . . although he doubted it. But he could at least avoid her for now.

He thought about Gina Barone and her refusal to talk to them the day before at the airport. There wasn't enough for them to force the young flight attendant to talk, but maybe some pressure could be put on her from a different angle. He picked up the phone and called Brandon Samson, the security guy at UAL who had helped them previously.

Samson picked up on the first ring.

"Hey, this is Jack Keller over in Rocklin County. You helped my partner and I a few days ago."

"Of course. How you doing this morning?"

"Okay, but a little frustrated with our investigation. I wanted to see if maybe you could give us a little assistance with our case."

Samson perked up. "Sure, I'll do whatever I can. Whatcha need?"

"We believe that a UAL flight attendant may know our person of interest. We attempted to talk with her yesterday but she totally shut us down, which of course makes us even more suspicious that she knows the guy. I'd like to do a little background check on her, but I don't have a home address."

"Hmmm, okay. And I'm guessing you want me to see what I can find out?"

"Well, if you could, that would be great. I ran her through all our systems here in Colorado but got nothing. So she must live somewhere else, but with these airline people—she could be living almost anywhere in the country."

"I'm not sure if I can really give out that kind of information . . . you know, officially. But give me just a minute and let me see what, if anything, I can do."

"Man, that would be great. I don't even need an address, just a hometown would be enough to go on. Maybe that'll help ease your mind a little bit on the search."

A minute later Samson came back on the line. "Jack, let me ask you a question. What's your favorite NFL team?"

Keller played along. "I'm from St. Louis originally, so I'd have to say the Rams."

"Yeah, they're pretty good. But you gotta love those Miami Dolphins, you know?"

"Oh yeah, absolutely. Hey, thanks so much for taking the time to talk football with me this morning, Brandon."

"No sweat, Jack. You have yourself a productive day."

Jack did a quick Google search, found the number to the Miami-Dade Major Crimes Bureau, and was soon chatting with a homicide detective named Diane McGrath.

"Good morning, my name is Jack Keller and I'm a homicide investigator from Rocklin County, Colorado. I was wondering if you could give me a little help this morning."

"Sure, what can I do for you?"

"I'm trying to track down a suspect in a rather nasty homicide that took place out here a few weeks ago. Our perp took a flight from Denver to Miami not long after committing the one-eighty-seven and hasn't been seen since. We have information that he got chummy with a flight attendant on that flight and we think she may know of his whereabouts. I have it on good authority this flight attendant lives in the Miami area. If I give you a name could you run her for me?"

"Of course, I can do that."

"Her name is Gina Barone. I don't have a DOB, but I'd say she's mid-twenties."

"Let me put you on hold and I'll get back to you in just a couple minutes."

"Thanks very much."

As Jack sat at his desk waiting for the Miami detective to get back to him, Mia poked her head in his cubicle.

Jack looked up and greeted her. "Hey, good morning, Mia."

"Hey, what are you working on?" Mia asked a bit suspiciously, seeing the murder book open on his desk.

"I'm on hold with a detective down in Miami. Got a lead on Gina Barone."

Mia stood there, trying to hide her frustration. Once again Jack was going off on his own without keeping her apprised.

"What do you mean, a lead?"

"Look, we need to track down the flight attendant. After getting such a cold reception from her the other day, we know she's gotta be hiding something. I called the security guy at UAL and he gave up the fact that she lives in Miami. I'm on hold right now while they see if they can come up with something on her."

"You did all this without checking—"

Jack held up his hand to quiet Mia. McGrath was back on the line.

"I just talked with our records division and gave them the name of your flight attendant. Got an address for her, but I actually got a little more than that."

"Like what?" Jack asked, intrigued.

"The records clerk I spoke with says she actually knows your flight attendant. They went to school together."

"Wow, what are the odds?"

"It gets better. The clerk tells me your subject's father works for Miami-Dade."

"You gotta be kidding me."

"Nope, it's your lucky day, detective. You should go out and buy yourself a couple of lottery tickets."

"What's her father's name? And can you get me a phone number for him?"

"Sure."

Jack scribbled down the contact information for Gina, as well as a name and phone number for her dad.

"Does she pop up in any of your databases?"

"Nothing more than a speeding ticket from a couple years back. And there are no calls to her residence in Opa-Locka."

"A model citizen, huh?"

"From our end it appears that way, but from what you're telling me, maybe not so much."

"Hard to say what, if any, her involvement might be in our one-eighty-seven. But my gut tells me there's something definitely there."

"Go with it, investigator. Gotta ride that hunch."

Jack hung up the phone and turned back to see an angry Mia.

"Jesus, Jack. It would have been nice if you'd clued me in on all this before you go calling all over the country."

"Calm down, Mia. This all happened really fast. I came in early and had a thought . . . I went with it and it paid off. I planned on briefing you when you got in. Now that you are here, do you want to know what's going on, or do you just want to throw a bitch fit?"

Mia's anger was only partially due to Jack's actions that morning—it was more for the problems he had caused given his relationship with Lisa Sullivan. Those frustrations were clearly spilling over into their conversation. She looked around the bullpen—it was deserted.

She let loose. "First off, knock it off with the bitch fit crap. I'm your partner and I expect to be treated with respect. If I had gone off like this without telling you I'd be hearing about it for the next two weeks. You can't ride solo, Mia, blah, blah, blah, but when you do it, and I react to it, I'm some kind of bitchy female. So go fuck yourself, Jack."

Jack didn't respond, but just looked at his partner. He didn't think any good would come arguing with her or trying to defend his actions that morning, so he let it go. But Mia wasn't done.

"And on top of all this, the Lennox trial is underway and so help me God . . . if that case goes south, I will personally wring your fucking neck."

"What the hell are you talking about, Mia? We've got him dead to rights; it's a slam dunk. Calm yourself, woman."

"Do we, Jack? Is it a slam dunk? 'Cause I can think of something that could derail the entire case in a heartbeat. Because of your stupidity, Lennox could walk. He could get away with murder. And that would be on you, Jack."

Jack looked at his partner. There was no use arguing with her. She had made her point—it was obvious that she was still upset about the relationship between him and Sullivan. It was best to move on.

"So do you want me to tell you what I learned this morning about Gina Barone?"

Mia was fuming. She needed to take a few minutes before she could continue on the Tolken case.

"Yeah, you bet your ass you're going to fill me in. But first I'm going to get some coffee. Stay the fuck where you are."

Mia kept him waiting a good fifteen minutes before walking back to his cubicle.

"So what did you find out?" she asked tersely, arms folded across her chest.

"Barone lives in Opa-Locka, outside of Miami—I've got an address for her and best of all, I learned a little something about our favorite flight attendant."

"What's that?"

"Her father is a Miami-Dade cop."

Mia took this in. What an incredible coincidence.

"So what's our next step?"

"I got a phone number for dad so I say we call down there and talk to him. Let him know that we want to speak to his kid, and that we've been unsuccessful in our efforts to contact her. Say we think she may know someone that we're looking for, et cetera . . . nothing ominous, just need to have a word with her."

"Well, let's hope he's not one of those cops that does anything and everything to protect his kid."

Keller looked at Mia and just shook his head.

She had scored the final point. She changed gears.

"Speaking of Miami, I spoke with Jameson yesterday. Asked him more about the money."

"And?"

"He tells me the guy was slick. All those years working in a bank gave him some real insights into how to work a shell game with offshore accounts. The initial trace of the money showed it going into twelve different bank accounts here in Colorado. But none of the funds stayed in any of those accounts for very long. In fact, bank transfer authorizations were put in place at the time he opened the accounts. So when the money from Tower got moved to these accounts, the funds were wired out, typically within a few minutes. Normally that's not possible, but when you have the authorizations Timbers had, you can make it happen."

"So the local accounts he set up were just a vehicle to move the money offshore quickly?"

"Exactly. And he was able to do this by using cashier's checks. There's no hold on a cashier's check so the money moved almost instantly."

"And where did the money go once it left the local accounts?"

"That's where he gets really good. He moves the funds into six different offshore accounts. Three in the Caribbean, two in Europe, and one in Malaysia. None of these countries have agreements with the US to share banking information. So, once the funds were deposited, the trail goes cold. Most times when we see money stolen, it gets moved to just one or two places, which gives us a pretty good idea where the person may be hiding. But with Timbers, you add this to the private pilot's license factor and who the hell knows where he could be."

Jack responded, "We know that when he left Colorado, his first stop was Miami. And that jives with the accounts set up in the Caribbean. And it also matches up with where Gina Barone lives. Maybe he killed Tolken once she had completed her role in making the money disappear. Maybe he and this flight attendant are in cahoots and the plan all along was to do away with Tolken."

Mia grew concerned. "What's interesting is our APB went everywhere, including South Florida, but we got nothing."

Jack answered, "Which tells me that dad may not know anything about his daughter and her choice of friends. Look, we've both spent our time in patrol—you know there's not much attention paid to posters of wanted subjects from out of state unless there's a direct tie to your jurisdiction. The flyer could have been shown during patrol briefings or hung on the squad room wall. But with all the people that disappear in South Florida every week, who know's if anyone paid it any attention."

"Or he saw it and didn't recognize Timbers; or he saw it, did recognize him, and is protecting his daughter and her friend for whatever reason."

The irony wasn't lost on Mia, but she had said enough already.

"So do we want to call the dad? That's the big question."

Jack looked at his watch, noting it was a little after eight. He wanted to be in the courtroom at nine when things were set to resume, but he knew that time schedules often slid during trials.

"We run the risk of tipping him off, but my gut tells me he's probably not aware of his daughter's choice of friends. Or maybe he knows Timbers through the daughter, but is blissfully unaware of his background. I say we call him, and there's no time like the present."

Mia took a seat in the chair across from Jack's desk.

"Let's do it."

Jack dialed the direct line to Tom Barone's office. Tom picked up on the first ring.

"Barone."

"Good morning, my name is Jack Keller. I'm an investigator with the Rocklin County Sheriff's Office in Castle Springs, Colorado. My partner and I are working a homicide case and we were wondering if we could get a little help from you."

"I'm a patrol supervisor. Have you spoken to anyone in our homicide bureau?"

"Actually, I did—Diane McGrath. She's the one who gave me your name and number."

"I'm not sure I'm following . . . you need to talk to me about a Colorado 187?"

"Yeah, let me explain."

"Okay . . . " responded Barone, starting to get a bit irritated at the vagueness coming from the investigator in Colorado.

There was no easy way to ask, so Jack just started in.

"Do you have a daughter named Gina Barone?"

"Yes, I do, but I'm not following. What does that have to do with anything?"

"We believe your daughter may know someone we are looking at for a murder that took place in our jurisdiction a few weeks ago. And we need to talk with her about it."

"There must be some mistake. My daughter has never been in any trouble. She's a flight attendant and—"

Keller cut him off. "We don't think your daughter is involved, per se . . . just that she likely knows the perp. In fact, we're pretty confident that she met him on a flight from Denver to Miami a few weeks back."

Barone considered what Keller was saying. His thoughts instantly went to Chris Houston. He's from Colorado, and the pieces fit.

"What's the name of the person you believe did the 187?"

"Jonathan Timbers. But we're certain he's using an alias."

"Can you tell me a little about the case? What did this guy do, exactly?"

"A month or so ago Timbers murdered a young woman in our jurisdiction. He also happened to abscond with seven million bucks from his employer in the process."

Barone took a second before responding. "Sounds like one bad dude."

"That he is. What complicates things is that the guy has his pilot's license and is highly mobile. In fact, the way he killed the woman was by pushing her out of an airplane. She landed in a fucking pine tree."

Barone's blood ran cold. It's gotta be him, he thought, remembering Chris said he had a pilot's license.

"Jesus."

"We sent out an APB a couple weeks ago, but you know how that goes . . . they can get lost in the shuffle."

Silence. Barone was trying to process what he had just been told. Could his daughter's boyfriend be the guy they were looking for?

After several seconds Barone responded, "Yeah we get a million of them, being down here in South Florida, and the Caribbean isn't far . . . "

"Totally understandable. Look, we get our fair share here as well, ski country and all, and frankly, they don't pan out too often. I can only imagine how crazy it gets for you guys down there."

Jack was trying to put Barone at ease. He needed him to be cooperative and the last thing he wanted was to have him turn defensive.

"Would you happen to have access to APBs sent to Miami-Dade over the past few weeks?"

"Yeah, I can access them. We get so many we put them on our in-house intranet system. Everyone here can access them. What agency are you from, again?"

"The APB came from the Rocklin County Sheriff's Department"

Barone signed in to the intranet and did a search on the agency name. Within seconds the flyer popped up on his screen. His heart sank when he saw the photo.

Wanted for questioning in a murder investigation in Colorado.
Considered extremely dangerous.

There was no doubt—the photo was Chris Houston. He had to warn Gina! He considered calling her right then and telling her to get away from Chris Houston—she was in danger!

The voice interrupted his thoughts.

"Barone, are you still there?"

"Yes, yes . . . I am. I found the APB. I was just reading it over."

"Is that the man your daughter knows?"

"Yeah, it's him. I know him as Christopher Houston."

Jack scribbled the name down.

"What can you tell me about him?"

"She met him a few weeks back, and like you said—it was on one of her flights. I've met him once, he spent a weekend at my place down in

Key Largo. He mentioned that he was from Colorado, and was a pilot . . . it all fits."

"What else did he tell you?"

"Just that he was from Colorado and worked in commercial real estate. I remember him talking about having a client interested in buying some property . . . in Fort Lauderdale, I think."

"When was the last time you talked to your daughter?'

"A couple days ago. She called me between flights just to check in. We're pretty close."

"Look, we need to scoop him up pronto."

"Of course. I'll do everything I can, but I think I should bring my supervisor in on this."

"That's fine, I appreciate that."

"Let me go find him—can I call you back in ten minutes?"

Jack agreed and gave him his cell number.

CHAPTER 34

Tom Barone sat at his desk, stunned at what he had just learned. Given the information the Colorado investigator had provided, there was little doubt that his daughter was involved with a killer, and the thought terrified him. He knew the two were spending all their time together and that "Chris" was staying at her place.

They needed to get Houston into custody immediately. But what if things got violent? The guy was clearly dangerous, and Tom didn't want Gina around when the arrest went down. Houston could be armed, he could take Gina as a hostage, who knew—almost anything was possible.

The best course of action would be to have him taken down when Gina was at work. He wasn't sure if she was on her days off or not, but that was easy enough to check. He picked up his cell and sent her a text, asking her if she was working.

Her response was almost immediate.

No, Chris is taking me flying today. We just took off :)

His heart sank when he read it.

He dialed the number to his lieutenant who in turn told him to contact the fugitive detail immediately. By chance he knew the sergeant that ran the unit so he dialed his number.

"Roy Guzman."

"Roy, it's Tom Barone."

"Hey Tom, how've you been? How's life down in the Keys?"

Barone skipped the pleasantries. "Look, I've got a situation. I just got a call from a homicide investigator in Colorado regarding a subject they are looking for in connection to a murder out there."

"Yeah, go on . . . "'

"I recognized the guy—he's dating my daughter."

"Oh, shit. Are you sure?"

"I'm about ninety-nine percent sure. No, hell . . . I'm one-hundred percent sure it's him."

Barone ran the situation down, including the text he had received from Gina indicating that she and Chris were in the air.

"All right, I'll get the entire team together. Tom, we'll find this guy. Any idea what airport he might be flying out of?"

"Not really, but Gina lives in Opa-Locka and I know there's a municipal airport there. But I can't be sure; he could be using any airport in South Florida."

"Okay, I'll call Opa-Locka and see if they have a rental plane operation there. If they do, I'll see if the guy rented a plane there this morning. Either way, I'll have my team paged and order them to report immediately."

Barone thanked Guzman and called Keller back. He explained that he had contacted the fugitive team and that they would soon be staging. He didn't tell them about Gina's text or that fact that Houston and his daughter were likely in the skies above South Florida.

Keller thanked him and asked for the name and number of the person leading the fugitive team so he could stay informed of their progress in nabbing Timbers.

He briefed Mia. "They're getting their fugitive team together right now. Going to try to grab him today."

"Wow . . . I can't believe it. I'll let Mick know. Keep me posted."

"I will. Are you going to the courtroom this morning?"

"No, I wasn't planning on it. I've heard enough from that dickhead Kramer."

"I think I'll head over there for a bit. But if things break with Miami-Dade, I'll come back to the office so we can start to coordinate Timbers' extradition."

After he got off the phone with Barone, Guzman googled *plane rental, Opa-Locka Florida*. He immediately got a hit and dialed the number on the screen.

"My name is Roy Guzman and I'm with the Miami-Dade Police Department. I need to know if someone named Chris Houston rented a plane there this morning."

"Is this official police business?"

"Yes, it is. And it's urgent."

"Hold on, I'll get Mark Lunn. He's my supervisor."

A minute later Guzman was able to confirm with Lunn that a Chris Houston had rented a plane just an hour earlier.

"What kind of plane? And I'll need the tail number."

"Can I ask what this is regarding?"

"No, I just need that information."

"All right, give me a second . . . let's see . . . okay, it looks like Mr. Houston rented a Cessna one-eighty-two. Said he'd be out about three hours. Tail number N43782. He paid with a credit card. Do I need to worry about the credit card? Is it stolen? Am I going to get paid for this rental?"

"Okay, listen to me. Is there a way to communicate with him in the plane?"

"I can't do that, but the tower can. Unless he's out of our airspace, then no."

"Okay, thanks for your help. We're on our way."

Roy Guzman and six members of the Miami-Dade fugitive team arrived at Opa-Locka Airport and quickly located the Fly-Away Rental Company. The office was housed in a small brick building in a row of businesses not far from the runway.

The detectives entered the building and Guzman asked for the supervisor. A minute later, a man in his late fifties came to the front counter.

"Sergeant Guzman? I'm Mark Lunn. We spoke earlier."

"Mr. Lunn, we have a situation and we're going to need your assistance."

"Of course. What do you need?"

"First off, can you tell me if Houston was alone?"

Lunn turned to the clerk who was standing by, listening to every word.

"Ron, was the guy alone?"

"No, he had a woman with him."

Guzman's heart sank as he thought of his friend Tom Barone. Given the text message, he knew there was a high likelihood she was with Houston, but he was somehow hoping that wouldn't be the case.

He looked back at Lunn. "Did Houston file a flight plan before departing?"

"I'm sure he did. Let me find it."

Lunn queried a computer on the counter.

"Yes, he said he was going to do a sightseeing trip out over the Keys."

"How much fuel did the plane have when he took off?"

"It was full. We always refill the tank when a plane is returned. Kind of like a rental car."

"How far could he fly with the amount of fuel he had?"

"The fuel capacity in that plane is fifty-five gallons. If he flies at a normal speed he'll burn about twelve gallons per hour, so he could safely fly for three or four hours before he'd have to refuel. So that would put him at about three to four hundred miles, depending on conditions."

"Mr. Lunn, Houston is a wanted fugitive, and we need to take him into custody as soon as he lands."

Barone glanced over at Ron and saw that the clerk was listening to every word.

"Can we go someplace private where we can talk?"

"Sure, come on back to my office."

The detective team followed Lunn back to his office and crowded in.

Guzman continued the conversation. "It's imperative that we take Houston into custody as soon as he returns. The woman with him is an innocent person in all this and is most likely unaware he is wanted. We need to get her clear from Houston before he knows he's going to be arrested. He's a fugitive on the run and there's no telling what he might do."

"I understand. We'll do anything you need to assist you."

CHAPTER 35

"Hello, is this the Eyewitness News tip line?" he whispered, secluded in an unoccupied office.

"Yes, it is. Do you have some news you'd like to report today?" asked a young woman with a cheery voice.

"My name is Ron, and I work at the Fly-Away airplane rental place at Opa-Locka Airport. Some big news is about to break here."

"Really? Tell me more about it . . . "

Guzman left Lunn's office and gathered the fugitive team together.

"At this point, it's critical that we don't do anything that could tip off Houston that we're on to him, so all communication should be on band two or use your cell phones. Keep in mind this guy could disappear very easily in that plane and that he's got an innocent subject with him. And just to let you know, that woman is the daughter of a Miami-Dade officer."

Everyone stared at Guzman. He nodded but didn't say anything further.

Guzman continued, "We've alerted the Opa-Locka PD and let them know what we have here. They've offered any and all resources to us. I've asked them not to discuss any of our operation on their police frequencies. I don't think Houston has the capability to monitor their frequency, but we're not taking any chances. According to the flight plan he filed, he's not expected back here for another ninety minutes. But you never know; he runs into bad weather, or whatever—he could be landing before that so we need to be prepared. So here's what we're going to do—"

Guzman stopped mid sentence and nodded to the person who had just joined the group.

"Everybody—meet Tom Barone. He's a Miami-Dade patrol supervisor and it's his daughter, Gina, that's up in that plane."

"That asshole isn't calling me back."

"Kit, give the guy some time, I'm sure he's busy."

"I've given him a year and a half. He never called me back before and he's not calling me back now."

"I don't know what you can do about it."

"I know exactly what I'm going to do about it."

Kit grabbed her phone and did a quick Google search. She pressed a button and the line rang through.

"Good morning, Channel Eight Action News. How can I direct your call?"

"Angela Bell, please."

"She's on air right now, but I can connect you to her voicemail."

"You do that."

The detectives took their positions at various locations around the Opa-Locka Municipal Airport. Each was hidden, out of sight from any aircraft approaching the airport. The last thing they needed was for

Chris Houston to see officers on the ground as he was making his final approach to the runway. The plan was to wait until the plane taxied back to the rental agency. Once Houston and Gina left the plane and walked into the office, Houston would be arrested. Two officers would handle the arrest while two others would quickly shuttle Gina safely away from the scene. Now all there was to do was wait.

CHAPTER 36

Angela Bell finished up her noontime newscast and was back in her office looking online at the different newswires. Her next newscast wasn't until four. As she scrolled through the breaking news stories, she picked up her phone to see if there were any voicemails. She heard the familiar *beep* indicating new messages, so she dialed the number.

"Hello, Angela. You don't know me but I'm a big fan of yours and I only watch Channel Eight. I'm calling to tell you there's something fishy going on with that trial, the one with the fellow accused of killing his business partner. Me and Ralphie was watching the news yesterday . . . "

Angela rolled her eyes and was about to delete the message when the caller caught her attention.

" . . . and we saw that Jack Keller guy with that woman—the really pretty one. Anyway, I remembered that I seen them together a while back, before any of this trial stuff happened. They were at the Mountain View Café off Interstate Seventy. I'm a waitress there and it looked like they were breaking up. She was crying and all, and I remember it 'cause she threw an iced tea in his face. So I called the sheriff's department and I talked to Keller, 'cause there was a reward and all, and I thought maybe I, you know, would get some of that money for telling them what I seen. Anyways, I thought you'd want to know, and like I was telling Ralphie, there's something not right with all this. My name is Kit Bumgartner and my number is 303-555-7748. Oh, and I really love your show."

Angela Bell sat at her desk, stunned, her mind spinning with possible scenarios involving Jack Keller and Lisa Sullivan. They were together after the Lombard killing? Could they be involved romantically? Is this what Mia's text message to Mark was all about? Did they know about this relationship? As she was considering the possibilities and what it could mean for her career to break such a huge story, she stopped. My God, was Mark involved in some kind of cover-up?

Angela quickly dialed the number Baumgartner had left on the voicemail.

"Hello?"

"Ms. Baumgartner, this is Angela Bell returning your call."

"Oh, hi. Thanks for calling me back. I love your show. Me and Raphie watch you all the time—"

"Well, thanks for that. I appreciate it. Now tell me more about Detective Keller and Lisa Sullivan. You said you saw them together?"

Kit Baumgartner explained in great detail what she had witnessed that day at the Mountain View Cafe. Once the conversation had ended, Angela grabbed her cell phone and composed a text message to Mark.

Call me ... its urgent.

As Roy Guzman watched the skies, he noticed an aircraft several hundred yards south of the airport, hovering in place. Couldn't be Houston, he thought, it had to be a helicopter to stay in one place like that. He grabbed his binoculars and focused his sights on the aircraft.

"Damn it!"

"What is it, sarge?" asked a member of the team.

"It's a damn news chopper with the Eyewitness News logo on the side. How in the hell did they know about our operation? I swear, if the Opa-Locka PD broadcast our location on their frequency and some newsie picked it up on the scanner, there will be hell to pay!"

Guzman quickly made his way to Mark Lunn's office.

"We've got a problem. There's a news helicopter out there and I'm afraid if Houston sees it it could blow our cover. Is there anything we can do to bounce them out of here? Maybe some rule that requires them to be a certain distance from the airport?"

"Not that I know of but let me check with the tower."

Lunn placed the call, spoke to Dona Lange—the lone air traffic controller, and explained the situation. She considered what Lunn was asking, then answered, "If the news chopper is out of our airspace, there's not much we can do to shoo them away. Law enforcement could make that request, and they may or may not cooperate. It's impossible to know."

Lunn relayed the information to Guzman.

"The problem is we don't know what they're doing up there. They could be over a traffic accident on the highway for all we know. Or it could be that they overheard Opa-Locka PD on their scanner and they're on to us. But either way, if Timbers sees that chopper up there he could get nervous and change his plans to land."

Lunn replied, "Can't you just call Eyewitness News and talk to them?"

"Not really. If it is something unrelated to us, like a traffic accident, then basically we'd be letting them know we've got something going on over here. That'll get their attention faster than anything."

"So you're kinda screwed either way, huh?"

"Yeah, pretty much."

Guzman changed subjects. "I think we could oversee this operation more effectively if Barone and I were up in the tower, communicating directly with air traffic control."

"Of course, makes perfect sense. No need having a third wheel like me in the conversation. I'll walk you over there."

"Thanks for all your assistance."

CHAPTER 37

Mark Archer was in a staff meeting when he saw the text from Angela. He excused himself from the room and dialed her cell.

"Hey, what's up? Everything okay?"

"I need to see you, Mark. Like right now."

"What's wrong? Are you okay?"

"I'm okay, but I need to see you. Can we meet somewhere in thirty minutes?"

"Geez, Angela . . . I'm in the middle of a staff meeting. Can't it wait until tonight? We could meet for dinner—"

"No, we need to do it right now. Meet me at Bean Crazy in Lone Tree. You know the place."

"Okay, I'll be there in thirty."

Mark returned to the conference room and apologized, explaining that something had come up. He left the room and headed toward Lone Tree.

Angela arrived at Bean Crazy, looked for Mark, but didn't see him. She ordered a cup of decaf and took a seat near the back of the small coffee house. A few minutes later, Mark walked in.

"What's going on, Angela?"

"Sit down. We need to talk."

Mark looked at her and saw a look in Angela's eyes he had never seen before.

She spoke in a voice that was barely a whisper.

"I got a phone call this morning from a woman telling me some things about the Lombard murder case. I need to ask you about it. And Mark, I need the absolute truth."

Mark lowered himself onto the chair across from Angela and took a deep breath. This can't be good, he thought.

"Go on."

"The woman told me that she saw Jack Keller and Lisa Sullivan together eighteen months ago in a café way outside of town."

"Okay . . . "

"This was after the Lombard murder. She said it looked like they were very familiar with each other, and it looked like Keller was breaking up with her."

"That's ridiculous, Angela. This woman sounds like some crazy lunatic," replied Mark, shifting uneasily in his chair.

"Maybe, but she was certain the two were together. She's a waitress at the place and she said Sullivan threw a glass of iced tea in his face. That sounds pretty personal to me."

"Maybe he was interviewing her about the accident. Ever think of that?"

"Since when do investigators meet with a beautiful, young murder suspect in an out-of-the-way café seventy five miles away from their jurisdiction? And it sounds like Mia wasn't there, so why would he meet her alone like that?"

"I don't know, but I'm sure there's a reasonable explanation."

Angela looked at Mark. He wasn't budging. She was hoping he'd come clean, but that wasn't happening. She contemplated the consequences of what she was about to say.

"Mark, listen . . . a few days ago, when you stayed over, I saw a text message on your phone."

"What? You were looking at my messages?" he responded, incredulously.

"Yes—I mean . . . only one. I know, there's no excuse for it and I'm sorry. You were in the shower and I was still in bed. I heard a message hit your phone so I glanced over and saw it was from Mia. I thought it might be about meeting them in the restaurant and I was . . . I was just curious."

Mark's heart sunk. He knew exactly the message Angela was referring to. Oh, God, he thought, things were coming unraveled fast. His only hope was to shame Angela into silence.

"Damn it, Angela. I can't believe you would do that! I trusted you, and thought our relationship was better than that. How can I trust you when you pull a stunt like this?"

"I know, and I'm so sorry. But that doesn't explain the text from Mia. She said that the secret about Keller could come out and that Lennox would walk free. And that the sheriff's career could be ruined. My God, Mark—what is going on?"

Mark sat for several seconds, not responding to Angela's questions. He looked for any sign that Angela's resolve might ease, but she was was adamant.

"Okay, I'll tell you what's going on. But only if we agree that everything I say is off the record. You can't go public with any of it."

"Mark, you know I can't agree to that until I at least hear what this is about. Give it to me in a nutshell and I'll see if the off-the-record approach will work."

There it was. What Angela was asking Mark to do would require the ultimate trust. More than the Lennox case hung in the balance—so did their future together.

Chris Houston radioed the tower and reported he was five miles out. The controller, Dona Lange, cleared him for landing, and immediately turned to Guzman and Barone, who had taken seats next to her, and let them know. Their attention quickly focused on the skies directly east of the airport. Guzman continued to check on the helicopter and saw it was still there, hovering in place.

Eighteen hundred feet in the air and five miles east of the airport, the small Cessna chugged for home.

"You want to land it, Gina?" teased Chris through the headset.

She laughed. "No, I'll leave that to you, but thanks!"

Gina had thoroughly enjoyed the flight. It was her first time being in such a small plane, and Chris let her have the controls for several minutes over the Atlantic. She caught on quickly, and using the rudder pedals and the yoke, she was able to maneuver the plane quite a bit. As a flight attendant she had received some rudimentary pilot training so much of it was familiar to her. She quickly caught on to reading all the control instruments and would give Chris readings when asked. She enjoyed the feeling of power she got from controlling the plane; it gave her a sense of complete freedom. She hoped she and Chris would go flying on a regular basis.

They were a half mile from the runway at an altitude of two hundred feet when Chris noticed a helicopter hovering in place off to his left. He took a long look at it, and could see the Eyewitness News logo painted on the side of the bird. Chris suddenly grabbed the yoke and the plane quickly accelerated. After a few seconds he maneuvered the Cessna upward and pointed the nose due south.

"What are you doing, Chris? I thought we were going to land."

"Didn't like the way we were coming in."

Gina didn't say anything, but watched as Chris headed away from the airport, picking up speed. After a minute or so she could see that he wasn't making any effort to head back to the airport.

Puzzled, she asked, "Where are we going? Don't we need to land?"

"Don't worry, we will. Just want to take a little different route."

"What the hell is he doing?" Guzman shouted.

Dona Lange, wondering the same thing, replied, "Weird he would abort his landing like that—his approach was textbook."

"That fucking Eyewitness news chopper. I'm going to call for our bird. We can't do anything from the ground. Damn it!"

Guzman radioed Miami-Dade dispatch and requested the air unit. He realized he had made a tactical error by not having their chopper moved into the area as a precaution. He hadn't anticipated this scenario, a definite mistake on his part. He explained the situation to the watch commander on duty, who informed him they could have a chopper in the air within five minutes.

He turned his attention back to the traffic controller. "Can he be tracked on radar?"

"Sure, we can do that. And any other airport in South Florida with a control tower has that same capability."

"Okay, let's keep an eye on him. Once our chopper is up I'll need you to convey the location information to my pilot."

"No problem."

CHAPTER 38

Mark started in, "Jack Keller and Lisa Sullivan do have a relationship, but it's not what you think."

"Go on."

"It doesn't impact the case against Scott Lennox. It's all immaterial, really."

"Then why did Mia's text say Lennox could walk if the truth about Jack came out?"

"I think you can chalk that up to Mia being a bit overwrought about the case. It's her first big trial and she was just overthinking things. It happens . . . "

"What, exactly, is the nature of Keller's relationship with Sullivan? If not romantic, then what?"

"It doesn't matter, you just have to trust me that it's immaterial to the case."

"Come on, Mark . . . I need more than that."

"And I just can't give you more than that. You trust me, don't you?"

"Of course I trust you, but this is work. I have a duty and responsibility as a journalist to find the truth. If there's something out there that the public isn't aware of, then I'm going to report on it. It's that simple."

"No, it's not that simple. There are people's lives at stake here, Angela. It's not just about television ratings, it's real stuff. Real people with a lot at stake."

"That's pretty insulting, Mark. I think you know me better than that. I'm not one of those reporters who puts the story above everything else. I know there are gray areas, and in some cases, you sit on a story because a greater good will come from it. But you aren't giving me enough to make that judgment. I need more information before I can make the call to kill this story."

"So, you really don't trust me," Mark replied, shaking his head slowly. "I'm telling you that this is a non-story and yet you have to hear more about it before you get to make the decision as to whether or not you put the story out there? Who made you God?"

"No one made me God, but we do have something called freedom of the press in this country—you've heard of that, right?"

Things were getting nasty.

"Yes, I believe I have, perhaps back in high school . . . maybe in a civics class?"

Angela ignored the sarcasm. "So, what are we going to do here, Mark ? Are you going to give me more or am I going to have to do the story without the RCSO giving their side of things? I can interview the woman on camera and she can lay it all out there for the world to see."

"Wonderful. Put some woman on the news without corroborating her story. Great journalism there, Angela."

She ignored the dig and continued.

"Or I can go talk to Keller, or maybe the sheriff . . . "

Mark looked at Angela. He knew he couldn't let her talk to Keller or McCallister. His would have to tell her the whole story and hope she saw it his way. It was his only chance.

"Okay. Here it is . . . "

After a couple minutes, Chris settled into a nice clip, keeping it at a steady 120 knots. He checked his fuel level gauge and saw he still had more than half a tank. He did the calculations in his head, and determined he had enough fuel to go at least another two hundred miles. He wasn't sure what that news chopper was doing by the airport, but he wasn't going to take any chances.

As he watched the small plane disappear in the sky to the south, Tom Barone tried his best not to think about the heinous murder Jonathan Timbers had committed in Colorado.

Guzman radioed Captain Barry Rainey, the pilot of the Miami-Dade PD helicopter. He explained the situation, telling Rainey that Timbers had aborted the landing, picked up speed, and was heading due south. Rainey calculated that Timbers probably had a twenty-mile head start, and said he would contact the other South Florida police agencies with air units to let them know what was transpiring in the skies above them, and to be on the lookout for the Cessna. Rainey hoped he could track down the Cessna and trail it until it landed.

Mark filled in Angela on the Keller/Sullivan fiasco, leaving nothing out.

"Wow, that's unbelievable."

"If this gets out then Lennox, a cold-blooded killer, walks."

"I understand that, Mark. But at the risk of sounding cavalier, that's not my problem."

"But what good does it do to publicize all this? At best, the judge will declare a mistrial, at worst he'll enter a directed verdict of not guilty. Lennox will walk out the door a free man and we'll never be able to touch him. Meanwhile, Keller will be ruined and so will Mick."

"I understand all that, but the public has a right to know!"

"Do they? Do people really need to know how sausage is made? If they did, that business would go under in a heartbeat. Look, our criminal justice system is the best in the world, but it's not without its warts."

"Agreed, but people have a right to see the whole system, warts and all."

"And if we show them a few of the warts in this particular case a lot of really bad things will likely happen. And for what? To show what a father will do to protect his daughter?"

"Keller took an oath as a police officer, and he certainly violated the promises he made to the people of Rocklin County."

"Okay, so ask the people of Rocklin County which they would rather see happen—a killer walking free or a cop getting away with a couple of shortcuts to help out his long-lost daughter?"

"Not the point, Mark, and you know it."

The fugitive team stayed in their respective positions in case the plane returned to the airport. Barone and Guzman remained seated in the control tower.

Barone had an idea and he shared it with his boss. "I could text my daughter and ask if she and Houston want to join me for dinner tonight. See if I can start a dialogue with her and maybe glean some information."

"Yeah, let's do it," responded Guzman.

Tom Barone typed out a text.

> Are u guys still in the air? Wanna join me for an early dinner 2nite? I'm in Miami.

He hit send and then he waited.

Gina turned to Chris. "My dad just texted me, and asked if we wanted to join him for dinner tonight. He says he's in Miami. You want to do that?"

Chris looked at Gina, a suspicious look spreading across his face. "He texted you just now?"

"Yes, I told him we were going flying today. He's probably working today and figured dinner might work."

Chris considered Gina's dad's text. Was it a coincidence he was texting her just now, or was he pumping her for information? Was that news helicopter hovering near the airport because they thought something newsworthy was about to happen, or were they covering something totally unrelated? Chris contemplated turning around and heading back to Opa-Locka. Maybe make another pass and see if the chopper was still there. But he felt he couldn't risk it and so he considered his options.

"So, should I tell him we can meet for dinner?"

"No, I don't think we'll be able to do that."

"Really? I think it would be fun. Come on, Chris . . . "

He didn't respond, and began banking the plane to the east, toward the vast, blue Atlantic.

CHAPTER 39

There was no use arguing any further. Both had pled their cases, and neither had budged from their respective positions.

"So what are you going to do?" asked Mark.

"I have no choice but to report it. I'm sorry, Mark."

"I guess the story is more important to you than us? I really thought we were going to work out this time."

There, he had said it.

Angela looked at Mark, grabbed her purse, and walked away.

Judge O'Brien called for an afternoon break a little before three. Luke, Lisa, and Jack found an empty conference room down the hall from the courtroom and each took a seat.

"So what's the time frame look like from this point forward, Luke?" asked Jack.

"Testimony should wrap up this afternoon and then we should be doing closing arguments in the morning."

"That's great, and you're doing a terrific job."

"Thanks, Jack. I think it's gone well. And Lisa, you've been a rock up there. I couldn't be more proud."

Jack nodded in agreement and looked at his daughter. She had grown up so much during the two years since they had been reunited.

Soon, the three made their way back to the courtroom and got ready for the afternoon testimony. Jack found a seat for himself while Luke took his seat at the prosecution table. Lisa sat in her usual seat in the front row, directly behind Luke. The courtroom filled quickly and soon the bailiff was asking everyone to rise.

Tom Barone stared at his cell phone and saw no response to his dinner invitation.

He turned to Guzman. "Nothing back from my daughter. That's not like her; she's usually quick to respond to my texts."

"Okay, let's give it some more time. We're doing all we can right now. We just need to be patient."

Easy for you to say, thought Barone. It's not your daughter in that plane. His thoughts drifted to the poor woman in Colorado. The asshole had pushed her out of a plane and now, he wondered, could his daughter be facing the same fate?

Mark Archer had no time to waste. He ran to his car and headed back to RCSO headquarters. In his mind he ran through the possible scenarios likely to play out once Angela went public with the story. God, it was going to get ugly, he thought.

The first order of business was to brief the sheriff. The DA would also need to be informed, but Archer would let Mick do that. Dave Baxter had made such a spectacle of himself during the trial, pontificating to news reporters each day on the courtroom steps. This was going to be a very bitter pill for him to swallow. Archer thought about Mia and how she had shared the entire fiasco with him in confidence only to have it about to blow up in her face. He would have to tell her what had happened with Angela and the text message.

And then he thought about Keller, and the fallout for him. "Fuck him," he mumbled under his breath.

Archer grabbed his cell phone and called Lucinda, the sheriff's administrative assistant, letting her know he would need to speak to Mick as soon as possible. She said he was in a budget meeting but that she would pull him out when Mark arrived back at the station.

As Angela headed back to the studio the reality of the situation set in. Tears began streaming down her face as she thought about her relationship with Mark. She loved him, but she had just made a decision that caused him to believe she put more value on her career than on him.

Was that true? she wondered. Did she care more about her career than she cared about Mark?

On the surface she didn't think so, but then the evidence was pretty clear—she had just walked away saying she was doing the story. She knew the price of that decision, and yet she still chose the story over Mark.

He'll come around, she thought, trying to reassure herself. Over time he would come to understand why it had to be this way and he would forgive her. Her relationship Mark wasn't over, she would make sure of that. But, deep down, there were doubts. Her mind flashed back to twenty years earlier and she saw herself sitting back in the courtroom in Denver. The judge's words still echoed in her mind. There would be no justice for her father. Her family was devastated.

CHAPTER 40

The Cessna was soon over water heading toward the Caribbean and Gina was getting anxious.

"What are we doing Chris? I thought we were going back to the airport."

Chris looked at Gina. "Change of plans, I'm afraid."

"Change of plans? What are you talking about? Let's just go back to the airport and meet my dad for dinner."

"Not going to happen. We can't go back there."

Gina's demeanor changed immediately. She knew intuitively she was in trouble.

"Chris, what's going on! You're starting to scare me. I want to go back—now!"

Chris didn't respond. Instead he pushed the throttle forward, accelerating to full power.

Gina looked at Chris and clearly saw a change in him, seeing a side she'd never seen before. She knew she was in danger and that she needed to do something. She waited for Chris to look away for a moment to text "911" in response to her father's text.

Chris caught her and grabbed the phone, looking at the screen. It was too late, the message had been sent.

"You fucking bitch!" he raged.

"Chris, what's going on? Tell me now!" she responded angrily.

No response.

"I want to go back to Opa-Locka. Take me back—NOW."

"Not going to happen, Gina. You fucking ruined everything!"

"What the hell are you talking about?"

A weird calm came over Chris. He knew what he had to do. It was a fait accompli.

"Look, I gotta tell you—I haven't been totally honest with you."

"Oh, God."

"I might as well tell you, I guess I owe you that much."

"Tell me what?"

"The police in Colorado are looking for me, but not as a witness to a crime."

Gina stared at Chris. Up until a few minutes ago, she saw him as the man she loved. Now she was thousands of feet over the Atlantic with a man she suddenly didn't know. She gulped hard and asked, "Why are the police looking for you?"

"Let me start by telling you my name is Jonathan, not Chris.

Gina felt sick to her stomach, the bile rising up in her throat.

"God help me . . . "

"And I'm sure as hell not a realtor."

Doing her best to control her emotions, Gina shifted in her seat and turned toward Chris, "Go on . . . "

"I worked for a large bank in Colorado, and I embezzled some money. They're looking for me in connection to that crime."

"My God, Chris. How could you do this to me? I loved you, and I thought you loved me."

"Things aren't always as they seem. I don't know what else to tell you."

Tears began to stream down Gina's cheeks. She gathered herself and asked, "So where are we going? Can you at least tell me that?"

"You'll see soon enough. Just sit back and relax, enjoy the ride."

Gina knew she was in a desperate situation, but her options were few. The Cessna was now a few miles off the coast. Chris seemed certain of where they were going; he hadn't made any effort to shift the plane's direction.

A moment later Chris reached over and activated the autopilot on the control panel. He then looked over at Gina, but didn't say anything.

"Why are we on autopilot?"

As the plane continued on its course, Chris unbuckled his seatbelt and turned toward Gina.

"What are you doing?" Gina asked. Her fear was quickly growing.

Chris didn't say anything, but reached over and quickly unbuckled Gina's seatbelt. Then, in one fell swoop he reached over her and tried to open the door. Gina, realizing what was happening, instantly grabbed the yoke in front of her to prevent Chris from pushing her out of the plane. Fortunately, the door was difficult to open given the force of the wind at their speed of 120 knots.

"My God, stop it!"

She let go of the yoke and began fighting for her life. She managed to land a fist to his chin, which infuriated him. He tried to grab her around the throat, but before he could get a good grip, Gina reached over with her left hand, grabbed his crotch, and squeezed as hard as she could. All those self-defense classes her father had made her attend were suddenly paying off. Momentarily incapacitated, Chris let his guard down and she punched him several more times in the head. She needed a weapon of some sort and suddenly remembered that she had a corkscrew on her keychain. She quickly reached into her purse on the floorboard between her legs. While keeping a death grip on his crotch, Gina drew her arm back and drove the corkscrew into Chris's right temple with all her strength. The hit was direct and the corkscrew penetrated an inch or more, causing blood to spurt from the side of his head. From her self-defense training as a flight attendant she knew that a serious blow to the temple could be fatal. She looked at Chris and realized she had very likely delivered a death blow.

Mark Archer pulled into the parking lot at RCSO and made his way into the building. He wasn't looking forward to the conversation he would be having with his boss, but it was part of the job and he knew it was best if Mick heard everything from him and not someone else. He was the only person at RCSO who had all the pieces of the puzzle.

"I texted him that you needed to speak to him," said Lucinda, seeing Mark coming toward her desk.

"Can you let him know I'm here and I'll be in his office?"

"Sure."

Lucinda had been Mick's admin assistant for more than five years. She knew all the members of the RCSO command staff and could tell from the look on Mark's face that something major was up.

"Everything okay?"

"No, not really."

"Anything I can do?"

"Not yet, but all hell is going to break loose in a few minutes."

Lucinda reached into her desk drawer and took out some hand lotion. She quickly applied it onto her hands and began rubbing vigorously. Mark had seen her do that before—it was a tell she had. Grab the hand lotion when things were getting difficult.

Mark took a seat in Mick's office and tried to compose his thoughts. How was he going to break this news to the sheriff?

Seeing *911* pop up on his cell phone screen, Tom Barone was consumed by fear. He began praying, whispering, "Please, God, I beg of you. Save my daughter." Tears filled his eyes.

Guzman leaned over and put his arm around his shoulder to comfort him. Lange looked at the two men and started to get emotional herself.

Just then, a voice came over the radio, choked with fear.

"My God, someone please help me—how do you land a plane?"

Tom Barone was too stunned to speak. He was overjoyed at hearing the sound of his daughter's voice, but was terrified at what she was asking.

"Gina, this is Roy Guzman—a sergeant with Miami-Dade. I'm here with your dad. Tell us what happened."

Gina took a few seconds and then tried her best to explain the situation. Her voice was quick and high pitched—bordering on hysterical.

"He tried to push me out of the plane. I fought back and I think I killed him. I had no choice! He's in the seat next to me. I'm going to have to land this plane but I have no idea what to do!"

"Okay, we'll get someone on the radio who can talk you down. The important thing is to remain calm. You can do this, Gina."

"How can I land this plane? I've never done this before," she responded frantically.

Guzman could hear Gina start to sob. He knew he had to give her confidence that she could pull off a landing. It was the only hope for a successful outcome.

"Gina, lots of people have landed these little Cessnas . . . this happens more often than you think. And your dad tells me you're a flight attendant, so that should help. It's all going to be fine. We'll get you down."

It was a lie, but he didn't know what else to tell her.

"This happens all the time?" she asked incredulously.

"It happens, Gina. And we're going to get you down safely, but you need to remain calm and do exactly as you're told. Can you do that?"

"I don't think I have much choice."

Guzman held his hand over the mouthpiece and asked Lange to find someone who could talk Gina down safely.

"Already did. He's on his way," she replied.

Guzman turned his attention back to Gina.

"Okay, Gina, we're getting someone to help you. It'll just be a few minutes. Are you in control of the plane right now?"

"No, it's on autopilot. Chris activated it just before he attacked me. He was going to push me out of the plane. I really had no choice, I had to fight back."

"Of course you did, Gina. And it sounds like you did an incredible job. No one here is going to question what you did. You're a hero, Gina. The guy was a bad dude. You're a strong woman, and you're going to successfully land this plane."

Lange spoke to Gina, "I have the best flight instructor in South Florida coming right over. He was working on his plane in his hangar, which is very close by. He should be here any second, and when he arrives I'll be turning things over to him. Do you understand?"

She managed a feeble "Yes."

Just then a booming voice filled the room.

"You're damn right you've got the best flight instructor, but I'm a little insulted you made it just South Florida."

All attention turned to the man speaking.

"It's my understanding that we've got a young lady up in a Cessna who needs a little help."

"Her name is Gina," answered Lange, handing the man a headset.

"Hi, Gina, my name is Steve Low. I'm a flight instructor and I'm going to help you land that plane."

No response.

"Gina, are you there?"

CHAPTER 41

"What's going on, Mark? Lucinda said it was urgent we talk."

Mark stood up and closed the door.

"Sheriff, we have a situation and I need to tell you about it. It's not good."

"That sounds ominous. What is it?"

"It concerns the Lennox trial."

"Something happen today in court?"

"No. In fact, no one in court knows what I'm about to tell you."

"Okay, tell me what you got."

Archer looked at his boss and decided that he'd just come out with it. There was no use sugarcoating it.

"I just met Angela Bell for coffee and she told me that she has information that Lisa Sullivan is Jack Keller's daughter."

"What?" Mick answered incredulously, almost rising out of his chair.

"She says that Sullivan is Jack's daughter and that he acted inappropriately during the investigation, essentially helping her elude capture."

"What the hell are you talking about?" Mick responded angrily.

"From what I've gathered, Jack may have been protecting her, essentially using his position to shield her from prosecution."

"You mean it's true? I'm going to kill that son of a bitch!"

He grabbed his phone. "Lucinda, find Jack Keller and tell him I need to see him immediately."

Mick looked at Mark. "How long have you known about this?"

Mark looked at his boss. He'd never seen him this angry, but it was certainly understandable.

"A couple of weeks. Mia came to me and—"

Mark stopped dead in his tracks. It was a slip up and there was no taking it back now.

Mick slumped in his chair. "You're telling me that Mia knew about this as well?"

"Not in the beginning, but after Lennox was arrested she learned about the relationship between Keller and Sullivan."

For a moment, Mark thought Mick was going to be sick.

"I'm sorry, sir. I just wanted you to hear this from me. I believe Channel Eight will be breaking the story at the top of their next newscast."

Mick slowly reached for the phone.

"Lucinda, have Mia come to my office as well."

Mark continued, "We need to prepare for the fallout from all this. I might suggest you call Dave Baxter and let him know what's coming. His office is going to get bombarded by the media. And, of course, so will we."

Mick sat there, taking it all in, his head spinning.

"Judge O'Brien will declare a mistrial. I don't see any way around it," Mick said quietly.

"That's probably the best thing we can hope for—maybe get a new trial with a change of venue. But I'm more concerned about the judge finding Keller's actions so egregious that he issues a directed verdict of not guilty. There is a very real possibility Lennox will be a free man by the end of the day."

"My God, Branch Kramer will be on the front page of every newspaper in the country after this all comes out. People will hail him as a fucking genius," Mick added.

"And there will be no justice for George Lombard and his family."

Both men sat in stunned silence, contemplating what was before them.

"Yes, I'm here," Gina finally answered, her voice barely audible.

"Okay, darling. I'm going to get you down. That's a promise and I never break a promise. Now the first thing I need you to do is tell me where you are. Are you over land or water?"

"I'm over the ocean. The plane has been on autopilot for several minutes. I think we're headed toward the Keys."

"Good, Gina . . . very good. Okay, we're going to get you turned around so I'll need you to turn off the autopilot. But first I'm going to give you a quick lesson on some of the controls you'll be using to bring that plane in for a perfect landing. You with me so far?"

"Yes, I think so."

Guzman leaned over and whispered, "She's a flight attendant, so she has some familiarity with aircraft."

Low nodded at Guzman.

"Good, we'll do this together. Now I need you to tell me what some of the instruments say on the dashboard. There should be one that reads *altimeter*. Do you see that?"

"Yes, it says I'm at sixty-five hundred feet."

"Excellent! And look at your speed . . . do you see that one?"'

"Yes, it says one hundred and twenty knots."

"Great job, Gina! So tell me, do you have any experience flying a small plane?"

It was a long shot, but Low thought he'd at least ask.

"Not really, but an hour ago Chris let me fly the plane. He gave me a quick lesson on the controls and he said I did pretty well. And I'm a flight attendant for United so I'm used to flying and I've had some training on how to read the instruments. Just not in a tiny plane like this and I gotta say . . . I'm not a fan."

It was a small attempt at humor by Gina and Low saw that as a positive sign.

"By the time I get you down on the ground I'll have you signing up for flying lessons with me."

"Yeah, well . . . let's not get carried away."

"You'll see, Gina, you'll see. Oh, and you owe me a nice steak dinner when this is all over."

"You get me on the ground safely and I'll buy you that dinner."

"Perfect. Now give me a minute or two so I can check on a couple things. I'll be right back, Gina."

Low asked Lange if the tower had notified the other airports about the Cessna given he'd be bringing Gina through the crowded airspace around Miami. She confirmed that she had put the word out. Guzman radioed Barry Rainey and let him know that the plane had been located and he could cancel the APB he had issued to all other law enforcement aircraft.

"Okay, Gina, I'm back. But before we get started I have to ask you another question."

"What is it?" she asked.

"Why is that I can only get one bag of those little peanuts when I fly commercially? Geez, I pay an arm and a leg for my ticket and all I get is a dime pack of roasted nuts? It doesn't seem right, Gina. It just doesn't seem right."

Gina laughed, "I'll bring that up to the bigwigs at United. I'm sure they'll listen to me."

"You do that. Okay, listen . . . it's time to disengage the autopilot and get you turned around. You ready for that, young lady?"

"Sure, why the hell not?"

A nice chemistry was forming between the two, something that Low knew would help them both get through the ordeal they were facing.

Tom Barone managed a small smile at Gina's comment. It was a sign his daughter wasn't going to give up without a fight.

Low continued, "Okay, do you see the autopilot on the dash? In a minute I'll need you to push the button in the lower right hand corner.

It's marked AP . . . do you see it?"

"Yes."

"Once you push the button, the AP will disengage and you'll be flying the plane. Just keep everything steady at first, like I explained a few minutes ago, and then we'll get you turned around. We've got plenty of time and plenty of fuel so we can take our time getting you down. So, let's go ahead and disengage the AP."

Gina reached over and pushed the button. She could feel a change in the plane but it wasn't significant. She then took hold of the yoke and began to take control of the plane.

"Okay, I did it. Now what?"

"You have a hold of the yoke?

"Yep, I'm flying this thing," she responded, hesitantly.

"Okay, I need you to start to turn around and come back over land. When you flew earlier today did you learn how to maneuver the plane?"

"Yeah, I did. I think I can do that. Let me try."

As Gina banked the plane, the shift in direction caused Chris Houston's dead body to fall against her. She let out a little scream.

Low became concerned. "Gina, everything okay up there?"

She did her best to push the lifeless body back against the door. After several hard shoves she managed to get Chris somewhat wedged between the door and the yoke. The amount of blood from the body was extensive, much of it pooling in his lap and at his feet. But he seemed to be securely in place so she returned to the task at hand—getting the plane turned back around toward Miami.

"Yeah, I'm okay. It's just that . . . never mind."

Thirty seconds later Gina had the Cessna headed in the right direction.

CHAPTER 42

Once again, Jack felt his cell vibrating in his pocket. Hoping to get word from Miami that Jonathan Timbers was in custody, he stole a quick look at the screen.

Please come to the sheriff's office immediately

Shit, he thought. Still nothing from Miami and now the big boss needed him. He slipped the phone back in his pocket, left the courtroom, and headed to the RCSO.

"Okay, I'm heading back towards land."

"That's fabulous, Gina. You're a natural! So, let's drop the altitude to six thousand feet and keep your speed at one hundred twenty knots. How much fuel do you have? Do you see that indicator on the dash?"

"Yes, it says I have just under a half tank."

"Perfect. Plenty of fuel."

In reality Low was concerned about having that much fuel onboard given the likelihood of a rough landing and subsequent fire. But the Cessna wasn't designed with the capability to dump fuel like a large commercial airliner. But he didn't let on to Gina.

"Air traffic control is going to clear the airspace as you come back to Opa-Locka. So that's a big help. Gotta get all those damn United pilots out of the way."

"Yeah, good luck with that. So, what's next?"

"Looking at the radar it looks like you're about five miles from being back over land and about twenty miles from Opa-Locka Airport. They have a nice long runway here so you don't have to be perfect to nail the landing. You should be arriving here in about twelve minutes or so. Meanwhile, let's go over some of the things you'll need to know for landing this puppy."

Mia arrived at Mick's office a minute after getting the call from Lucinda. She knocked on the closed door and was told to come in. Upon entering, she saw Mick and Mark Archer sitting there and the looks on their faces told her something was very wrong. Her heart skipped a beat and instantly she knew.

"Close the door, Mia."

She took a seat and looked at Mick. He looked devastated, like he had just lost his best friend.

"I'm sorry, Mick. I should have told you."

"Yeah, you should have told me," Mick replied, his anger in check.

Mark spoke up. " I just met with Angela Bell and she knows about Keller and Sullivan—"

Mia instantly cut in, "What, you told her? You told her what I told you in confidence?"

"No, Mia, I didn't tell her. She read the text message you sent me a couple days ago and figured things out on her own."

Mia shook her head in disbelief.

"I'm the fucking sheriff! How could I not be told any of this? What the hell were you two thinking keeping this from me?"

Mark responded, "Sheriff, it was my decision not to tell you. We didn't want to burden you with this. The trial was going well, things would be over in a few more days, justice would be served, and Lennox would go away for a very long time. If we had told you, we would have put you in a very untenable position. I couldn't do that to you, and I take full responsibility."

"It's not your fucking call, Mark! I can't believe this. The two people I trust the most and both have deceived me!"

Mia interceded, "Mick, we did this to protect you. If you knew about this then you'd be put in the position of having to decide what to do. If you decided to come clean with the truth then Lennox would walk free. If you don't say anything, Lennox would get convicted but you have this awful weight on your shoulders knowing there were shenanigans going on with Keller. So, we kept it a secret, feeling confident that the trial would proceed and justice would be served. We never thought it would come out."

"But then Keller gets away with his bullshit?"

Mia continued, "Yes, that was the price we'd pay. But better that than seeing a cold-blooded killer walk free. Think of Lombard's family."

Just then, Mick's phone buzzed.

"Jack Keller is here to see you."

Gina was a quick study and had managed to maneuver the plane into the proper position to begin the descent into Opa-Locka. Low knew that was the easy part; the critical time would be putting the plane down successfully on the runway. He didn't share his thoughts with Gina or any of the people he was with, but he knew that the odds getting her down without major injury to her or anyone else were slim.

He had gone over the landing strategy with her several times on the way back toward Opa-Locka, but it was a lot to remember and most pilots had instructors with them to take over the controls if a landing wasn't going as planned. Obviously, Gina had no such luxury.

"Gina, how you doing?" he asked, trying to get a read on her current mental state.

"I feel like I'm in the movie *Airplane*, where the pilot with very little experience has to land the jet in Chicago."

Low laughed. Gina was fine.

"Love that movie. Remember Lloyd Bridges up in the control tower? I promise you I'm not sniffing glue or doing cocaine."

"Well, that's a relief," responded Gina with a small chuckle.

"Okay, let's get you down on the ground. As you approach the airport you'll notice some emergency folks on the ground. They are just there as a precaution. I have no doubt you're going to put this puppy down, but I didn't want you to get concerned when you see the equipment."

"Thanks for letting me know. Let's hope they send some cute firemen."

Low shook his head in amazement at Gina's composure. He looked at Tom Barone and smiled. Just maybe they could pull this off, he thought.

In reality, Gina was terrified, but she had no choice but to try to land the plane so she was going to give it her best effort. She also didn't want her father see her die. She knew he was at the airport and would witness the landing.

"You're about eight miles from the airport, Gina, so I need you to drop your altitude to about four thousand feet. Do you remember what to do?"

"Yes, I can do that."

"Okay, let me know when you're there."

A couple of minutes went by and Gina told Low she was at four thousand feet.

"Great job, Gina. Keep your headings; your approach is perfect."

"It's not the approach I'm worried about," she responded, nervously.

"Hey, every good landing begins with a proper approach. And right now, you're perfect."

Low looked over at Barone and the other members of the Miami-Dade fugitive team. They had all come in from their positions around the airport and now stood crowded together in the small tower. There was no more Chris Houston to worry about and their focus had shifted to a fellow officer's daughter in the sky. Barone looked a little calmer than he had twenty minutes earlier, but was still obviously filled with fear for his daughter.

"Okay, Gina, let's take it down to two thousand feet and ninety knots. Let me know when you're there."

A half minute later Gina spoke, "Okay, done."

"Good. You're about four miles from the airport. Keep your headings steady."

"Okay, I can do that."

"You're doing great, Gina. Wind conditions are calm at the airport so that's a good thing. You can just bring her on in. You're cleared for landing."

Gina took a deep breath. "Here goes nothing."

"Okay Gina, you're two miles out, so bring her down to five hundred feet and seventy knots. And it's time to activate the landing gear. Do you remember how to do that?"

"I think so. Let me find the switch."

Gina looked at the instrument panel and found it.

"Okay, pressing the switch now. I can feel it going down."

"Great, now we just gotta bring her in, Gina. You can do this!"

Gina's hands were shaking and she felt like she was going to be sick. Just hold it together, she told herself. It's almost over.

"Okay, I can see the runway straight ahead. I'm just aiming right at it."

"Perfect. You're a natural, Gina. You're doing fabulous."

Low looked out the window of the tower and could see the plane headed straight for the runway. She looked to be about a mile out.

"Gina, you're about ready for touchdown. So let's aim directly at the white lines on the runway and begin to ease her down, drop to a hundred feet and sixty-five knots. That'll be your landing speed."

Gina dropped the Cessna down to one hundred feet and took dead aim at the white lines.

"Okay, you need to do full flaps, just like I told you earlier. Do you remember how to do that?"

"Yes, I'm doing that now."

"Perfect, now just apply steady back pressure on the yoke and use the rudder pedals to keep yourself level. You can do it, Gina. You're almost there!"

Low looked out the window at the runway directly in front of him. He could see the emergency vehicles all in place, ready to assist as necessary. Gina was now over the runway but was still fifty feet off the ground.

"Gina, you need to get lower. Push on the yoke and get her on the ground. You can do it!"

But Gina pushed too quickly on the yoke and the plane began a nosedive.

"Too steep, Gina—you're too steep!

CHAPTER 43

Angela pulled her car over onto the shoulder of I-25. She was too teary eyed to see the road. She would take a few minutes to compose herself and then proceed to the news station to break the biggest story of her career. Sitting there, her mind went to that fateful day twenty years earlier and the words from the judge played in her head.

Ladies and gentleman of the jury, some new information has come to my attention concerning this case and I have no choice but to declare a mistrial. I apologize for the inconvenience, but it can't be avoided. You are all hereby dismissed. Thank you for your service.

In her mind's eye, she replayed the scene in the courtroom. She saw the defendant stand up and raise both arms in victory. The bastard looked over at her and her family and extended his middle finger in their direction. Angela's brothers both bolted toward him but were tackled by the bailiffs assigned to the courtroom. There were fifteen seconds of chaos before order was restored. The devastated Bell family left the courtroom to wait for a new trial for their murdered father. But a new trial never came and the defendant was ultimately freed. The case haunted Angela every day.

She reached for her cell phone and typed a text.

Mark, we need to talk.

Jack Keller took a look around Mick's office as he entered, assessing the situation. This can't be good, he thought.

"Boss, you wanted to see me?"

"Sit down."

Keller took a seat next to Mia and looked at the sheriff.

Mick didn't waste any time. "It has come to my attention that you're Lisa Sullivan's father. Is this true?"

Jack felt a surge go through his body. He had been discovered and he knew there was little he could do.

"Why do you think that?"

"Jack, I'm asking you a simple question. Are you Lisa Sullivan's father?"

Jack had no choice. After several seconds of silence he answered, "Yes."

"And you kept this fact from all of us and used your position as an RCSO investigator to help her avoid being arrested in connection with the Lombard murder—is this true?"

"Look, sheriff, I can explain."

"Answer the fucking question, Keller!"

"Yes, it's true. But there were extenuating circumstances, and—"

He was interrupted by Mark's cell phone. Mark checked the screen. "It's Angela. She wants to talk."

Mark stood and walked out the door. He found an empty adjacent office and called her cell.

The emergency vehicles reached the plane just seconds after it hit the ground. The entire fugitive team, along with Tom Barone, ran from the control tower toward the downed plane. As he was running Tom looked to see if there were flames coming from the wreckage. He knew the fire personnel would quickly extinguish any fire resulting from the crash, but the idea that his daughter could burn to death was too much for him to bear. No flames were visible, thank God.

As he reached the mangled plane he began yelling for Gina, but there was no response. His fear was becoming reality; his daughter was dead in the wreckage of a plane sitting there on the runway. Fire personnel, unsure what they would find, held him back. But it wasn't enough and he had to be restrained by several officers.

"Let me go!" he screamed.

"Tom, no . . . let the firefighters do it. They know what they're doing," shouted Guzman, grabbing Barone around the waist.

"I need to save her, let me go!"

Just then a faint voice came from the mangled wreckage.

"Dad . . . help me."

"Did you hear that? She needs me. Let me go!"

Guzman let go of him and Barone rushed toward where the voice was coming from.

"Gina, are you okay?"

"No, I'm hurt, Dad. I can't feel my legs."

The fire personnel began quickly working their way to the cockpit. After a minute or so one of the firefighters yelled for the hydraulic shears as it was too difficult to reach Gina through the wreckage. Other firefighters quickly spread fire retardant material on the gas that was spilled all around the plane. It was fortunate that the fuel hadn't erupted in flames on impact with the ground.

After a few minutes they were able to reach Gina and start to assess her injuries.

"Don't move, just tell us what hurts."

"My arm and my head. And I can't feel my legs."

"Okay, we'll have you out of here shortly. Don't worry, we're going to take care of you."

Tom moved into the wreckage to where he could see his daughter. Her head was bleeding, but she was alert and talking.

"Gina, thank God you're alive," he cried.

Gina looked at her father and began to cry. She had never seen him so upset, and it shook her to the core.

"I love you, Dad."

"I love you, too, sweetie. I love you, too."

CHAPTER 44

A very relieved Mark Archer walked back into Mick's office. "I just spoke with Angela and she seems to have had a change of heart."

Mick looked up, "What do you mean, a change of heart?"

"She's not going to do the story. Said she won't go public with it after all."

"Thank God—that's great!" Mia exclaimed.

"I don't understand. Why would she pass up the biggest story of her career?" asked Mick, a bit suspiciously.

"I don't know if you guys know this, but Angela's father was murdered during a robbery in Denver about twenty years ago. The Denver PD caught the guy but he got off on a technicality. The experience made Angela very sensitive to the plight of victims. In fact, that's how we met a few years ago—at a victim's rights event up in Denver."

Keller took in what was happening, but didn't speak. He wanted to see how this all played out. But he knew he wasn't off the hook, not by a long shot.

"Well, maybe we dodged a bullet. But that doesn't mean we're home free," replied Mick, looking directly at Keller.

Mia jumped in, "But now we can allow the trial to proceed and Lennox will get convicted and sent to prison. That's the bottom line."

Mick was still staring at Keller.

"Jack, you need to leave. Go wait in the outer office with Lucinda. I'll let her know when you can come back in."

Keller stood and left without a word.

Mick turned to Mia and Mark. "Look, just because Angela's not going to do the story, it doesn't mean we're all good here. We have some serious decisions to make."

Mark spoke up, "There's no decision to make, Mick. We proceed as if nothing is wrong. Look, this is exactly why we didn't want you to know about any of this. Mia and I were willing to shoulder the responsibility."

"Yeah, well thanks for that, but as the sheriff, it's my responsibility to deal with the good, the bad, and the ugly. Angela may be backing off the story, but we have a duty and obligation to the court to tell what we know."

Mia responded angrily, "But Lennox will go free if we do that."

"Let the chips fall where they may. If he walks, he walks. I don't see how we can continue with this cover-up, and that's exactly what it is—a fucking cover-up."

Mark looked at his boss. On one hand he was proud of him. Such an idealist, he thought. Mick was determined to do the right thing, at least right in his mind. But, on the other hand his boss was a bit naive, still very new to the job of being sheriff. Mick needed to learn politics were an important part of the job and being pragmatic was the key to survival. The district attorney certainly knew this, and Mark brought the conversation around to that.

"If you do proceed and go public with all this, you'll need to let Dave Baxter know your plans. You don't want to broadside him; the fallout for him will be enormous. It will cost him his job."

Mick looked at Mark, but didn't respond.

Mia spoke up. "Mick, think about it for a minute. You tell the world about this and these are the things that will happen: Lennox gets away with murder, the RCSO and the DA's office get absolutely reamed, and you take the brunt of the fallout. If we just let it go, then Lennox gets convicted, the RCSO and the DA's office look good, and justice is served. The only downside to this is that Keller gets away with one, but you can deal with him internally."

"I don't know. It just doesn't seem right."

Mark and Mia looked at Mick. It seemed he was softening a bit. Maybe the practical side of Mick McCallister was starting to kick in. Mark perceived the opening and decided to take it.

"Look, Mia's right—we should proceed as if nothing is wrong and then you lower the boom on Keller. Fire his ass and be done with him. Let him tell people that he decided to retire, just like he did in St. Louis ten years ago. They forced him out and so can we. Keller sure isn't going to blab this around. Mick, we gotta do this for George Lombard and his family. If we don't, think about the repercussions for them."

Mick responded, "How do we know Angela won't change her mind? If she does the story then everything comes out, including the fact that we covered the whole thing up."

"She won't change her mind. She understands the ramifications of all this, and after speaking to her just now, I'm very confident that she'll stay quiet. She was in tears on the phone with me, talking about her father's case. She said she doesn't want the same thing to happen to the family of George Lombard. Those were her exact words."

Mick leaned back in his chair and stared at the ceiling in his office. It was decision time and both Mark and Mia waited anxiously to hear what he would say.

"All right . . . we'll do it your way."

He reached over and picked up his phone.

Tom Barone rode in the ambulance that transported Gina to the Jackson Memorial Hospital in Opa-Locka.

She was conscious but in a great deal of pain. A paramedic was busy tending to her, monitoring her vital signs during the ten-minute trip to the hospital. Tom was relieved when Gina started moving her lower limbs—there didn't appear to be any obvious signs of paralysis.

His voice trembled with emotion as he spoke to his daughter. "I prayed for you, Gina. Five minutes ago I got down on my knees and prayed that you would land the plane and survive. God answered my prayers."

Tears welled up in Gina's eyes. "Your prayers worked, Dad. I knew I had to try to land that plane. I didn't want you to see me die."

Tom reached over and took Gina's hand. "I'm so proud of you. And I am so sorry for what you had to endure up in that plane. You're a hero, Gina. Chris Houston was a bad guy and you put an end to him. He won't be hurting anyone anymore."

Gina reflected on what happened on the plane. She closed her eyes and could see the fight with Chris unfolding in her mind in slow motion.

"I guess all those self-defense classes you made me go to paid off, huh?"

"Yep, they sure did."

They rode to the rest of the way to the hospital in silence, holding hands and thanking God for answering their prayers.

CHAPTER 45

"Lucinda, tell Keller to come back in my office."

Mick turned to Mia and Mark, "If you'll excuse me, I'm going to have a private chat with Investigator Keller."

Mia nodded but didn't say anything. She didn't want to think about the conversation she knew she'd be having with Mick later that evening.

The two stood and headed out the door. They encountered Keller as they were leaving, but no one spoke.

"Sit down."

Keller took a seat and looked at his boss.

Mick took a long look at him before saying anything. Jack didn't flinch; he had a pretty good idea of what was coming.

"Before I say anything, I'd like to hear from you about what possible motivation you had pulling this stunt."

Jack looked at Mick for several seconds before responding.

"You don't have kids, do you, sheriff?"

"No, I don't."

Jack continued, "I have—or had—two kids. My son, who is deceased, and a daughter. It's a long story but my daughter and I became estranged more than thirty years ago, and through an incredible set of circumstances we found ourselves reunited twenty months ago. I saw an opportunity to help her and so I did, pretty much like what any parent would do."

"Most parents don't hold a position like yours, Jack."

"That's true. But still, a parent will do what they need to do to protect their kid."

"Even if it means obstructing justice? Betraying a trust? Violating an oath you took as a police officer?"

"I've seen parents throw themselves in front of speeding cars to save their child. Parents who used their body to shield their child from a spray of gunfire. It's biology, I think. And no offense, sheriff, but unless you're a parent, you may not understand that."

"Don't be condescending, Jack. What you did is unconscionable. I can't condone it under any circumstances."

"I understand that. You gotta do what you gotta do."

"I need your gun and your badge."

Keller slowly stood up, removed his Baretta from its holster inside his coat, and placed it on the desk. He grabbed his badge from his wallet and placed it next to the gun. He stood there, but didn't speak.

"I'm placing you on paid administrative leave effective immediately. First thing tomorrow I will file papers to have you terminated. I will have a deputy escort you to your office so you can gather your things. You will be led from the building and you are not to return. If you come back inside I will have you arrested. Do you have any questions?"

"No."

"Good. Now leave my office. Wait with Lucinda for the deputy."

Keller turned to leave, but stopped as he reached the door. He turned back at Mick.

"Just so you know . . . I'd do it all again."

"Get the fuck out of my office."

Jack waited at Lucinda's desk for the deputy escort. Mick had let her know what was happening and she had called for a deputy. Keller sat quietly in the chair; Lucinda knew better than to try to start a conversation with him. The moment was both awkward and sad, but Keller had been through it before in St. Louis.

After a few minutes Deputy Christina Raymond arrived and Lucinda directed her to Mick's office. She walked out a few minutes later, looking pretty uncomfortable with the assignment she had been given.

Sensing the young deputy's apprehension, Keller stood and said, "You've got a job to do; let's get to it."

Fifteen minutes later, after collecting all his belongings, Jack left RCSO headquarters for good. He walked away from the building and didn't look back. He thought about heading to the courthouse, but it was already after five and he was sure the trial proceedings would have recessed for the day.

After he left RCSO he made a quick stop at Mountain Pacific Bank, withdrawing three thousand dollars in cash from his personal money market account. He returned to his car and placed the call from his cell phone.

"Hello, this is Investigator Keller. I'm trying to reach Katherine Bumgartner."

"Yeah, this is her. Nice of you to call me back. I've been waiting for almost a year and a half."

"Yes, let me apologize for not getting back to you sooner. The George Lombard murder investigation is a very complex case and I've been working on it nonstop for almost twenty months. But I have some good news for you. I reviewed my notes from your earlier call and I was able to get a portion of the reward for you."

"Really? Oh, that's great. Hold on a sec . . . Ralphie, come quick—I got us some big news!"

Jack continued, "As you may remember, the total reward offered in this case was ten thousand dollars. Now, we did receive critically important information from several other callers and so we are having to split the reward four ways."

Before Kit could object, Keller lowered his voice. "You'll be pleased to learn that you are receiving the largest portion—a total of three thousand dollars."

"Ralphie! What I seen at the café that day is getting us three thousand bucks!"

Jack continued, "Now, there are a couple of rules about the money."

"What kind of rules?" asked Kit, suddenly concerned that there may be a hitch to getting her cash.

"The RCSO always pays its rewards in cash. This way you, the tipster, can never be traced, which is important because in a murder case, well . . . you can never be too careful."

"Um, sure—I guess that makes sense. So when do I get my money?"

"I can give it to you this evening. But you can't tell anyone about it, ever. It's for your own safety, really."

"Ralphie—he says I get the cash today!"

Keller met with Kit and Ralphie Bumgartner in the fresh produce aisle of the SavCo market in Highlands Ranch. Kit could hardly contain her excitement as Keller, wearing dark sunglasses for full effect, handed her the envelope with the cash. He cautioned her again about keeping the reward payout a secret, putting the fear of God in her by making something up about it being a felony if she spilled the beans to anyone.

Once the Bumgartners left with their money, Jack slowly walked toward the front of the market. The events of the day were catching up to him and reality was setting in. His career as a cop was over; it was almost certain no other law enforcement agency would ever hire him. His age was an issue, but, more importantly, he knew the odds of getting a good recommendation from the RCSO were nil.

As he neared the exit of SavCo he stopped and looked at the tall display of merchandise next to the checkout station. He shook his head.

What were the odds? An entire wall of Southern Comfort, there for the taking. He had more than ten years of sobriety under his belt, a daily hard-fought battle, but Southern Comfort had always been his liquor of choice.

He reached for a bottle. He took it in his hands and studied it like it was a piece of beautiful art. He tucked it under his arm and walked to the checkout aisle.

CHAPTER 46

After leaving Mick's office, Mark Archer headed up I-25 toward Denver. He knew Angela would be finished with the five o'clock newscast and he wanted to see her. He arrived at the Channel Eight studios just before six, parked in the visitors lot, and badged his way through security. He saw Angela in the newsroom and walked over to her.

"Is there someplace private we can talk?'

"My office."

Mark followed Angela through the newsroom to the row of offices at the back of the building. Angela closed the door behind them and they each took a seat.

"Angela, I just want to thank you for what you did today. I know it was a very difficult decision but I really think it's the right one."

Angela replied, "I'm not so sure it was the 'right decision,' as you put it, but it's one I can live with. I couldn't watch Lennox go free."

"And that's exactly what would have happened. I think your father would be proud of you."

"Maybe, maybe not. He was proud of my work in television. He always said 'do the right thing, always' . . . and now, here we are. On one hand I feel I did the exact right thing, but on the other hand I feel like I've totally failed as a journalist."

"I can understand that. But making sure a murderer is held to answer carries more weight than what you do in the newsroom. I'm not minimizing your role as a journalist, but keep in mind, Jack Keller didn't plant evidence or do anything else that would result in an innocent man going to prison. The right guy is going down for his crime. And that wouldn't have happened if you didn't do what you did today."

"And in my heart, I get that. In my mind, I'm not so sure."

Mark looked at Angela, trying to get a read on her. She was second guessing herself a bit, but that's normal, he thought. She had just made her biggest decision ever as a reporter, and it would take some time to balance things out in her head.

"Let's reverse things for a second and say you decided to go with the story. The judge would have declared a mistrial this afternoon, or worse, and you'd be sitting here, a hero to your peers, for breaking this huge story. Journalistically you'd be on top of the world, but how would you really feel?"

"Like shit. I'd be sitting here regretting what I did. Thinking about my father and what happened in his trial twenty years ago."

"Angela, you did the right thing."

"I know. It'll just take some time to get my head wrapped around it."

Mark changed gears. "Can I take you out to a nice dinner?"

"Actually, what sounds best to me is dinner at home. I don't care if we grab a pizza, I just want to be alone with you. Is that all right?"

"Of course—no argument from me. Let's go."

Mia arrived home, poured herself a large glass of wine, and took a seat on the living room sofa. Mick was still at the station and, according to a note left on the kitchen table, Chuck was out running errands. She was content to have some time alone; she needed to think about the conversation she knew she'd soon be having with Mick. She had never seen him as angry as he was that afternoon in his office, but it was certainly understandable.

A few minutes later she heard the front door open and looked up. Sasha ran to the entry barking but quickly calmed down when she saw it was Chuck. He reached down and greeted her, then looked up to see Mia sitting on the sofa. He made his way into the living room.

"You sitting here all by yourself? Everything okay?"

"Not really, Dad. It's been a really rough day."

"Uh oh, I'm sorry to hear that."

"Thanks. I expect Mick here soon. And I'm sure he and I will be talking about some things."

"Is there anything I can do?"

"Not really. It's work stuff, but I appreciate the offer."

"When he comes home, Sasha and I will clear out to the basement. Give you guys some privacy."

Mia looked up at her father and gave him a half smile. "Maybe it'll be better if you're around."

"Geez, Mia—is it that bad?"

"I don't know for certain, but there's a very high likelihood Mick fired Jack Keller today."

"What? How in the hell . . . Never mind, you don't have to tell me anything."

"It's all right, Jack had it coming."

Chuck didn't respond immediately, thinking about the day months earlier he had been caught by Keller as he followed him around Castle Springs.

"Well, you know how he played fast and loose with the rules. Things tend to catch up with people like Keller."

"That they do."

Sasha began barking, interrupting the conversation. Mia went to the door and looked through the peephole. She saw Mick walking up the steps to the porch so she swung open the door, letting him into the entry. He made no effort to kiss or embrace her and both stood for a few moments looking at each other but not speaking. Chuck walked into the foyer to greet his future son-in-law and could instantly sense the tension between the two.

Chuck spoke, "I think I'll let you guys have some time alone. Sasha and I are headed to the basement to watch the Rockies lose another game."

Mia turned to Mick, "Can I get you a drink?"

"No, thanks."

Mia motioned for Mick to follow her and she led him into the living room. They sat a few feet apart on the sofa.

Mick started, "We need to talk about what happened today."

"I know, I should have told you as soon as I learned about Keller and Sullivan."

"Yeah, you should have. And I guess that's what bothers me the most. You didn't tell me the truth from the beginning."

"But you do understand why I did what I did, right?"

"Yes, in a convoluted way you were trying to protect me. I get that. You didn't want to put me in the position of having to make the decision. You were trying to save me from that. But my God, Mia . . . if I can't trust you . . . "

"Protecting you was my only motive in all this. I thought we'd get through the trial, get a conviction, and everything would be good. Each day I prayed no one would learn the truth. I never thought a reporter would figure out what Keller had done."

"And it was a text message you sent to Mark?"

"Evidently. It was on the night you proposed, when we ran into Mark and Angela at the restaurant. You had told me that night that the DA was making a big spectacle of himself with the trial and I guess it just got me worried again about the whole thing. I texted him saying I wanted to talk with him and evidently his snoopy reporter girlfriend read it."

"And things unraveled from there," Mick added, looking past Mia at the fire in the fireplace.

"Yes, but I really don't see how Angela figured everything out from just the text. I didn't say specifically what Keller had done. But somehow she put the pieces together and figured it out. And that's when she confronted Mark."

"Yeah, well, she's no dummy. I don't know how she did it, and I seriously doubt we'll ever know. That's probably something she won't even tell Mark."

"I am so sorry, Mick. Please forgive me."

Mia moved toward Mick, reaching out for him. But Mick shook his head, keeping an arm's distance between them.

She stopped and looked at her fiancé.

Mick replied, "I'm sorry, but I need some time to wrap my head around all this. I just feel very betrayed."

Mia sat silently on the sofa, thinking about the huge mistake she had made keeping the secret from Mick. Her intentions were honorable but it seemed there was no convincing Mick. Her emotions were mixed—scared, yet a bit angry—unsure why he couldn't understand she did this out of love for him. She was just protecting him, for God's sake.

After a half minute of silence, Mia slipped the ring off her finger and handed it to Mick.

"Maybe you should take this back."

Mia looked at her fiancé and from the expression on his face she instantly knew.

Tears rolled down her cheeks. Mick slipped the ring into his pocket, leaned over, and gave her a hug. He walked to the door and let himself out. Mia curled up in a fetal position on the sofa and cried herself to sleep. Awful, blood-filled scenes from Columbine soon filled her dreams.

CHAPTER 47

The following morning, closing arguments took less than two hours. Luke Dominic outlined his case against Scott Lennox in a methodical, systematic way while Branch Kramer relied more on theatrics. It was all he could do, given the weakness of his case. At this point he was just trying to keep his client from receiving a lethal injection courtesy of the state of Colorado.

Lisa sat in the front row directly behind the prosecution's table. She kept glancing over her shoulder; it was nearly eleven and her father, who had missed very little of the trial, was nowhere to be found. She was a bit surprised by this, certain that he wouldn't want to miss closing arguments.

Once both attorneys were finished, Judge O'Brien gave the jury their deliberation instructions and dismissed them to the jury room. Luke and Lisa huddled together and discussed what was next.

"Look, I don't expect a long deliberation, but with juries you just never know. I've got your cell number so when I hear something I'll call you immediately. Where do you plan to be the rest of the day?"

"I'll probably go to the library. I've escaped there a few times during the trial and haven't been bothered."

"Okay, I'll be in touch."

After a very rough morning, Jack Keller arrived at the courthouse just before noon. Finding the courtroom vacant, he slipped into an adjoining courtroom and spoke with the bailiff, who advised him that the Lennox case had gone to the jury.

With nowhere else to go he decided to pay Luke Dominic a visit at the DA's office and get a quick rundown on the trial proceedings. He walked through the criminal justice building to the elevator and took it to Luke's office on the fifth floor. As he approached the employee's entrance he remembered he no longer had an RCSO ID that would allow him quick access to the office. Frustrated, he turned and walked to the public entrance.

"Jack Keller, here to see Luke Dominic."

"Is he expecting you?"

"Not exactly, but it shouldn't be a problem."

The clerk at the window gave Keller a quizzical look as she dialed Dominic's extension.

"I'll buzz you in. Do you know where his office is?"

"Yes, I do."

She pressed a button and the door buzzed. Jack grabbed the door and let himself in. He walked through the large foyer and headed down the hall to Luke's office. He poked his head in and saw Luke working at his desk.

"Hey, Jack, we missed you in court this morning. I thought you'd be there for closing arguments."

"Yeah, sorry about that. Had something come up this morning."

"You okay? You look a little tired."

"I'm fine, no problems here. So tell me how the closing went."

"It went well. Kramer did a nice little tap dance, but when you got nothing, you do what you gotta do," replied Luke with a chuckle.

"Yeah, he'll be lucky if he keeps his boy from getting the juice."

Luke studied Jack.

"You sure you're okay? Can I get you some water or something?"

"No, no—I'm fine. So where did Lisa go after the jury went to deliberations?"

"She said she wanted some quiet time and that she'd be at the library. I told her I'd call her once the jury comes back with something."

"Okay, well give me a call as well, would you mind?"

"Sure, no problem, Jack."

Keller headed out of the criminal justice building and walked down the street to the library. His steps were deliberate—he was certainly feeling the aftermath of the night before. He found Lisa sitting off in a corner reading a magazine.

"Well, good morning. Do you come here often?"

Lisa laughed. "Actually, yes . . . it's kind of my sanctuary. I've been here several times during the trial and have yet to be recognized."

Lisa looked at her father. Something seemed amiss.

"I missed you in court this morning."

"Yeah, sorry about that. I talked with Luke and he said things went well. Now we just wait on the jury."

"The waiting is the worst part. Here, take a seat," Lisa added pointing to a chair next to hers.

"So, how are you holding up?" Jack asked.

"I'm doing okay . . . just want it to be over."

"Yeah, I know. I'm so proud of you, Lisa. You've been through so much and you're so strong. I can't believe the changes in you over the past twenty months."

"Sometimes I have a hard time believing all this happened. It's like a nightmare, except that I don't wake up from it. I think about George Lombard every day and I dream about him at night. I am so sorry for my involvement in his death. It was so unnecessary."

"Look, you can't undo the past. You just have to move on and make the best of the situation."

"I know all that, and I really need to start considering where I go from here. I've been thinking about going back to my old job in nursing. Maybe become an RN. I'm not sure the hospital in Rosebud will have me back, but I'm sure I could find something. Even if it means moving away from Colorado."

Jack looked at his daughter. He didn't want to lose her again. Their reunion twenty months ago had followed nearly thirty years of no contact.

"You never know what the future may bring. Keep your options open."

"I'll do that. Hey, are you sure you're okay? You look a little out of sorts this morning."

"Look, there's something I need to tell you."

As Lisa opened her mouth to reply, her cell phone vibrated. She looked at the screen.

"It's Luke."

CHAPTER 48

Jack and Lisa quickly made their way back to the courthouse. As they approached, they saw the entire street lined with news trucks, each with its antenna reaching to the sky. News helicopters hovered fifteen hundred feet above and more than a dozen reporters had already staked out positions on the steps of the courthouse. Jack marveled at the speed with which the media could assemble for a juicy story. The cops could learn a thing or two from them, he thought.

As they started up the steps of the courthouse, Cherry DuLaney, a reporter from Channel Nine, recognized them and bolted in their direction. Jack saw her coming, grabbed Lisa's arm, and shuttled her quickly up the steps and away from DuLaney. A dozen other reporters saw what was happening and moved up the steps to head off Jack and Lisa.

"Lisa, what's the verdict going to be?" shouted DuLaney.

"Do you feel responsible for the death of George Lombard?" shouted another reporter.

Jack knew from experience that if they stopped now they would be surrounded, so the key was to keep moving and ignore all the questions. He tightened his grip on Lisa's arm and continued toward the door.

"Don't answer any questions," he whispered.

"Don't worry, I wasn't planning to!" she answered.

A minute later they slipped inside the doors of the courthouse and made their way to the conference room down the hall.

Jack texted Luke, telling him where he and Lisa were, and a few minutes later a bailiff knocked on the conference room door. He told them the hallways were lined with spectators and reporters and that he would escort them to courtroom ten. With the bailiff's help they managed to get into the courtroom without being accosted any further.

Luke, who was inside seated at the prosecution's table, saw the two enter and waved them over. "I don't want to get ahead of myself, but the fact that the jury took less than three hours to reach a verdict is a pretty good sign. I think we'll have some really good news here shortly."

Jack responded, "Yeah, I agree. I've never had a case where the jury comes back this quickly with anything but a guilty verdict."

Lisa looked at the two men and tried not to get her hopes up. Her insides were churning.

Suddenly, all three turned their attention toward a loud commotion coming from near the doorway. Two reporters from competing news stations were pushing and elbowing each other to get the best vantage point to videotape those entering the courtroom. The judge had allowed one pool camera to cover the court proceedings inside the courtroom but there was no such limitations on media access outside the courtroom. The hallway was fair game and these two reporters were going at it, complete with loud expletives.

Luke was just about to comment when he noticed the two bailiffs assigned to the courtroom moving toward the scuffle.

Jack turned to his daughter, "You need to decide if you want to give a statement to the press once the verdict is read. They're going to hound you, but it's totally up to you whether you want to speak to them or not."

Lisa looked at the two men but didn't say anything.

"It's your call," agreed Luke.

"Well, let's see what happens in here and then I'll figure out what I want to do."

As people continued to file into the courtroom Jack took his usual seat near the back. Lisa sat directly behind Luke and tried not to pay attention to all the craziness around her. Luke positioned himself at the prosecution table and tried his best to remain calm. His nerves weren't helped any when he saw District Attorney Dave Baxter enter the room. Baxter approached Luke and extended his hand.

"Regardless of what happens here, I want you to know that you did a great job. I appreciate all the hard work. You presented a great case."

"Thank you. I appreciate that. Now I'm just ready for the verdict."

Luke knew his boss wouldn't be nearly as supportive if the jury came back with anything other than a guilty verdict. A politician through and through.

"All rise. Court is now in session, the Honorable Richard O'Brien presiding."

Everyone stood and the crowd quieted down.

Judge O'Brien took his place on the bench and said, "Good afternoon, everyone. Please be seated. It's my understanding that the jury has reached a verdict in this case. I'd like them to be brought into the courtroom at this time."

The jury members filed in and took their seats in the jury box. All eyes were on the seven men and five women, with everyone trying to get a read from the looks on their faces. Luke couldn't pick up any obvious telltale signs.

The judge continued, "Ladies and gentlemen of the jury, have you reached a verdict in this case?"

The foreman, a man in his sixties, stood and replied, "Yes, we have, Your Honor."

"May I see the verdict?"

The foreman handed a form to the bailiff, who presented it to the judge. Judge O'Brien studied the form for a few seconds, then handed it to the clerk to be read.

The judge continued. "In the matter of Scott Lennox versus the state of Colorado, what say you?"

"We find the defendant, Scott Lennox, guilty of the crime of first-degree murder."

A collective gasp could be heard in the courtroom. Lisa put her head down and began to cry, relieved that the ordeal was finally over. Luke sat stoically at the prosecution table while Keller pumped his fist. Lennox sat at the defense table, showing no emotion.

"This is an outrage!" shouted Laura Lennox, sitting in the second row, not far from where Lisa was sitting.

"My husband didn't kill anyone—it was her!"

The woman was standing now, pointing directly at Lisa.

The judge spoke up immediately, "Bailiff, remove this woman from my courtroom!"

Within seconds, one of the bailiffs had Laura Lennox by the arm and started to lead her away, but she didn't go quietly.

"He's innocent! Tell the truth, you bitch!" she screamed, staring at Lisa.

Judge O'Brien slammed his gavel on the desk. "Madam, you are in contempt of this court. You are remanded to county lockup."

It was a minute or more before the buzz in the courtroom finally subsided.

Once calm had been restored, Judge O'Brien continued, "I want to thank the jury for their hard work on this case. Capital murder cases are difficult and this jury handled their duties very well. The next step in the process is to determine the proper sentence for Mr. Lennox. That, too, will be handled by this very same jury. I would like you all to return in two weeks to start on that part of your deliberations. For now, this courtroom is in recess."

As he was being handcuffed, Scott Lennox managed to catch Lisa's attention. Lennox looked directly at her and mouthed the words, "I will get you for this." She sat in her chair, stunned, and tried to gather herself.

Jack, Luke, and Lisa stayed in the courtroom while the others filed out. There would be plenty of reporters waiting for them outside and they were in no hurry to face them. Besides, Dave Baxter was having his time in the sun on the steps of the Justice Center. Branch Kramer quickly climbed into a waiting limousine and fled the scene.

"What's the matter, Lisa?" asked Jack, seeing that she was upset.

"It's Scott . . . he just threatened me."

"What?" responded Jack and Luke, simultaneously.

"He looked at me as they were leading him out the side door. He said, 'I will get you for this.'"

"That son of a bitch. They can't give him the juice soon enough for me," responded Jack, angrily.

"I'll bring this to the attention of the court. A threat like that will not be taken lightly by Judge O'Brien and I'm sure he'll factor it into the sentencing," added Luke.

"Good. Now let's get out of here," Jack replied.

For weeks Jack had been promising Lisa that once the trial was over the two would have an opportunity to spend some time together to celebrate. They dodged the reporters through a back door of the Justice Center and were soon on their way.

Jack grabbed a handful of Advil and chased them down with a bottled water sitting in the truck's cup holder.

"Are you all right, Dad?"

Jack's head was pounding. He wasn't about to tell his daughter why.

"Yeah, I'm okay. Just tweaked my back a little bit yesterday and it's bothering me," he fibbed.

"You just took a lot of Advil. Be careful—that stuff can cause stomach problems."

"I'm fine, sweetie. No worries."

Fifteen minutes later Jack pulled into the parking lot of the Centennial Airport. He glanced around and thought back to his previous visit to the airport just six weeks earlier. He and Mia had come out to check on the CSI team as they processed the plane Jonathan Timbers had rented to kill Vanessa Tolken. Jack thought back to the case, unaware of what had transpired the day before over the skies of South Florida. Tom Barone had called and left a voicemail message on Jack's office line about what happened, but it was a message that Jack would never hear given his termination from the RCSO. He tried not to think about the sudden end of his career. Right now he just needed to focus on his daughter.

He looked at Lisa sitting in the seat next to him and said, "I am so proud of you. You did it—you put away Lennox and in a couple of weeks he'll probably get the death penalty. He can't hurt you now, despite that weak-assed attempt to intimidate you. It's over, sweetie. It's in your past now. You can get on with your life."

Lisa looked at her father. She knew what he said was true, but she still felt in shock over the whole experience. It wasn't joy or happiness she was feeling at the verdict, but rather a sense of sadness. Her thoughts went to George Lombard.

"I know, Dad. I just need time to process this whole thing."

He took her hand. "You're right—it'll take some time, but that's to be expected."

As Jack was saying this his cell phone chirped. He reached in his pocket, fished out his phone, and read the text message.

Lisa waited until Jack slipped his phone back into his pocket.

"So what are we doing at the airport? Are we going somewhere?"

"Come on, follow me."

Jack and Lisa climbed from the truck and Jack began walking toward a large hangar a hundred yards away, his arm gently around Lisa's waist.

"Dad, what are we doing? If we're going somewhere I don't have anything packed. You should have told me."

"Don't worry about it."

As they approached the hangar, Jack steered his daughter to an area with several private planes parked just off the tarmac.

"Where are we going, Dad?"

"You'll see."

Jack slowed as they walked through the collection of planes, each anchored to its respective tie-down space. There was one plane that stood apart from the others: a large, shiny, white aircraft with a Gulfstream logo painted on the side. Jack steered Lisa to the plane, stopping at the bottom of the stairway.

"Dad, tell me what's going on!"

Just as Jack was about to answer they heard the door of the Gulfstream swing open. Both looked up and saw a man standing in the doorway of the plane several feet above them.

Jack didn't say anything and it was a second or two before Lisa could muster any words.

"Oh, my God—Peter!"

Peter stood there, a big smile spreading across his face. He quickly climbed down the stairs and turned toward Lisa. She stood there frozen, too stunned to move.

"Hello, Lisa."

"What are you doing here?" she stammered.

"I got your letter a few weeks ago, and it really touched my heart. I wanted to be here for you when the verdict was read. I've been following the trial on the news and Jack's been keeping me apprised the past several days. I flew here to Colorado the instant he told me a verdict was reached."

Lisa looked at her dad, who just smiled and shrugged. "Peter wanted to know what was going on so I gave him regular updates. Nothing wrong with that, is there?"

"No, of course not. I'm just shocked that you're here," she replied, looking at the man who had broken her heart on the beach in Mexico ten months earlier.

Peter answered, "How are you doing? I can't even imagine how difficult this whole thing has been for you."

"Better now that it's over. Although Scott threatened me as he was leaving the courtroom."

Peter responded, "What?

Jack jumped in, "Yeah, that asshole has some kinda balls."

An angry Peter replied, "Can something be done about it?"

Jack continued, "The prosecutor has been informed about what happened. He'll tell the judge."

Peter motioned toward the plane behind him, "Let's go where we can have some privacy."

Jack answered, "You two go ahead. I need to get something from my truck. I'll be back in a few."

Peter and Lisa climbed the steps of the Gulfstream while Jack headed for his truck. Soon he was sitting alone inside, his head still pounding from his binge the night before. He closed his eyes and knew he was at a point where he could easily relapse back into the life of an alcoholic. More than ten years of sobriety down the fucking tubes, he thought. Was last night going to be a one-time thing or the start of another ugly chapter in his life?

He grabbed a bottle of champagne from a cooler in the back seat and held it in his hands. Not his drink of choice but it would do in a pinch, he thought. He had purchased the champagne in the event Lisa and Peter wanted to celebrate the verdict and their reunion. Jack knew he could pop it open and down the bottle in a few minutes. No one would be the wiser.

He reflected on all that had happened the day before with the sheriff. Now unemployed, he didn't know where his life was about to go—all he knew was that he wanted his daughter to be part of it. He stared out the window at the mountains in the distance. Did he want to make alcohol part of that relationship?

Jack made his way back to the plane and climbed the stairway to the cabin. The Gulfstream was beautiful inside, large enough to accommodate a dozen or more passengers. The walls were paneled in wood and the leather chairs were large, similar to the recliner Jack had in his living room. A long antique rug covered most of the floor. It was certainly unlike any plane Jack had ever flown on. Peter and Lisa were sitting together near the back talking quietly. Peter was holding her hand.

"Nice ride, Peter. Hey, I thought the occasion called for a little champagne. Can I interest either of you in a glass?" Jack asked, holding up the bottle.

Peter looked at Lisa and she nodded.

"Absolutely," Peter replied.

Jack popped the cork and handed each a glass. He grabbed an iced tea he had also brought from the truck, poured it into a glass, and raised it in a toast.

"To the start of a new life."

The three clinked their glasses together.

"Hear, hear," Peter answered, turning to Lisa.

Lisa raised her glass and smiled at the two men in her life. "Cheers."

The three took sips from their drinks and enjoyed the moment. After a few seconds, Peter said, "Look, I know that there's a lot of media attention on this case right now and that you're likely to be hounded for a while. I don't know what you want to do with respect to all that but I'd be happy to take you and Jack back to Puerto Peñasco. You can take some time to sort through things without anyone knowing where you are. It could give you a bit of a respite from all the craziness of the next few days."

Lisa looked at Jack, unsure what to say.

"No harm in a little getaway. Let things settle down here for a bit. The media will lose interest in a few days and be on to the next salacious story. It might give you a chance to catch your breath."

"I could fly you back whenever you wanted. A few days, a week, or whatever. It's totally up to you," added Peter.

Lisa nodded, taking it all in.

CHAPTER 49

"Sheriff, Jack Keller is here to see you."

"Send him in, Lucinda."

Three weeks had passed since Mick had sent Jack packing.

Keller was still on paid administrative leave, and Mick was anxious to complete the termination so he could be rid of him. But before he could do that, Keller was entitled to a hearing, and that was the purpose of the meeting.

Jack walked into the office and nodded at the sheriff.

Mick wasted no time.

"Take a seat."

"Sheriff, I know you're a very busy man, so I'll get right down to it."

"Please do," responded Mick, anxious to get the whole thing over with. The anger he felt at Jack was palpable.

"I'm here to ask for my job back. I feel that termination is too severe a punishment for what I did. Other than a few minor scrapes, my record here at the RCSO is exemplary. And no one in the history of the department has enjoyed the clearance rate I have in homicide cases."

"That's never been in question, Keller. You're not being terminated for your work ethic or your clearance rate. You're being fired for insubordination and the fact that you can't be trusted. You lied to me, to your partner, and to just about everyone else you had contact with on the Lombard investigation. You're also guilty of obstruction of justice and if I had my druthers I'd turn the case over to the DA's office for prosecution. But I'm not going to do that. You need to go quietly off into the night and I never want to see you near this office again."

"It may be your right as sheriff to do that, but I'm not sure that's the best course of action in this case."

Of course you don't, you putz, thought Mick.

"You're entitled to your opinion. But what's important is what I think is the best course of action. The last time I checked, the residents of Rocklin County voted me into office, so I have the last say."

Keller sat quietly in his chair, looking at his boss, studying him, thinking about what his reaction would be to what he was about to say.

"I'm glad you mentioned the voters, sheriff. As I see it, you're terminating me because of something I did to protect my child. A loving, selfless act. And it seems to me that the people of this county, a good many of whom are parents themselves, might look at my actions differently than you."

Mick looked directly at Keller.

"Jack, you're going down a dangerous path here."

"Sorry you feel that way, sheriff. And you know, if you do terminate me then I really have no reason to stay quiet about all this. My motivation to keep this whole thing under wraps is gone. I mean, I could call a press conference on the steps of the courthouse and tell the world Lisa Sullivan is my daughter and how I helped her elude capture. Hell, I've got nothing to lose. If I go public it would almost certainly result in Scott Lennox being freed from prison, and be quite devastating to you, the entire RCSO, and the DA's office."

"Go fuck yourself, Jack."

Jack stood up and faced Mick. "If I go public, then your role in covering it up will also come to light. Nobody likes a cover-up. Perhaps this is something you should think about very carefully before making such a rash decision about my future with the RCSO."

Jack walked toward the door, and turned back to Mick. "You have yourself a nice day, sheriff."

ACKNOWLEDGMENTS

I have so many people to thank for helping me write my second novel. First and foremost my beautiful wife and best friend, Giselle, who read each section as I wrote it and offered me feedback. Her help was invaluable.

My three kids, Jessica, Michael, and Alyssa, each listened to me patiently as I ran ideas for plot lines by them. One of the most critical scenes in the story came from an informal conversation with Giselle and Alyssa during dinner one night on our back patio. The plot line, which I had been struggling with, suddenly became crystal clear. I had lots of moments like these.

I also want to thank Sunie Van Dueck, née Dahl, a woman I do not know. She was the successful bidder at an auction held to raise money for a dear friend battling cancer. Being the high bidder that day won her the chance to have a character in the book named for her. Congratulations, Sergeant Dahl!

One of the best things that happened to me in the process of writing this story was getting the assistance of Dara Murphy. Dara went over every word I wrote and corrected grammar, punctuation, etc. Knowing she was there to back me up enabled me to write what I was feeling and not worry too much about the technical stuff. She is one of the brightest people I know and is a wonderful new mom to baby Turner.

My friends at OMG Media in Monterey, California were once again a huge help to me. They kept the story on track and called me on stuff when it didn't seem to make the best sense.

Barry Rainey was also very helpful to me with the pilot/airplane storyline. His decades of experience flying commercially for a major airline as well as his experience in smaller aircraft paid great dividends for me. He took me flying one day so he could show me the ropes; we had a blast!

As with *Icy Betrayal*, my former co-worker and good friend Mike Palmieri was a great resource for me. His more than three decades in law enforcement, much of which was spent investigating homicide cases, provided me with insights time and time again. I worked for many years with Mike at the Oxnard Police Department and he's truly one of the best.

ABOUT THE AUTHOR

David Keith has nearly thirty years of experience in criminal justice and policing. As the longtime spokesman and community affairs manager with the Oxnard Police Department, he publicly handled high-profile cases including more than 200 homicides. Considered a leading expert in media relations, David has trained officers and staff from over 500 police agencies across the nation in media communications, community outreach, and crisis management.

David lives in Southern California with his wife, Giselle.